FALLEN STAR

"Perle?" I said loudly, pushing the door open. "Is everything okay? We really need to get back to the inn." No reply.

"Perle?" I repeated as Margo and I worked our way through the rows of dark seats toward the stage. The still quiet of the large room turned my gut to ice. "It's almost time for your lecture, Perle," I called, trying to offer calm compassion with my tone of voice.

I walked up onto the stage, where racks of scarves, shawls, hats, sweaters, and blankets hung ready for tomorrow. Even as I passed the tables of needle sets, Perle was nowhere to be seen.

"She must be backstage," I said, pointing to the wall of curtains. "Only, why can't she hear us?"

When I pushed aside the thick curtains, my heart jumped out of my chest. The whole world ground to a halt as I gasped in horror.

There, slumped up against the back wall, was Perle. Her head was cocked at a gruesome angle above what looked like a skein of red yarn wound around her neck, twisted tight around one of her needles in a lethal tourniquet. A set of the large needles lay at her feet, their mother-of-pearl beauty marred by bloody red smears on the tips.

Perle Lonager couldn't hear us—or anything—because she was dead.

On Skein of Death

A RIVERBANK KNITTING MYSTERY

ALLIE PLEITER

BERKLEY PRIME CRIME
New York

BERKLEY PRIME CRIME
Published by Berkley
An imprint of Penguin Random House LLC
penguinrandomhouse.com

Copyright © 2021 by Alyse Stanko Pleiter
Penguin Random House supports copyright. Copyright fuels creativity, encourages
diverse voices, promotes free speech, and creates a vibrant culture. Thank you for buying
an authorized edition of this book and for complying with copyright laws by not
reproducing, scanning, or distributing any part of it in any form without permission.
You are supporting writers and allowing Penguin Random House to continue to
publish books for every reader.

BERKLEY and the BERKLEY & B colophon are registered trademarks and
BERKLEY PRIME CRIME is a trademark of Penguin Random House LLC.

Knitting pattern by Starla Williams

ISBN: 9780593201787

First Edition: June 2021

Printed in the United States of America
1   3   5   7   9   10   8   6   4   2

Book design by George Towne

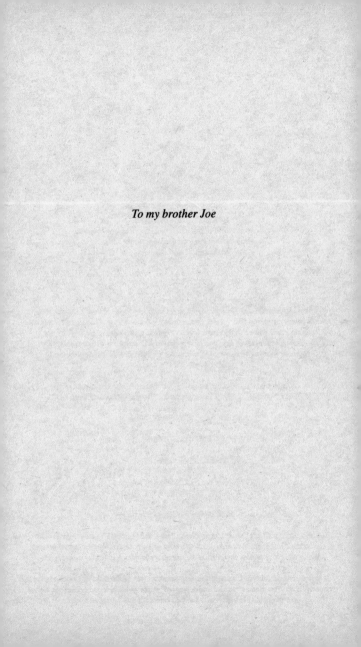

To my brother Joe

CHAPTER ONE

"So it's more than 'yarn'?" the young woman staring at my shop sign asked. "The letters . . . stand for something?" She didn't stare at the single word. Instead, I could tell she was wondering about the period after each letter.

My big wooden shop sign is one of the things I love most about Y.A.R.N. Like the shop, the sign is full of color and texture. It shows a ball of green yarn winding its way through the four letters to land—as all yarn should—on a pair of knitting needles. I had it hand-carved by a local artist, and when it first arrived, I spent a whole day just touching it. I ran my fingers lovingly over the carved lines and curves before I let them put it up. Now it sits nestled beside a big display window to stand out against the colonial charm of my brick storefront.

I stopped watering the potted plants on either side of my door and offered the woman my warmest smile. "Oh, you bet they do." Since that sign went up on opening day three months ago, there isn't a single moment I love more than telling someone what Y.A.R.N. means.

"What?" she asked.

I have answered this question a hundred times. I'd happily answer it a thousand times more. "Come on inside and I'll show you," I said as I pulled the shop door open. I'll admit I have had to learn to tamp down my raging enthusiasm at moments like this. In the shop's first weeks, I tended to go a little overboard and scare off unsuspecting customers. Now it almost always ends the same wonderful way.

"What's your name?" I asked as we walked inside.

"Caroline," she offered. She was dressed in trendy weekend yoga wear, a wildly designed combination of turquoise and peach. This was a woman who liked color. And if there's one thing Y.A.R.N. is overflowing with, it's color.

I gave her a moment to take it all in. "Welcome to Y.A.R.N., Caroline. I'm Libby Beckett." I gestured around the shop. Every wall is covered with stacked square cubbies holding all kinds of yarn. Soft pastels, riotous self-striping mixes, understated heathers, thick, thin, fuzzy, shiny—there's a whole universe of things just begging to be touched and explored.

Y.A.R.N. is a comfort space. More than just comfortable, the shop exudes comfort, with deep cushioned chairs, bright warm lighting, tables to gather at, and thick rugs underfoot. It smells like good coffee, frequently of baked goods, and of the particular but unidentifiable scent of creativity. Not a speck of chrome to be found here, just deep shelves and bins in every nook and cranny.

This isn't a place where you just duck in and grab what you need; it's a soothing haven where you linger and discover. Where you sit for an hour and no one cares—in fact we love when you do.

Y.A.R.N. is the thing I was born to do. Sure, I was good

as a pharmaceutical sales rep, but that was just a *job*. I think of Y.A.R.N. as the most excellent work of my soul. My prescription, if you will, for happiness—mine and everyone's.

Caroline was intrigued; I could tell already. I led her to the only black furnishing in the whole color-strewn shop: the giant blackboard that covers one wall. With one hand I gave her my friendliest handshake, while with the other I pointed up to the colorful list scribbled all over the chalkboard. "And here's the answer to your question."

I watched Caroline take in the kaleidoscope of words. Some are scribbled in a reckless manner; others are artfully drawn. I have always thought of my blackboard as graffiti of the very best kind. Only one version is painted to permanently stand at the top of the board—my original vision of what Y.A.R.N. stood for: *You're Absolutely Ready Now.* Maybe someday it will stop sending a zing through my veins when I read it, but that hasn't happened yet.

At the bottom of the board sat a little bucket of colored chalks painted with the invitation: *Add your own.* And my customers have over the months—some funny, some poignant:

You'll Always Remember Nice
Yellow Adds Romantic Notions
Yell at Ridiculous Negativity
Yielding Amounts to Relatively Nothing
Your Anger Rewards No one

There have been dozens. I want there to be thousands before I'm done . . . if I'm ever done.

Caroline took a moment to read several. "Cool." I could see her catch the notion that perhaps yarn could be more than just what Grandma kept around the house to crochet granny squares. No disrespect to granny squares—I'm thrilled they're coming "back."

"It's always so much more than yarn," I told her. I pointed to the perfect coordination of her top, leggings, and expensive cross-training shoes. Peach and turquoise are lush, creative colors, and Caroline had paired them beautifully. Even her hair band and shoelaces matched. "You've got a great eye for color. You'd love knitting."

"Really?" Her face caught that spark that shows whenever you open someone up to the possibility that they have some art inside them. It would be hard to come up with a moment that I live for more. Except for maybe that first bite of my friend Margo's coconut cream pie—that comes close.

"Absolutely." I guided her toward a basket of exquisitely soft and richly colored yarn over by the window: a collection of plush alpaca yarns in a range of ice-cream peach, sky blue, mint green, pale yellow, and sherbet orange that drew her touch like a sweet fuzzy kitten. "What do you do? Are you from nearby?" I asked as she fingered the beautiful skeins. Collinstown is such a picture-perfect Maryland town that we get lots of tourism, especially on gorgeous fall days like today.

"Just across the bay. I'm an entertainment reporter, which isn't nearly as glamorous as it sounds. I'm here to meet a friend for lunch over at the inn." She tilted her head in the direction of the Riverside Inn just across the street. "It was such a pretty day, I came early to just wander around."

In my head I had already selected four possible first-project scarf patterns for my new friend Caroline. "When's lunch?"

"Noon."

I checked my watch. "I can have you knitting before your first bite of salad. Want to try?"

Her eyes said yes long before she opened her mouth.

Like I said, I live for these moments. Out of the corner of my eye, I caught my shop assistant, Linda Franklin, smiling from behind the counter. Linda gets as much of a kick out of watching me do this as I get out of doing it. "I'm just here to ring up the sales you make," she says, but I've seen her in action. Linda is just as much of a yarn "evangelist" as I am. I wouldn't have it any other way.

Caroline turned out to be a natural—I seem to have a gift for spotting them—and she held up her fourth pretty-darned-near-perfect row twenty minutes later. "Look at that!" She grinned. "I didn't know I had it in me."

We'd already talked about how she could knit on the Metro into her DC job rather than scrolling through her social media (she gets enough of that at work). She confessed to frequent bouts of insomnia, so we talked about how soothing knitting can be in lonely hours. We'd chatted about how her niece would love a scarf in her school colors. When Hank, my English bulldog, who is Y.A.R.N.'s official mascot, walked up and fixed her with his big brown eyes, Caroline talked about how her French bulldog, Milo, might like a new sweater.

I grabbed a flyer for my big event coming up. "You need to come to this. Perle Lonager creates the most amazing patterns from Scandinavian motifs—mostly Norwegian, but some other cultures as well."

"That sounds interesting." Caroline liked the idea of culturally inspired designs, I could tell. She struck me as a smart and thoughtful person—just the type of knitter who would love Perle's work.

"She's doing a fashion show and new-product launch on

Saturday," I explained, "but we'll also have an exclusive dog sweater kit debuting at a smaller private workshop she's doing here in the store. That's on Friday before her lecture and dinner. You could make a whole weekend out of it. And"—I pulled out the sample version of the project that was almost finished for Hank to model—"you could have plenty of time to dive into something like this."

Caroline's eyes widened at how the sweater's clever use of zigzags, diamonds, and dots gave it a unique Nordic style. A little doggy ski sweater, if you will. "I could make that?"

"The great thing about Perle's designs is that there aren't a lot of special stitches you need to learn. Sure, some Norwegian *Lusekofte* sweaters are tricky, but Perle's patterns are great for beginners. It's all in the color combinations." I gave Caroline my most encouraging smile. "You could absolutely make that. I chose gray and white for Hank, but you could have a ball with all sorts of color pairings for your little Milo."

"Blue and yellow, maybe." Caroline ran her fingers over the bold rhythm of Perle's Nordic motif. A new knitter was born.

Sure, it was important to my business that I fill the room. Perle is one of the rising stars in our industry, and I had been working for months to line her up for this event. As the owner of a new shop, I needed some big successes to get my name out there, and this was my shot.

But more than that, I wanted to introduce Caroline—and lots of people like her—to the world of fiber arts and artists. It's the whole point of Y.A.R.N. As I watched Caroline's eyes light up, I wondered again why I had let this dream sit ignored for so many years.

Actually, I know exactly why. His name is Sterling, and

I'm not married to him anymore for that and a hundred other reasons.

As I walked Caroline out the door a bit later—after Linda rang up a scarf kit, needles, yarn, and two sets of tickets to Perle's events—I wasn't at all surprised that the young woman gave me a hug. I had no doubt that someday soon my blackboard would include whatever Caroline came up with for what Y.A.R.N. stands for.

I know there are some customer service experts who would tell me I just gave Caroline an authentic experience in my store, but I would tell you I shared what I know to be true: the yarn connects us. It's not old-fashioned; it's timeless (there's a difference, even if Sterling could never see it). I meant every bit of the hug I gave her back.

Hank woofed at my feet as he caught sight of Margo coming out the front door of the Perfect Slice pie shop she owns across the street. To Hank, Margo means food. To me, Margo has been a steadfast friend—and nonstop source of calories. She is one of those infuriating people who can stay effortlessly slim despite all the goodies she creates for a living. Were she anyone else, her figure and her perfect, shiny straight hair that falls obediently into a neat dark bob would make me want to hate her. After all, her obedient black locks make my blond waves look riotous, and her waistline . . . well, let's not go there. But I love Margo to pieces, and was thrilled for her when she opened the Perfect Slice five years ago. It's perfection that Y.A.R.N. opened just across the street, so we see each other every day.

Margo wiped her hands on her trademark green apron and smiled. I watched my best friend notice both the Y.A.R.N. bag and the bounce in Caroline's step as my new customer greeted her lunch date outside the inn. "You did it again, didn't you?"

I might have allowed myself a smug grin. "I did."

"I have customers, but you somehow manage to have a steady stream of *converts*." Margo crossed her arms over her chest. "I bet you even sold her tickets to the event, didn't you?"

"Two, actually. And she'll buy the dog sweater kit when it's ready, too. I guarantee it."

Her expression told me what she was going to say next. "You absolutely should run for president of the Chamber of Commerce."

As no big fan of George Barker, a real estate broker who was the current president, Margo had been on this particular mission since I moved back to Collinstown five months ago and opened the shop two months later.

"I've been a shop owner three months. I'm not qualified." That was an easier argument than "I don't want to." As much as I adore Margo, she can be a bit relentless.

She made a noise that, if we were in Georgia, would have translated to *pshaw*. "You are smart. You have common sense and tact. Even before you opened Y.A.R.N., your qualifications ran circles around George's."

This wasn't exactly true. George was very qualified. Overqualified. But George was one of those people who seemed to be constantly figuring out how to sell you something. Or deny you any advantage over their success. That gets old fast. So the way I saw it, my only virtue over George was that people didn't cross to the other side of the street when they saw me coming.

Then there was the fact that the Chamber president regularly interacted with the mayor of Collinstown. And since the current mayor was Gavin Maddock, that presented a bit of a problem. Gavin and I were still trying to figure out how to act around each other. Moving back newly single to the town where you grew up and opening a shop are complicated enough without having to negotiate your high school boyfriend as the town's mayor. Margo knew this, which was why she didn't bring it up.

Hank, whose extraordinary canine talent is knowing exactly when to change the subject, chose this moment to whine and bump his head into Margo's shin. This was his version of "Why is that cookie still in your hand when it should be in my mouth?"

It worked. "Oh, Hank, buddy, of course this is for you." Margo reached down and opened her hand to let Hank gobble up the shortbread circle. She is known for her pies, but her shortbread is almost as famous. Especially with Hank. Most days I am convinced she sends delicious smells wafting across the street on purpose. Every once in a while I catch Hank sitting in the window and I swear he is staring across the street, dreaming of Margo's shortbread.

I can hardly blame him. My bathroom scale offers daily proof that Margo's pies are my coping mechanism of choice—next to yarn, that is.

"How close are you to filling the room for Perle Lonager?"

"We're on track to sell out, I think." Lots of local people had been supportive and bought tickets for the dinner and lecture I had planned, but my true goal was to bring knitting enthusiasts from all over the area into the shop for the pair of workshops I had set up. Perle had stopped doing most promotional appearances. The fact that I'd managed to convince her to come here and do not one but three events should have put Y.A.R.N. on the map in the fiber arts world.

Not that it had been easy. Perle had been living up to her reputation for being difficult to work with. Still, I knew she was worth it. Any request Perle made—and she had made quite a few of them—I found a way to accommodate.

Margo had come up with one of the best special touches. "I'll have the Danish Dream Cake ready for tasting this afternoon. Should I bring it by?"

I already knew it would be delicious, but I never turned down the chance to eat anything Margo brought over. "I'll have the coffee on."

Margo leaned in. "So, has Gavin told you yet?"

"Told me what?"

She waved it away. "Oh, I shouldn't. It should be his thing to tell you."

Margo has always been utterly incapable of keeping a secret. "Tell me what?"

"He's making a declaration at tomorrow night's town council meeting. There's going to be a Collinstown Yarn Day as part of your big event weekend."

A town-wide day? For my shop's event? "Seriously? Where'd he get that idea?"

Margo's grin told me exactly where Gavin got that idea. "I knew you needed to make a big splash. What are friends for?"

"Margo—"

"And I may have mentioned that it might help convince you to keep George from winning a fourth term."

Like I said, relentless. It isn't always a bad thing. Just in this case.

"Collinstown Yarn Day. I like the sound of it." My brain started churning out ideas right away. "We might have just enough time to yarn-bomb the trees down Collin Avenue."

I pointed to the tree in front of the shop. A few friends and I had "yarn-bombed" it the week before the shop opened, meaning we knit up little patches of colorful fabric that got stitched around the trunk and branches. A tree sweater, if you will. I could easily envision a dozen trees up and down the town's main street sporting such decorations. Perhaps we could work in some of Perle's signature motifs. Perle would have to love it.

And Gavin would either love it or think it was the most ridiculous thing ever. At the very least, it would be another way to show Perle how much this visit meant to me and the shop.

Margo's voice pulled me from my plans. "He's coming over this afternoon to tell you. I think there's a certificate or something."

"Needles to the city instead of keys?"

Margo groaned, but she laughed. "Not exactly. Act like you didn't know, okay?"

If I had a dollar for every time Margo has asked me to "act like you didn't know," I wouldn't have needed Sterling's hefty divorce settlement to open Y.A.R.N.

We stood outside in the glorious fall sunshine for a few more minutes, chatting and gossiping about all the things there are to chat and gossip about in a small town like Collinstown. I feel so much more at home here than in the pressure cooker that is Washington, DC. It might be only an hour or so away, but to me it feels like a whole other universe. The spice of fall leaves and the tang of bay water in the air here are a bone-deep hometown memory for me. Every day something reminds me this was the right choice—hence *You're Absolutely Ready Now*—and I kick myself for not ditching the suit-and-salary job sooner.

The door pushed open behind me and Linda popped her head out. Normally Linda is unflappable, but at the moment she looked unnerved. "You've got a call," she said as she mimed putting a phone to her ear with one hand. Her eyes were wide and her lips pressed narrow. "It's Perle."

Perle Lonager did not call. I had been spending our entire relationship hunting her down, leaving unanswered phone messages and e-mails, foraging for information. That woman never once initiated communication. "Perle's on the phone?"

"Yep. And she sounds upset. Okay, maybe just really anxious, but I think it sounds more like upset."

I sent Margo an alarmed look, took a deep breath, and headed back inside to see whether Collinstown Yarn Day had just come unraveled.

CHAPTER TWO

Twenty minutes later, I leaned back against my tiny office wall and sighed in exhaustion.

Linda poked a curious face through the door. A five-feet-two bundle of efficiency, she has a head of strawberry blond curls that behave way better than mine and big expressive eyes. "Everything okay?"

"It is now." Ten minutes ago I might have given a different answer.

She leaned against the doorframe. "She sounded really perturbed."

I slid the pages of furious notes I'd taken during my conversation with Perle into the growing-fatter-by-the-day event file I'd been keeping. "You were right—she's really anxious. She asked to make a bunch of changes to the event. Nothing we can't handle, but it will take some doing."

Perle was a gifted young designer—one of the new,

mostly digital generation of knitters whose "cool factor" is shifting the craft out of the "past generation" vibe. I want her to succeed for both our sakes, but while I expected her to be sensitive and artistic, I hadn't expected this level of anxiety. "Whatever Perle wants . . ."

Linda shrugged. "And what does Perle want?"

I rousted myself up from the chair to head back out into the shop and toward the coffee machine. Caffeine was most definitely in order after all that cajoling and touchy personality management. "Well, for starters, she confirmed that Henrik is coming"

Henrik—who never seemed to need a last name—was Perle's muse of sorts. He was an exceedingly handsome Norwegian and Perle touted him as her familial link to the fascinating Nordic patterns that marked her work. Perle's biography cites her heritage as Danish, but the more intricate patterns of Norwegian knitting captivated her designing eye. To hear Perle tell it, meeting Henrik during her initial delves into the famous Norwegian *Selbu* mittens fueled her passion for all things Norwegian—and a certain tall blond "Viking" in particular. It wasn't hard to see that her success came from more than just clever use of traditional Norwegian motifs; Perle's audience was mostly female and Henrik was a *decidedly* fine example of Nordic male.

Linda's eyes danced. "Oh, goody. I mean, we all love Perle, but . . . Well, let's just say Henrik is the frosting on the cake—or is that the icing on the Danish?" She chuckled at her own joke. "You'll sell out for sure once we can announce he's coming." After a moment's thought, Linda asked, "Why wasn't he *always* coming?"

"Search me. When I worked up the nerve to ask, she was always a bit vague about it. They certainly act as if they're a serious couple, but I figured I didn't have enough leverage to pressure her."

Linda was right—Henrik coming was a big plus for my event. In fact, he didn't even need to come to the whole event. Even if he showed only for the lecture and dinner, it would help sell tickets.

"There's more, though," I went on. "She also wants us to publicize that she's making a big announcement at the lecture."

Linda reached for the largest ceramic mug hanging from the rack next to the coffee machine and handed it to me. "Good news all around. Henrik *and* a big announcement from Perle Lonager. The event can't help but be a hit now." She selected a more ordinary-sized mug for herself as I filled my giant one nearly to the brim and dumped in a compensatory amount of flavored creamer. "What's she announcing?"

The creamy-savory scent of pumpkin spice soothed my agitation as I took a lavish gulp. "She wouldn't say. Only that it was big."

"The announcement of a big secret. Sounds exciting."

"You'd think, but she sounded awfully nervous about it. She's too young to retire, too sought after to fail. . . . I'm not sure what it could be. Maybe it's about her next book."

Linda's eyes lit up with an idea. "Hey—what if Perle chose your event to announce that she and Henrik are getting married?"

"Here? I'd doubt she'd do that."

Linda gave a mischievous shrug. "But it's possible. We don't know for sure. We could simply start a rumor."

Just because it would work—brilliantly—didn't mean I was going to try it. I had no plans to chance offending our guest or her dashing muse even if it was the one thing most Perle fans would die to know.

From everything I'd seen, Perle and Henrik were madly in love. They made a charismatic pair who won fans easily. While she was the fragile and sensitive artist, he played the loyal and powerful protector to perfection.

The fact that he appeared to be a modern-day drop-dead-gorgeous Viking didn't hurt, either. Photographs of him in Perle's sweaters, the sleeves pushed up just enough to showcase muscular arms, only added to the appeal. Her pattern books boasted shots of his piercing blue eyes peering soulfully out from under Perle's slouchy beanies. Magazines held glossy photos of him jutting his strong chin into the distance as the wind tossed a Perle scarf over his broad shoulders.

My theory was that Henrik managed to personify many knitters' romantic fantasies. After all, what knitter doesn't secretly crave a handsome man who not only wears what she knits, but deeply appreciates it? That was Henrik—or at least how he appeared.

"The engagement. That's got to be it. I bet her next book is about weddings. Lacy shawls, veils. She could probably design and knit her own dress—she's that good," Linda declared, and took a sip of her coffee.

"I'm not so sure. She's bringing her publisher, too. I can't see why she'd bring him to an engagement announcement."

"But announcing an engagement could be perfect publicity for another collection of *Selbu*-inspired mittens." Linda lowered her voice as a pair of customers wandered into the shop. "Everybody wants more of those from her."

Selbu mittens, famous for their intricate snowflakelike patterns on the front and back, were indeed a traditional Norwegian engagement gift. It would be a stupendous marketing tie-in. Still, I thought Linda's imagination was working overtime on this one. Perle didn't strike me as the kind to go in for a gimmick like that. "I have no idea. All I know is that she asked me to arrange specific seats and accommodations for both of them."

"Shouldn't her publisher be handling the accommodations? Don't those companies have publicists for that sort of thing?"

I'd had the same thought, but I was fully ready to bend over backward to accommodate Perle. "We do whatever she wants." Besides, these last-minute changes worked in my favor. Linda was right—the event was sure to sell out once we could publicize that not only was Henrik coming, but Perle was planning some big announcement. It wouldn't matter that we had no idea what that announcement was.

"Elizabeth, we're here!"

The sound of my mother's voice broke the sweet reverie of success. My eyes, which had momentarily fluttered shut in pumpkin-spice bliss, shot wide open.

Mom.

I turned to see her and three of her friends trotting into the shop. Mom stopped and looked around. "Where is everyone? You said to get here early because the shop was going to be packed."

Forty-eight hours early? "Mom, today's Wednesday."

"Wednesday, October third." Mom blinked around as if maybe her eyes just needed to adjust to indoor light. "Where's Perle?"

I applied the I-will-not-be-frustrated tone that had become my nearly constant companion around Mom lately. "Perle's coming on Friday. I just got off the phone with her, as a matter of fact."

It never ceased to amaze me how my mother could wield such a powerful stink eye while being totally in the wrong. "You said Wednesday."

"No, Mom. I said Friday. It's always been Friday." I tamped down the urge to point to the flyer next to me on the counter, a copy of which I knew for a fact sat on her refrigerator door. Because I put it there. With the date and time circled. In red.

"So the dinner thing's not tonight, either?"

At least she remembered there *was* a dinner thing. "No, that's Friday night. I gave you everyone's tickets when we had lunch on Monday." That might have been a mistake. By Friday Mom was likely to have forgotten where she put them.

"Well," piped in Mom's friend Barb, "we're here now. We might as well sit down and enjoy ourselves for a bit." Barb gave me a what's-the-harm? smile as she and Mom's other friends Jeanette and Arlene plopped themselves down at the large circular table in the middle of the shop, where my customers often gather.

Mom sat down in the chair nearest me while Linda deftly took her cue to fill coffee mugs for the quartet of elderly knitters my mom calls "the Gals." "And where's my Hankie boy?"

At the sound of Mom's nickname for him, Hank waddled out from behind the sales counter to present his chubby head for a good scratching. Mom lavished him with coos worthy of the most adored grandchild—which in many ways Hank was.

I gave in to my urge to confirm dates and swiped four copies of the event flyer off the pile. "Okay, Mom, let's go over this again." I pointed to the listing of each event, one at a time. "There's the limited special appearance here at one on Friday. That's the event where we are debuting the dog sweater pattern and she'll sign your book." I placed a flyer down in front of each of the women. "Then there's the dinner and lecture at the inn that night, where she's going to talk about the Nordic cultures and motifs she uses in her designs. Then the bigger event will be in the theater at ten on Saturday morning. That's the one with the fashion show of her designs and where she'll debut those gorgeous wooden needles she's about to start selling."

"The ones you showed me with the mother-of-pearl in them," Mom recalled. "They're beautiful. I want the whole set as an early Christmas present."

"So you keep telling me," I confirmed. Perle—whose name was the Danish word for "pearl"—had recently found a way to honor her own heritage by creating a line of beautiful handcrafted knitting needles in the Danish woodworking tradition. The larger needles had an intricate mother-of-pearl design inlaid on the shaft, and every needle had a beautiful mother-of-pearl ornament on the blunt end. They were stunning. This event launched Y.A.R.N. as one of the first retail shops where the luxury needles would be sold. The needles were gorgeous and well-made; I was sure they'd be in high demand, despite their hefty price tag. "Everything's on the flyer as well as on the tickets I already gave you."

Perhaps among the four of them, they could manage a return trip at the correct time. I wasn't going to have any time those days to drive across the river and shuttle her here myself. Mom might have been having a growing number of "senior moments," but she still seemed competent behind the wheel—at least for now.

"Oh, good," came a deep voice from the door, "you've got a crowd in here."

I wasn't sure I agreed with Gavin's assessment that two customers and Mom's Gals constituted a crowd, but I was pleased for the distraction. "Hello, Gavin."

I had been back in Collinstown for five months, and Gavin and I still hadn't quite figured out how to deal with each other. We'd been a serious couple in high school, but college and life had peeled us off in different directions. And to marriages that hadn't lasted for either of us. Neither of us knew where to file the intersection of our old and current lives—friends, colleagues, old flames, awkward acquaintances, et cetera. Everything felt forced and uncomfortable.

He held up the large manila folder in his hand. "I have a surprise for you, Libby."

I remembered Margo's words and planted a look of surprise on my face. "Really?"

"I love surprises," Mom chimed in, followed by chirps of delight from the other ladies.

Gavin applied what I secretly called his Mayor Voice, all deep and officially resonant, as he extracted a sheet of paper from the envelope. "As mayor of Collinstown, I am officially proclaiming Saturday Collinstown Yarn Day."

I knew it was not much more than a silly promotional gesture, but I couldn't help but be charmed by the show of community support. Y.A.R.N. means so much to me. I take every success and failure personally. The weekend's events felt like my coming-out party as the woman I was supposed to be all along. Collinstown Yarn Day warmed me like a stamp of approval.

I smiled at Gavin as I pushed out a surprisingly choked-up "Thank you."

Gavin smiled with a touch of embarrassment as he handed me the fancy proclamation. "You can hang it in the window or something."

"You can frame it," Mom offered.

"We can celebrate it," Linda said. "Is there enough time to yarn-bomb all the trees along Collin Avenue?"

I stopped myself just before saying, "I had the same thought," since that would reveal Margo had spilled the beans. Instead, I widened my eyes and said, "What a great idea!"

Gavin looked a bit startled. "What's a yarn bomb?" Caution, rather than curiosity, filled his voice.

"It's what we did to the tree out front." I pointed through the shop's front window to the midsized maple trunk covered in cheery stripes of stitching.

"Oh. That."

I should not have been so amused at the please-don't-do-that look in the man's eyes.

Mom certainly was amused, too. "We can get started right now. We're here, after all. It's like it was meant to be."

Mom's favorite excuse for whenever she gets something mixed up is to turn it into an adventure or serendipity. It was never wrong; it was simply "meant to be this way." Frustrating as it can be, sometimes I think Mom is onto something.

Rising up from her chair with new vigor, Mom grabbed my elbow. "Whatcha got that we can use?"

Thinking of four elderly ladies gleefully decking out Collin Avenue trees in tiny tubular sweaters seemed like the perfect way to celebrate Collinstown Yarn Day. What better sight to welcome the crowds here to see Perle? My eye caught the phrase on the far right of the chalkboard: *Your Angels Relentlessly Nurture*.

"Linda," I said with a grin I truly felt, "why don't you take the Gals into the stockroom and see what we've got that they can use? There's that whole box of swatches, and they can use any large needles and yarn they can find back there."

The four women followed Linda, giggling like kids in on the best of pranks. Maybe that was exactly what they were.

Gavin waved the proclamation. "Am I going to regret this? Is Collin Avenue going to look like an aisle from IKEA?"

"IKEA is Swedish," I assured him. "And Yarn Day is a lovely idea. Thanks. I'll take all the PR I can get for this weekend."

He must have caught the hint of stress in my voice. "Everything okay?" He'd always been far too good at reading me, and time hadn't changed that.

"Let's just say that Perle is proving the classic artistic personality. I have to think she's done lots of these kinds of events, but she seems to be highly anxious about this one."

"Anxious?"

"She just changed a bunch of stuff at the last minute. Adding Henrik and her publisher as VIP guests, making a load of particular demands about where they stay and where they sit at the lecture, wanting to get into the theater space the night before the fashion show for some complicated setup—that sort of thing."

"Henrik?"

Barb walked by with an armful of chunky white and red acrylic yarn and a pair of needles the size of broomsticks. "He's that handsome Viking fella." She waggled her gray eyebrows as she emphasized "handsome."

"Nordic," I corrected. "Or Scandinavian. The only Vikings around these days are on television."

Gavin bounced his gaze between Barb and me before asking, "Perle Lonager has a spokesmodel?"

Barb giggled, but it wasn't entirely inaccurate. "'Boyfriend and muse' is probably closer to the truth," I explained. "Henrik is Norwegian, like most of Perle's designs, while Perle's own heritage comes from Denmark. They've been a couple for a while, and Linda thinks they're going to announce their engagement."

Barb's eyes shot wide open. "Are they?" I realized that whether or not I'd meant to, I'd just launched the rumor. Would I regret this?

I shrugged in reply. "Perle's not saying." As Barb took a breath to inquire further, I cut her off with "And I'm not going to ask."

Barb did a U-turn back to the rest of the Gals in the stockroom, eager to share the juicy news she'd just learned.

"Well, Jillian wants to come to the thing here," said Gavin. "If that's okay, that is. I know it's sort of a private deal, but she's all excited about the dog sweaters. If she can only go to the Saturday thing, I'll understand."

Now this was news. I had met Gavin's thirteen-year-old daughter and found her charming—well, as charming as girls get at that age. I didn't have to be a mother to know how young teens can be balls of conflicting emotions and unsteady attitudes. Never being able to have kids myself, I especially treasured the handful of young people who ventured into the shop.

"Of course." I didn't have to fake the enthusiasm in my smile. The idea of Jillian wanting to come to an event at Y.A.R.N. pleased me to no end.

Gavin shifted his weight as if this were some sort of touchy subject. "Evidently she wants to learn. You know, to . . ." He mimed using a set of needles as if "knit" was the *other* kind of four-letter word.

Once again I had to tamp down my "new convert" enthusiasm so as not to scare anyone off. "I think that's wonderful. And she absolutely can come to Perle's private session—and even the dinner lecture if you want." I stepped a bit closer just because he looked so awkward about asking. "But she won't really learn at the store event. She'll get inspired, and I'll make sure she gets a kit the right size for your dachshund, but I won't have time to show her that afternoon. If you like, we could set up a time for her to come in next week and I'll teach her myself."

He looked surprised. "You'd do that?"

I'd do that for just about anyone, but most especially for Jillian. She struck me as a sweet kid who hadn't quite found her feet after her parent's divorce. It hadn't been a smooth one. I'd come to a sort of gratitude that my prickly split with Sterling hadn't been complicated by children. I know shared parenting can be done well, but I have serious doubts my winner-takes-all ex had the capacity for it.

"I would absolutely do that. Especially for the mayor who just gave me Collinstown Yarn Day." I've always found it a smart tactic to keep things on a decidedly professional level with Mayor Maddock given our history.

He looked as if I'd handed *him* the keys to the city. "Great. We'll be there."

I expect most other single dads would just drop their daughter off with the friendly shopkeeper lady and duck across the street to the inn bar. Not Gavin. Despite the fact that it must have been a monster of an uphill climb to be the single father of a teenage girl, Gavin was all in. His greatest virtue had always been how hard he tried at things. If a man could be a virtuous workaholic, Gavin fit the bill. I got the distinct sense parenthood was confounding him these days and he needed a win. If Y.A.R.N. could give him one, I was all for it.

Still, I couldn't resist: "You're sure you don't want to learn?" I inclined my head toward the poster on the wall behind me. It was a kitschy book cover with a near-shirtless cowboy atop a fiery steed with yarn and needles. The title was *The Masculine Art of Knitting*. We sold copies in the store, but I confess most of them were as gag gifts.

Gavin's response was immediate. "Nope." After I shot him a look, he backpedaled to "I'll keep my attendance to an official capacity."

"Well," Linda said as she came up behind me, "you won't be here alone. I just got off the phone with a man who signed up. Talks like a young guy, too—asked if we were livestreaming any of it. He bought tickets for Perle's session here, the lecture dinner, and the Saturday show and demonstration—the whole shebang."

"A guy?" Gavin balked. "A young guy?"

"Hey, all the cool kids are doing it," I teased. "I do have men customers. I don't see why Perle wouldn't have men fans. I mean, Henrik is definitely male and he knits. In fact, the needle making could be classified as woodwork. Very manly."

"This guy even mentioned Henrik," Linda said. "Maybe he's really more of a Henrik fan than a Perle fan."

That caught my attention. "How would he know Henrik's coming? We didn't even know until just now. We haven't announced it."

Linda shrugged. "Maybe it's out on social media or something."

I didn't actually know for a fact that Henrik knit. He could have been just posing with props for all those photographs. Sterling had taught me that being exceedingly handsome enables some people to get away with all sorts of things.

"He even asked if I could tell him which hotel Henrik and Perle were staying at," Linda added. "He was full of questions."

Gavin and I exchanged wary looks. "We have his name, right?" The last thing I wanted was some sort of Perle stalker casting creepy shadows over my event.

"Nolan Huton. And of course I didn't give out those details."

Gavin ran a hand across his chin. "With only two hotels in town, it wouldn't be hard to figure out. And it sounds like this Nolan fellow really wants to know."

I cast my memory back to my last conversation with the designer. "Perle was sounding anxious on the phone. Maybe Nolan is the reason she's bringing the other two with her and wants them close by."

Gavin leaned in. "Do you want me to talk to Frank?"

I consider Police Chief Frank Reynolds a friend, but I saw no reason to take this up as an official matter. "No." I held up my hand. "Let's just keep an eye out for the guy and watch him when he shows up."

"It's not like he'll be hard to spot," Linda offered. "You and he may be the only men in the room. Not counting Henrik."

"Hey, Henrik counts," I teased. "If hot girls can sell cars, why can't hot guys sell knitting?"

"I'm not even going to try to answer that," Gavin replied. "But rest assured, I'll be here." His low-spoken words had the air of a promise of protection. Whether it was for Jillian, me, or all of us, I couldn't tell.

CHAPTER THREE

I walked outside an hour later to see what Mom and the Gals had been up to.

A burst of gratitude and happiness spread through my chest at what I found. Mom and two other women were chatting away as they wrapped the colored squares of knitted fabric around tree trunks and branches, stitching the coverings shut with long strands of white yarn.

Barb was among a whole new set of women—evidently Mom had called a few friends—sitting on a nearby bench. Each of them wielded large knitting or crochet needles, speedily stitching more squares and rectangles in a carnival of colors. The minute one piece was done, Barb passed it to the women wrapping the trees. I felt as if I were watching the world's most adorable assembly line.

"No, Rhonda, not there," Jeanette, said. "We just did three green ones on that branch. Pick a different color."

"Everyone's a critic," Mom grumbled as she snatched

back a forest green rectangle and accepted a yellow and white granny square from Barb instead.

"How far up the trunk do you want us to go?" said Arlene, who had already started on the next tree. At this rate the whole block would be finished well before Perle showed up. Looking down the street, I could see shop owners peering out the windows at the colorful commotion.

I was just about to answer the question with a plea for an elder-safe arm's-reach-and-no-higher rule to keep ladders out of the equation when the secretary from the insurance agency two doors down poked her head out the door. "Can you use things that are already knit?"

I turned to the woman. "Nancy, you never told me you were a knitter." I'd never seen her in the shop, so I have to admit I was surprised. I was sure I knew every knitter in Collinstown—or if I didn't, Mom did.

Nancy's face reddened. "I'm not." She reached behind her to produce a burgundy scarf. "But someone left this in the office a while back and I've never quite known what to do with it. Looks homemade."

I took the scarf Nancy held out. Any knitter worth her salt can tell immediately if something is hand knit or store-bought. Nancy was right to think this was hand knit. Which was good, because I don't think any of the Gals would have stood for someone just hacking up a mall store sweater and putting it into their project. "Definitely hand knit. What do you think, Mom? Can you put it to use?"

Mom's response was to take the scarf and stretch it out along the length of the tree branch she was decorating. I shouldn't have been surprised that the length and width were a perfect match. "Meant to be," Mom declared.

Mom's outlook makes me think that when you expect serendipity, you get it. The charmed nature of her life is what keeps me from getting worked up—well, too worked up—about her increasing little slips these days.

As if to remind me, Mom turned to me and said, "What day is your woman coming?"

"Friday," half the women said in unison.

Mom didn't miss a beat. "Well, then, we'd better use anything we can get our hands on."

Jeanette pulled out her cell phone. "I'll have the church secretary go through the lost-and-found box for anything that looks handmade."

"I've got three sweaters I know I'll never finish," said another woman as she and her giant crochet hook completed a bright pink granny square. "I'd rather they go to this than sit in my project box for another year."

I felt my smile widen. "You gals are nothing short of amazing. At this rate, the whole street will be done in no time." Collinstown Yarn Day was going to be spectacular.

Friday was spectacular, sort of.

Perle turned out to be as nervous as I'd expected—and then some. As we stood beside the shop door staring out over the heads of the knitters who packed the room, Margo gave me a look. "This can't be the first time she's done this, can it?"

I had been asking myself the same question. Given our phone conversations, I was expecting Perle Lonager to be a diva. Instead, she proved a bright young woman with straw blond hair, luminous fair skin, and ethereal green-gray eyes. She looked every bit the Nordic beauty. While Danish herself, she had become captivated with the intricate-looking designs found in traditional Norwegian motifs and devised ways to make them easy and accessible to both beginning and experienced knitters. I could never quite say how she did it, but Perle made the traditional look current without shedding one bit of respect for its tradition. I found her as captivating as her patterns, and my determination to bolster her young career doubled.

One on one in person, she was calmer and a delight to talk to. Henrik's affection for her was charming if a bit over-the-top, and part of me really did hope they would choose my event to announce their engagement.

Right now, however, Perle was a nervous wreck.

"I don't know what's got her so anxious," I replied. "She knows this stuff inside and out. And she spoke so eloquently about it just this morning when I settled them in at the inn. I know her publisher is going to miss this part because his plane is delayed, but that shouldn't worry her this much. Honestly, she looks like she's waiting for lightning to come down out of the sky and strike her."

"Maybe you shouldn't have told her about the mystery caller. I think it spooked her," Margo offered.

"Only Nolan didn't show. Which is weird because he sounded like it was really important that he come to all the events." I glanced around at the shop again. Every chair was packed; every space that could hold a folding chair had one stuffed into it. I'd even had to move a few displays of yarn into the supply room so we would have space for everyone. But the crowd was almost all women, and not one of the men gave the name Nolan Huton. Perle's mystery fan didn't seem to be here.

"You did ask her about him, didn't you?"

I sat down on the ledge of the display window, currently filled with knitted-up samples of Perle's designs. Two of her stunning mitten patterns—one with the classic eight-petaled *Selbu* rose design and the other using the diamond motif featured on her dog sweater—peeked out from an antique tin loaned to me from the store down the street. A pale blue sweater, beanie, and scarf, each with a white border of geometric snowflakes, lay over a miniature chair.

I'd positioned a large photograph of Perle and Henrik inside a blue and yellow ceramic mosaic frame to finish off the display. They made such a perfect couple—I was sure her publisher's marketing department was ready to make full use of that when those two did make it official. "I did ask her about him. She said she didn't know who he was, but I'm almost certain that's not true. She tried to hide her reaction the minute I said his name."

"So we may never know what that's all about." Margo looked over my head out the window.

"Probably not." I shrugged. "I didn't think it was my place to press her on it. If it was something awful, she'd have told me to deny him entrance, don't you think?"

Margo squinted. "Linda said he sounded like a young guy?"

"Linda talked to him, not me. She said she guessed him to be in his early twenties, but who knows for sure?" I noticed Margo's expression. "Why?"

She inclined her head to the sidewalk just outside our shopwindow, in one of those don't-look-now gestures. "There's a guy pacing up and down the sidewalk, looking in your window. He's been there for ten minutes. He seems artsy. Has that Viking look about him, too."

I scowled. "Meaning what?"

"He seems like what I'd guess a young male Perle Lonager fan would look like."

"Hey, no profiling my customers." I glanced out the window just as a young man tried very hard to casually turn in the other direction. Margo was right—he clearly was lurking outside the shop. Let's just say loitering is not a problem

I usually have. "I should go talk to him. Find out what's up."

"Does anyone have any questions they'd like me to answer?" Perle said from the small podium we'd set up for her workshop. Poor thing, her voice practically squeaked.

"How about 'Are you currently being stalked?'" Margo whispered. I swatted her discreetly with a hank of silk-bamboo blend sitting in a basket next to me.

When I rose to go talk to the young man, Margo stopped me. "Let me get Gavin to check on him. You've got to go play emcee with your celebrity guest."

I relented, thinking Gavin would seem like less of a threat than the shop owner pouncing on the poor guy. Perle had enthusiastic fans; this kid was probably just one of them.

I watched Margo tap Gavin on the shoulder and whisper in his ear as I walked up the aisle between the chairs to help Perle take questions from the crowd.

"So, your knitting patterns come from your heritage?" one attendee asked.

Given how this was part of Perle's brand, I was surprised the question seemed to flummox her. "No. Well, not really. My heritage is Danish. Lots of the Nordic cultures share similarities, but it's the Norwegian *Lusekofte* and *Setesdal* motifs I find most interesting. I do have some Danish patterns, too. But it's Henrik's Norwegian culture that has the incredibly rich tradition of these two-color geometric designs we all find so captivating." She pointed to two of the samples she had brought with her. Two cardigans— one dark and one light—were hung from a rack beside her. Each combined fields of small dots with contrasting geometric borders on the yoke and cuffs. A mesmerizing rhythm of X shapes, diamonds, stripes, and curly snowflake shapes graced each piece—black for the light sweater, white for the dark one, and each with a small punch of red on the border. When people think of "ski sweaters," it's often *Lusekofte-* and *Setesdal-*style sweaters they are picturing. "And of course," Perle added, pointing to a basket of similarly patterned mittens, "the *Selbu* mittens."

Henrik smiled and modeled his own vest of white snowflakes and zigzags against a black background. The shirt he wore underneath was unbuttoned so wide, I wondered why he bothered with it at all. I also wondered if teeth came that white naturally, or if Henrik just had a great dentist.

"Of course everyone finds *him* captivating." One woman elbowed her companion in the row just in front of us. "I know I do."

I rolled my eyes and Margo shrugged. Fans were fans, and tact couldn't always be assumed.

"My new needle collection draws exclusively from my Danish culture," Perle went on. "I'm very excited about that. Really excited. I do hope you'll come to tonight's lecture, because I plan to talk a lot about it."

I thought I saw a split-second silent exchange between Perle and Henrik before she went on to answer a question about the specific design on Henrik's vest. And I wondered if anyone else noticed the flash of alarm on her face when Gavin walked in the door four questions later with the young man beside him.

"Tell an old lady the truth," Barb said after Perle acknowledged her wildly waving hand. "I read those *Selbu* mittens used to be a traditional engagement gift. Are you planning to knit Henrik any of those mittens soon?"

I fought the urge to whack my head against the podium. I fought it harder when several other members of the audience chimed in with their eagerness to hear the answer.

I gave Perle the universal female I'm-sorry-about-this

grimace. Mom's friends should have known better than to press my guests for gossip.

I tried to think of a diversionary ad lib that would give Perle a chance to gather her wits to answer that question. Henrik beat me to it, stepping toward Barb. "You know, my hands are feeling a bit cold this weekend. What do you think? Should I ask her to knit me a special pair?" he asked with a wink and an entirely too silky voice.

"I think she'd have to be crazy not to," piped up an audience member from across the room.

Henrik put a hand on his chest as if humbled by the compliment. While he wasn't exactly a humble guy, he sure looked totally in love with Perle. It was adorable, and the crowd ate it up.

"Talk about inspiring design," came another call from back where Gavin and Margo were standing.

I groaned inwardly at how much the room laughed. I genuinely liked these two and didn't want them to feel like they'd walked into a crowd of tabloid reporters. The location of the comment's speaker, however, drew Henrik's gaze to the back, and I could see the moment when Henrik saw the young man. His shoulders stiffened—in fact his whole body stiffened. Surprise? Fear? Anger? He covered it up so fast, it was hard to say.

But not so fast that it wasn't now clear to me that both Henrik *and* Perle knew who this man was. This had to be Nolan, and neither looked happy he'd shown up. Should I deny Nolan admission to the rest of the event and refund his money? Perle's peace of mind surely had to take precedence over income from one fan's three tickets.

"What's *inspiring*," Perle said in a voice clearly designed to move things along, "are the dog sweater kits you all get first dibs on today. But you'll come back tonight to hear anything more about the special announcement. Now, who wants a kit before we sell out?"

That brought a rush from the crowd, including Jillian calling, "Dad, can I have one?" Before I could look up again from handing out kits, the young mystery man was long gone.

"Where'd the guy go?" I asked Gavin as I handed him the last small-sized kits I had managed to save for Jillian and her little dachshund, Monty. "I don't know. I couldn't get his name out of him. But he knows those two," he said, inclining his head toward where Perle and Henrik were speaking together in low tones. "Did you see the way they both reacted when they saw him?"

"They weren't happy to see him, whoever he was. I don't know what to do if he shows up at the lecture tonight or at tomorrow's workshop." I stared at Perle and Henrik, unable to shake the sense that something wasn't right. They were acting like a couple in love, but that was just it—it looked like acting to me.

Sterling and I had gotten into a massive argument the day we announced our engagement. Maybe the tension had gotten to those two and they were just keeping it together for the public eye. It wasn't any of my business. "She's my top priority over a single customer. I suppose I'll have to ask her what she wants me to do."

That didn't turn out to be a helpful tactic. Perle looked exasperated that I'd even asked. "Don't worry about Nolan."

"So you do know him?" I asked. It seemed a more polite question than "Is he stalking you?"

"I don't want to talk about it." Now a bit of the diva I'd expected was coming out. "I don't see how it's any of your concern. What is your concern is tonight's lecture and the fashion show tomorrow. It's important to me that the launch of the needle line go off without a hitch. I'd like to spend between now and dinner in the theater if you don't mind, setting things up. I've got some more needles to take over there."

I'd have thought she'd want to rest, given her nerves, but what the celebrity wants, the celebrity gets. "Absolutely. I'll take you both over there right now."

"Just me, if you don't mind." The request was aimed at Henrik rather than at me.

"Darling, is that a good idea?" Henrik clearly didn't think so.

"Just me," Perle repeated in a voice that told all of us Henrik's next choice of words might launch an argument. He held up a hand in surrender.

"Just you," I replied, offering a sympathetic look to Henrik. "Got it." I grabbed the keys to the theater a block away we'd secured to hold Perle's knitwear fashion show and the launch of the needle line. She was going to sign and auction off one full set of the beautiful needles as a finale to the show and to launch the line.

I tapped Linda's arm as Perle and I headed out of the shop. "Finish up for me here while I take Perle down to the theater, okay?" In a flash of inspiration I added, "See to anything Henrik might need in the meantime."

No one needed to ask her twice. "Gladly."

W hy would Perle want to be all alone in that theater? And I think I agree with Henrik—that's not a good idea with Nolan lurking around. He looks creepy." Margo glanced down the street toward the theater as she refilled my coffee cup. Now that the exclusive store session was done and the banquet room at the inn was all set up for tonight's dinner lecture, she and I were grabbing a slice of peace and quiet at the pie shop. It seemed a good plan to fortify ourselves with caffeine and extra portions of Dream Cake before the big night.

"Great artists need their alone time, I suppose." I ate carefully so as not to get any cake on the Perle-designed cowl I wore. The circular red scarf had an array of traditional white *Setesdal* designs—roses, diamonds, and zigzags. I'd gotten a compliment on how lovely the cowl was every time I'd worn it. Perle managed to create a garment that looked both historical and contemporary at the same time—timeless, I suppose.

It made me proud to play a part in furthering her career. After all, an artistic genius like that deserved a little coddling. The truth was, I liked the woman. "She was in a bit of a mood and clearly wanted to be left alone. So I just gave her the theater key and told her to give it back to me when we meet up at her room at the inn. She said she might need help to get some things downstairs to the banquet room tonight."

Margo smirked. "Doesn't she have hunky Henrik to do that?"

I had the same thought. "You'd think. It's sweet the way he dotes on her. Maybe it ruins the artist-muse dynamic if the muse does too much work for you."

Margo practically snorted. "Nonsense. Carl hauls stuff for me all the time." Margo's husband, Carl, was a stand-up guy and as nice as they come, but women would never drool over him the way they did over Henrik. Except for Margo, of course. Since Margo measured love in calories and she and Carl never chose to have little mouths to feed, her husband's waistline is as doomed as mine. Maybe more.

"Why wasn't it certain he was coming with Perle in the first place?" Margo asked as she sank her fork into the rich cake. "Their press makes it sound like they're inseparable. They look inseparable."

"Some scheduling wrinkle. I think it has to do with the publisher coming now, too. Bev at the inn told me Derek Martingale finally checked in about half an hour ago, so at least we're okay on that front."

Margo leaned in. "Will he tell you what it is Perle is announcing tonight? He must know."

"I haven't had the chance to ask. But it sure feels like something big. The publishing house even sent out press releases about my event. New York publicists writing about Y.A.R.N.—can you imagine?"

Margo smiled. "This is going to be a great weekend for you, Libby."

"Everyone seems to think so. I haven't met Mr. Martingale yet, but he did send me an e-mail insisting that I stock even more of Perle's books than I'd originally ordered."

Margo toasted me with her coffee mug. "A three-event weekend, with the first event already a success. You're going to hit it big with this. I can feel it."

"I sure hope so." I checked my watch and polished off the final bit of cake. "Well, I'd better get on over to the inn and help Perle with whatever it is she needs."

Margo looked past my shoulder. "Who do you think that could be?" Margo pointed out her shopwindow to where a well-dressed man was coming out of my shop at a near-frantic pace. The man dashed across the street, pushing through the pie shop door seconds later. "You're here," he announced in panted breaths. "Linda said this is where I'd find you. Derek Martingale."

My pulse rose at the panicked look on his face. "Hello, Mr. Martingale. What can I do for you?"

He pushed his glasses up on his nose. "Find Perle. Because I can't."

CHAPTER FOUR

I stood up to meet Martingale's worried eyes. "I'm sure Perle is done at the theater by now. She must be in her room at the inn. I was just heading over there."

"No, she's not." His voice pitched up as he pointed toward the inn. "I knocked on her door before I came to your shop. She didn't answer her door. Or the phone in her room. Or her cell phone." He ran a hand through his slick haircut and glanced around the shop as if Perle might pop up from behind the counter. "I was hoping maybe she was with you."

I started leading Derek toward the door. "I'm sure it's nothing. Maybe Perle was running the blow-dryer or something and didn't hear you." Or maybe she and Henrik were . . . making up after their spat. It wouldn't have been the first time I'd heard of a celebrity doing something unusual to gear up for a public appearance. "Let's go over there together and we'll get her down to the banquet room, simple as that."

It wasn't simple. Not at all.

Repeated loud pounding on Perle's door succeeded only in bringing Henrik out of his room next door. "Isn't she answering?" he asked. He was pushing up the sleeves of a beautifully knit gray turtleneck sweater. Evidently he was just finishing getting dressed, as his hair was still wet and he was barefoot.

"No." Derek came close to shouting the answer. "Where is she?"

"We were just"—Henrik made what I can describe only as a very worldly face—"*preparing* about half an hour ago."

I pretended not to catch his meaning. "We're just a bit worried. We don't want to rush her. Do you happen to have a key to her room?"

His look of shock made little sense, given his last remark. "Of course not. Perle treasures her privacy." He walked over and pounded on Perle's door. "Perle, darling?" He went on in his native language, but the urgency that filled his voice when she did not answer needed no translation.

"I'm telling you, she's not in there." Derek squared off at Henrik as if he were somehow hiding the reason for Perle's absence behind his back. "If she's not at the theater, where is she?" Derek demanded.

I hadn't realized Margo had left until I saw her coming up the stairs with Beverly Thomas, the manager of the inn. "I brought Bev up with the master key just in case we need her."

That's why I adore Margo—she's always one step ahead with just what you need. "Let's get that door open," I pleaded. Perle shouldn't have been at the theater. She was supposed to be downstairs greeting guests in thirty minutes. Unless she was meditating with noise-canceling headphones on, I feared nothing behind that door was going to bode well for my event.

"Maybe you should go finish getting dressed," Derek snarked to Henrik as Bev slipped the key into the lock.

"After I find out what's happened to my Perle."

Not wanting to wait for this testosterone standoff to get any worse, I made sure I was the first person in the room when Bev swung the door open.

I stared around the empty room in startled disbelief. Perle was not inside.

We'd booked one of the nicest suites at the inn for Perle, and she'd spread herself all across the space. All her books, as well as volumes on Nordic textiles, were open and piled up on chairs and tables. Several woven baskets holding yarn in her traditional colors—red, black, white, blue—stood ready to come down to the banquet hall. Some fruit and crackers were half-eaten on the small coffee table in front of the room's plush sofa. In short, it looked exactly like the room of someone getting ready for an arts lecture—minus the lecturer.

The suite held two double beds. One bed was rumpled, but several sets of Perle's debuting needles were laid out on the room's other bed. I'd seen most of the smaller sizes, with their mother-of-pearl balls, squares, and triangle ornaments on the blunt ends, but these also included a few gorgeous examples of the larger sizes. The diameter of these needles—some as thick as broomsticks—allowed for exquisite inlaid mother-of-pearl design work on the shafts. Even in my panic, I could see how these needles were as much art pieces as they were craft supplies. Knitters would love these.

Piled up against the wall were large pasteboard photos

of *Selbu* designs and the traditional *Setesdal* sweaters Perle
had talked about in her workshop. They were similar to the
two pieces she'd shown in the shop, but also showed a variety of colors. In one, stylized white snowflakes popped
out against a field of deep blue on a cardigan; in others,
black diamonds danced with X shapes across the neck of a
black pullover. There were also red, brown, and green vests,
hats, and scarves. They looked amazingly complex despite
using just two or three colors. All the intricacy came from
their marvelous latticework designs on the yoke, collar, and
cuffs. One board showed an enlargement of the shapes and
pattern that decorated her needles. A laptop and several file
folders sat on the desk in the corner.

I ignored them and looked around the room for some
sign of what had happened. A beautiful dress in an eye-
catching red hung on the closet door, set out in preparation
for Perle's appearance. Several pieces of—of course—lovely
pearl jewelry were laid out on the nightstand ready to ac-
cessorize. Shoes and a scarf sat waiting nearby.

The only thing missing was the woman herself. Where
would Perle be this close to her big night?

I began poking around for her cell phone, her handbag,
or any other sign that she'd just ducked out for a moment.
The shower stall looked wet enough to have been recently
used—perhaps by Henrik?—but as far as I could see, she
hadn't yet dressed for the event.

"She wouldn't still be at the theater, would she?" I was
asking myself as much as anyone else in the room. Apart
from causing genuine concern for this brilliant young
woman's well-being, a Perle no-show also spelled huge
problems for me. Could some sort of accident have happened? A fall down the stairs on her way to the parking lot?

A surprise encounter with our mystery man? It didn't look to me as if she'd been planning to leave, and that spun my imagination in various unwelcome directions.

I didn't want tonight's big announcement to be that Perle Lonager had gone missing.

Henrik went to the window and looked out. "Our rental car is still here." His words were tight and fast. "She likes to take her time getting ready for appearances. This isn't like her. At all. Something is wrong."

The five of us all looked at one another. Something was definitely wrong. This didn't feel at all like a simple case of Perle losing track of time. And she couldn't have gotten lost on the two flights of stairs down to the banquet room.

Wandering about the room for any clue, I came across Perle's hotel key sitting partially hidden behind one of the needle sets on the bed. I wondered why she would leave without taking her hotel key—until I remembered that she and Henrik had connecting rooms. She must have ducked out while Henrik was in the shower, fully intending to be back while he was still in the room. But to where?

It took only a minute to realize what was missing: the key I'd given her to the theater for tomorrow's event.

"The theater key isn't here," I said, daring to feel a small wave of relief. "That must be where she is. Maybe she just needed something from over there at the last minute."

"Perle doesn't do 'last minute,'" Henrik insisted. "She must be upset about something for tonight. You'd better let me finish getting dressed and go get her."

"I think *we'll* just head on over and get her," Derek said in a you-should-have-been-doing-that-and-not-what-I-think-you-were-doing voice.

Those two weren't helping. This was my event. I was

taking charge. "You," I said as I pointed to Henrik, "get some shoes on and meet us at the theater."

Derek looked like I'd just demoted him to second place, but I wasn't having any of it. "You," I said to him as I scrawled my cell phone number on a notepad I found on the nightstand, "stay here and call me if she shows up. And if she does, get her ready as fast as you can.

"Bev," I said as I walked out the door, waving for Margo to follow me, "are there guests in the banquet room already?"

"Just a few."

"Can you go downstairs and calmly let them know things may be slightly delayed? Find Gavin and ask him to get the dinner started. Have him make some speech about Collinstown Yarn Day if he has to. We'll just start without Perle and buy ourselves enough time to get her back here and ready."

Margo and I headed down the stairs at full speed. I said a quick prayer that my event hadn't unraveled yet—had just hit a small snag.

"She wouldn't be late to her own event, would she?" Margo asked as we reached the bottom of the stairs.

"She might," I answered as we headed out the inn door in the direction of the theater. "My friend with a yarn shop in LA had a movie-star knitter in for a book signing. The woman showed up two hours late. And drunk."

"Her customers must have been furious."

"You'd think," I replied as we stepped off the curb, "but knitters rarely get upset about delays—it's just time to pull out your knitting and knock off a couple of rows."

"Let's hope that's true for your crowd."

Margo and I broke into a full run by the end of the block. Dashing down the street in heels proved a bit of a challenge, but I had enough adrenaline surging through my system to carry me clear to Delaware.

"Artists," Margo panted with an optimistic look as she rounded the corner toward the side door of the theater right beside me. "Always losing track of time, right?"

"That had better be all this is." I wasn't having much luck ignoring the growing clang of alarm in my stomach. Poor Perle had been having trouble keeping an even keel even before whatever this was; making her race to get ready wasn't going to enhance her presentation skills. And if she was nursing a massive case of cold feet, I wasn't sure I could talk her out of it. If she was upset about something, I didn't cherish the idea of walking into a room full of one angry designer and dozens of pointy sticks.

As we reached the door, I spied the key still hanging from the lock. That wasn't my idea of good security—especially given her anxiety—but at least I knew we'd found our young star. "She's in here!" I said behind me to Margo.

"Perle?" I said loudly, pushing the door open. "Is everything okay? We really need to get back to the inn." No reply.

"Perle?" I repeated as Margo and I worked our way through the rows of dark seats toward the stage. The still quiet of the large room turned my gut to ice. "It's almost time for your lecture, Perle," I called, trying to offer calm compassion with my tone of voice.

I walked up onto the stage, where racks of scarves, shawls, hats, sweaters, and blankets hung ready for tomorrow. Even as I passed the tables of needle sets, Perle was nowhere to be seen.

"She must be backstage," I said, pointing to the wall of curtains. "Only, why can't she hear us?"

When I pushed aside the thick curtains, my heart

jumped out of my chest. The whole world ground to a halt as I gasped in horror.

There, slumped up against the back wall, was Perle. Her head was cocked at a gruesome angle above what looked like a skein of red yarn wound around her neck, twisted tight around one of her needles in a lethal tourniquet. A set of the large needles lay at her feet, their mother-of-pearl beauty marred by bloody red smears on the tips.

Perle Lonager couldn't hear us—or anything—because she was dead.

CHAPTER FIVE

This can't be happening." This was the last kind of excitement I'd ever want for my shop. Police were combing the theater, now bedecked with crime scene tape and glinting under the flashing lights of patrol cars and the ambulance that would take Perle's body to the county coroner's office. My heart ached at the collection of colors in front of my eyes: black-and-white police cars, red lights, blue police uniforms—all of Perle's signature colors now used to announce her death.

We were trying to keep this out of the view of anyone at the Riverside Inn, but that was impossible. Gavin, bless him, was struggling to keep some semblance of control over the Perle fans there, but it was a lost cause. The drama of Henrik dashing through the inn looking like disaster had struck—because it had—stirred up a commotion even Gavin's best Mayor Voice couldn't hope to contain. Many of them abandoned the line into the event to follow Henrik to the theater before we could stop them. They now stood behind barricades Chief Reynolds had thrown up as quickly as he could.

It was a tragic scene in every way. When Henrik learned the fate of his beloved, the poor man lost all composure. An officer could get him to calm down for only brief moments before he dissolved once again into fits of grief and rage. "We were going to announce our engagement tonight," he wailed. The scene broke my heart.

"I don't think we can get prints off the yarn," Chief Reynolds advised. "But perhaps we'll find some on one of the needles or elsewhere on the scene. She had to have struggled as all that yarn was going around her neck."

I swallowed at the disturbing thought of being strangled by something I loved so much. How awful had Perle's last moments been? Who would do something so malevolent with something as beautiful as yarn?

"This is terrible," I moaned. I wanted Y.A.R.N. to take its place in fiber arts history, but not like this. "Will people blame me for leaving Perle alone with some crazed fan lurking about?" I looked over at Derek Martingale a few yards away. He had been on the phone and pacing for half an hour. "Is her death somehow my fault?"

Frank put a hand on my shoulder. "Don't think that way, Libby."

Out in the theater lobby, a paramedic tried to give Henrik a bottle of water. The poor man howled and tossed the bottle aside.

"So, nothing else was amiss when you entered the building?" Frank asked, taking notes.

I felt like it would be decades before Perle's empty eyes above that red yarn left my memory, if ever. "Nothing except that the door was open. Well, it was closed but unlocked. I found the key I'd given her still hanging in the lock."

Evidence technicians were already dusting the door, the key, and all kinds of surfaces. I winced as I watched an officer remove the set of large beautiful needles that were at Perle's feet and slip them into an evidence bag. My stomach lurched as they removed the hank of red yarn—twisted so brutally tight around her neck with another, smaller needle—and slipped that into a bag as well. The sight of Perle's lovely creations—the last she would ever design—being treated as criminal evidence was enough to make me lean light-headed against the wall.

"I don't know that we'll be able to establish a time of death any more accurate than what we already know," Reynolds said. "You last saw her after the workshop at your store?"

"Yes, I walked her over here," I replied. "She didn't want me to stay. I thought she just wanted some time away from everyone. She seemed anxious. She wanted me to leave her alone." I felt like I had to keep repeating that, as if I had to prove I hadn't somehow neglected Perle Lonager's safety.

"Any idea what made Ms. Lonager so anxious?"

"We wondered if it was Nolan Huton," Margo offered.

I had told Reynolds about the eager young man who'd purchased tickets to all three events and how we were almost certain he was the one who had lurked outside the shop without coming in.

"Henrik and Perle both knew him," I added. "They said they didn't, but it wasn't hard to see from the way they reacted when we brought him inside. And I don't think they liked him. Gavin didn't get a chance to confirm his name, but Henrik and Perle seemed to know who he was."

"Does his name mean anything to either of you?" Reynolds asked.

"No. He's just one of the event attendees," I replied.

Chief Reynolds tilted his head in the direction of the still-wailing Henrik. "But you think he knows him."

Henrik was literally sitting on the ground with his head in his hands. "Seems so, but I'm not sure you're going to get anything lucid out of him at the moment."

Reynolds frowned in Henrik's direction and clicked his pen. "What's this Henrik's last name?"

I looked at Margo and Margo looked at me. "I don't think any of us know. He just goes by Henrik."

"Like . . . Cher, huh?" Chief Reynolds asked dubiously.

"So, this Nolan fellow. You said he disappeared at the event in your shop. Did he show up at the inn for the lecture?"

Since we hadn't made it to the banquet room, neither Margo nor I knew. Linda and Bev were going to be handling checking the guest list.

"He had a ticket. Linda will know for sure."

"I'm going to want to have a talk with him. And Martingale. And Henrik, whenever he pulls himself together."

That didn't seem like it would be anytime soon. I had to say, I felt like sinking down to the ground myself as I looked back toward the stage. My event had become a disaster. There were serious business considerations about that, but I could barely think about them in light of Perle's death. Such a bright young life extinguished in such a ghastly manner. My heart hurt for the designs that would now never be made, how her beautiful patterns and needles would cease coming into the world. I had wanted Y.A.R.N. to be part of expanding Perle's career, not the place where it came to a terrible end.

I needed to do something—anything—to start putting it right. "How much longer until I can get on that stage? There's yarn, and clothes, and needles and . . ." The hopes

I'd had for this weekend seemed to wrap around my throat and squeeze.

I felt Margo's hand on my shoulder. "Hey, give yourself a minute here. You've been through a lot." Suddenly it felt as if Margo's hand was the only thing holding me upright. Margo turned to the chief. "Do you need Libby for anything else? Otherwise I think we should get her out of here. Take her back to the shop."

Reynolds suddenly looked more like a grandfather than a police chief. "I'll take care of it from here. I'll call you when we've finished processing the scene and you can pack things up."

It wasn't even my stuff to pack up. Maybe Henrik would insist on doing it. But I had a bone-deep craving to help Perle in any way I could. My fingers even itched to go back to the shop and start knitting another Perle-designed sweater for Hank. As if that could somehow honor her memory— which, I suppose, was as fitting a way as any. I've written only one or two patterns in my career and I'd want knitters to stitch up my designs long after I'm gone.

I let Margo lead me out of the theater and down the sidewalk, putting one foot in front of the other in a fog of sorts, until I felt her stop. "What on earth?"

I looked up to see a small crowd lined up outside Y.A.R.N. They probably didn't know where else to go or what else to do any more than I did under the circumstances. Several of my regular customers were there, offering hugs to one another and murmuring in shocked tones. Caroline was there with a friend, and she looked horrified by the night's events.

As I crossed the street, I noticed Derek Martingale stood at the head of the line, cranking out phone calls. I hadn't even noticed he'd left the theater.

"Elizabeth, dear, are you okay?" Mom said, hugging me. "It's dreadful."

"I'm so sorry," said two customers. "Is she really . . . dead?"

"I'm afraid she is." I felt my voice catch on the pronouncement. Her vibrant face and creations called to me from the shopwindow. How had this gone so horribly wrong?

Caroline put her hand to her mouth and clutched the brand-new knitting bag she'd bought from me only days earlier. She looked like I felt—as though the only thing she could think to do was to be among Perle's yarns and designs. I'd watched her at the store event earlier today. She'd been captivated. I was so thrilled to have been her envoy into the knitting world.

An unfamiliar woman beside Derek asked, "Are you going to open the shop?"

I blinked. All other reasons not to aside, it was long past shop hours. "Am I *what*?"

"Are you going to open?" she repeated. "We want to buy anything Perle you've got."

I thought they had the same impulse as me, that they wanted to hang on to something from Perle's brief life to keep her vision going. That was until the unfamiliar woman's companion said, "If you've got any of those needles, they're going to be worth a fortune now."

My regular customers sent up a howl of shock at the nerve of these women. "How dare you!" Barb scolded. "That's a thoughtless thing to say."

I loved that my customers defended Perle's memory so fiercely. No Y.A.R.N. regular would ever behave like these women. Y.A.R.N. was a community, and my customers had welcomed Perle as if she were one of their own.

These women weren't my usual store customers. They

weren't my beloved "YARNies," as Margo liked to call them. No, this small flock of fiber vultures were Perle "fans" in for the event—though I would never call them true fans.

I swallowed the urge to growl "You heartless beast" at the woman, managing to choke out, "I hardly think so," instead.

Derek looked up from his phone. "I'm having more books express shipped. They'll be here tomorrow. Do you have any way of getting more kits here by then?"

Suddenly Martingale's energetic youth took on the appearance of a spoiled brat. "You want me to open up shop and sell her stock *now*?"

One of the "fans" held up her smartphone. "They've got some of her books in a store in DC. They open tomorrow at ten."

Derek gave me a shrug that said, "You want the sales or not?"

Most of the crowd turned to stare at them. "She just *died*!" Barb scolded. "Aren't you ashamed of yourselves?"

"Was it an accident or . . . ?" a woman asked, running her finger across her throat. She had the bald-faced nerve to sound intrigued. Suddenly I felt like running back to the theater and telling Chief Reynolds to demand an evacuation of Collin Avenue.

"I think you should leave right now," Caroline declared.

"So you're not going to open." Derek looked annoyed.

"No, I'm not going to open. What's the matter with you people?"

"Where do I get my refund for tomorrow's event?" the first woman asked. I didn't even bother to answer. I simply pointed very clearly to the closed sign on the shop door and jammed my key into the lock.

"How is Henrik?" Caroline asked.

I left the key in the door—with a pang of memory that Perle had done the same—and walked over to Caroline. "He's very upset," I replied. "He seemed to love her very much." I directed my next remark to Derek. "It's a terrible loss."

"Well, of course, it's terrible," he said. But that last word never quite reached his eyes. "We'll want to honor Perle's memory in every way we can. But, Libby, you can't argue with fans who want a chance to keep her work alive. What's wrong with wanting to have some of the art she loved so much?"

"Not tonight," I shot back. "How about we show a little respect and restraint, given what's happened?"

"We were just here to support one another and Elizabeth," Mom said. "Not crash an estate sale."

My customers chimed in with their agreement and Derek held up a hand in surrender. "I can't tell you what to do." He was trying hard to look contrite, but if you ask me, he thought I was missing a golden sales opportunity.

I looked straight into Derek's beady little eyes and said, "You may be Perle's publisher, but to me you're an arrogant, reprehensible jerk. Everyone, just go home." I walked inside with Margo insistently at my heels, and pulled the shop door shut behind me. I made a big point of yanking down the shade.

The inside of the shop felt as quiet as a church. All the chairs—still in rows around the shop—sat like empty pews. I took a deep breath as Margo and I sank down in the closest row. We sat silently taking in the solemn aftermath of Perle's death.

Only, I couldn't sit still. After half a minute I began to wander around the shop, touching the softest yarns, reaching for the tactile comfort knitting had always provided me.

When Sterling left me, there were days when all I could do was make one stitch, and then another, and another, until I slowly accomplished one small row. Knitting pulled me one step at a time up the steep slope of my failed marriage until I could remake my life. Knitting was my bread crumb path home out of the scary woods. Margo was right—I needed to be here.

I ended up facing the one shop wall where I'd hung a dozen *Selbu* mittens all on a line like artful laundry. They were all Perle's clever designs, intricate, elegant, and yet still cozy. What's more cheery and comforting than hand-knit mittens? *Selbu* mittens were originally made by young Norwegian ladies as the traditional engagement gift to their future grooms. By introducing a whole new batch of contemporary knitters to this culture, I couldn't help but think Perle had tried to bring more love into the world. Who could ever cut that work short? And why?

Pulling my favorite of the designs—a brown and white mitten with a coffee cup whose swirling steam brilliantly transformed itself into one of the traditional *Selbu* snow-flake swirls—I slid my hand into the mitten's soft warmth. "You're not all gone," I whispered to the yarn. "You've left so much beauty behind."

Something hard and determined settled just under my ribs, and I clenched that mittened hand into a fist. "We'll figure it out. We'll honor your work and your life by figuring out who did this." I hadn't really known Perle, nor could I say I'd loved her, but I did love what she stood for.

I knew right then and there that somehow, someway, I'd make sure the mystery of Perle's death would be untangled.

CHAPTER SIX

I didn't sleep much Friday night. I love my colonial cottage house, just the right size for Hank and me. Mom had moved out of our family home into a modernized town house across the river, but I wanted to return to Collinstown and live in a historic home like this.

Normally I sleep like a baby, even when Hank ends up snuggled against me and snoring in my face. At first I was worried I'd feel alone when I chose this as my new home away from the sprawling suburban magazine-cover house I'd shared with Sterling. That never happened. From my first hours in this tidy brick homestead, its perfection has been my companion. Whoever said, "Being alone isn't the same as solitude," probably lived someplace like this.

Now, as I plodded my way through my first sleepless night in this house, the creaky noises of the old structure bothered rather than comforted me. I pulled Hank close, cuddling him like a large drooling teddy bear until I finally nodded off from sheer exhaustion.

My dreams were a frantic tangle of stressful scenarios. Me running through dark hallways. Perle's lifeless body floating in front of me. Pressing hordes of hard-hearted knitters lurching toward me like zombies with outstretched hands clutching yarn and jagged needles. In other words, far from the stuff of restful slumber. I woke just before dawn Saturday morning feeling as if I'd run the Boston Marathon in snowshoes.

I lay in bed for twenty minutes, giving myself any number of arguments as to why I needed more sleep. It was the morning of what should have been Perle's fashion show and the launch of her exquisite needle line. The normally rousing display of sunrise creeping across the river felt invasive instead of inviting.

By the time a decent dose of sunlight came through my curtains, I had given up. I pulled on the coziest bathrobe I owned, donned a pair of gorgeous hand-knit socks, turned on some peaceful chamber music, and settled onto the couch with a cup of coffee. With Hank beside me, I dug out the pair of beautiful needles Perle had given me upon her arrival and a ball of fuzzy yarn in a delicate ballet pink. Without really thinking of much of anything, I cast on two dozen stitches. I knit row after row as I watched the brilliant sunny morning unfold, trying to stitch solace into what I knew would be a harrowing day.

Hank sensed the shift in my mood. I firmly believe dogs notice such things and have an innate instinct to minister to us. In those hollow weeks after my divorce, Hank never left my side. He knew what I needed most was to feel his loyalty.

So many well-meaning friends lobbed purpose-filled

words at me just after I split with Sterling. I didn't need words—Sterling was always full of words. Hank communicated more with his eyes and the way he'd lay his chubby jowls on my thigh, which I preferred to the dozens and dozens of roses Sterling had sent my way in apology throughout our relationship. Let's just say I'd seen my share of compensatory flora as it all went to pieces. In fact, I knew it was really over when the "sorry" roses simply stopped coming.

Next to Hank, what got me through those first fragile days was the handful of true friends who came here to my still-empty little cottage and knit. Half the time they were sitting on thrift store furniture rather than the antiques that fill the place now, but I don't think they would have cared if they were sitting on lawn furniture from the dollar store. They brought themselves. And casseroles, and cupcakes and several boxes of obscenely expensive chocolates. It is always a fine thing to have a friend who knows how to indulge well.

Speaking of indulgence, Margo brought me a pie every day for a week. She did not blink an eye when I ate half for breakfast. If I opted to eat the other half for lunch, she just found a fork and joined in.

She and the other sweet souls showed up without any expectations. They sat on my couch next to me in my frumpy sweatshirt that might or might not have been what I had on the day before. They ignored my beyond-messy bunned hair, lack of makeup, and baggy yoga pants. We simply knit. Wordlessly creating together, which helped to remind me I hadn't lost myself in the gruesome process of separating from Sterling and his high-powered shiny family.

That need for companionship, more than anything else, was what pushed me to slip my key in the door of Y.A.R.N. Saturday morning. And I wasn't at all surprised to see

Linda and three other regular "YARNies" waiting outside the door for me to do so.

"Did *you* sleep?" Linda asked. The circles under her eyes spoke the "Because I didn't" she left unsaid.

I pushed open the door and let everyone in. "I only know I dozed off a bit because I had awful dreams when I did." I switched on the lights out of sheer habit, even though the glorious fall sunshine filled the shop from the front windows. The irony of the morning's beauty only sharpened my sense of tragedy. Today was supposed to be a victory on so many levels—for both me and Perle—and I felt every inch of how far it fell short of that goal.

Linda, bless her, headed straight for the coffee machine. As the three regular customers set their bags on the shop's center table, Linda pulled two cans of whipped cream out of her handbag. "I figured we needed these."

I hugged Linda. I'm not saying life's troubles can be solved by a can of whipped cream, but there is something soothing and even hopeful in the indulgence of a sweet, fluffy cloud on top of your coffee. Or cocoa. Or tongue. To be honest, I don't trust anyone who eats pumpkin pie without it.

As the regulars went about setting out mugs, and the scent of brewing coffee filled the air, I reached into my own bag. I extracted the whopping to-do list I'd begun before dawn and been adding to in the hours since. There were three dozen tasks on that pad of paper, and not one of them was pleasant.

I sat down—or perhaps it's more accurate to say I sank down—at the table. "I sent out an e-mail at six this morning to everyone on the fashion show ticket list. There are about fifteen with no e-mail, so we'll have to call those." I slumped farther down into my chair. "I'm not sure I've got it in me to say, 'Perle Lonager's body was discovered yesterday evening,' that many times." I couldn't even bring myself to fathom saying the much simpler "Perle has died," let alone the more awful "Perle has been killed" to anyone.

"Do you have to?" Jeanette, a sweet retired French teacher who knit the most beautiful socks I've ever seen, asked. "Can't you just say something like 'due to unforeseen circumstances'?"

I pushed out a weary breath. "An unforeseen circumstance is a canceled flight or a broken leg. I don't think murder qualifies."

My whole body flinched at the word "murder." I still couldn't quite wrap my head around the idea. A murder is a deliberate act. That meant someone wanted Perle dead. What could possibly drive anyone to a hateful feat like that? Under any circumstances, much less not half a mile from my store and during my event. I'd never known anyone who had been murdered, and I didn't want to start now.

Irrational as it was, I couldn't help thinking the crime was against me as well. That someone meant to hurt me, or at the very least wanted me to suffer the consequences of the deed. An in-the-crosshairs feeling buzzed under my skin no matter how I tried to talk myself out of it.

Usually I love my walk to work, drinking in the fresh, crisp air and the charm of our small town. I love that any walk anywhere in Collinstown means friendly waves to six or seven neighbors as you go.

Not today. This morning I had driven. I couldn't bring myself to walk, knowing I'd be fighting the nonstop urge to look over my shoulder with every step. Perle's killer was out there. And could be anywhere. The thought skittered up my spine to land in a dull, throbbing headache no aspirin would touch. Murders just didn't happen in Collinstown. Or, at least, they hadn't up until now.

Linda took one look at my tired, squinted eyes and retrieved the printout from the table in front of me. "Don't you make those calls. I'll handle it."

I didn't have the will to fight her. "It's such an unpleasant task," I moaned.

Linda squared her shoulders. "I used to be a loan officer, for heaven's sake. I know how to deliver bad news."

For the hundredth time since opening Y.A.R.N., I was grateful for Linda. No one was more thankful than I that a corporate finance downsizing had spit her out of a glossy office and she had landed, energetic and efficient, on my doorstep. Still, those calls were only one item off my too-long list. I looked down at it, trying to decide which item I felt capable of tackling first. "We'll need a sign to post on the theater door."

Arlene looked up from the ball of yarn she was pulling out of her bag. "Let me take care of that. I just finished taking a calligraphy course."

"Thanks, Arlene."

I have actually left customers in charge of the shop while I have run to the bank or ducked down the street on a quick errand, and now you know why. They're far from just customers. They consider Y.A.R.N. their shop as much as mine, and I honestly believe they'd protect it with their lives—even if the zombie apocalypse of last night's dreams actually happened.

"What do you want it to say?" Arlene asked.

I had to think about that. "Perle Lonager has died" was too jarring. "How about just 'Today's event has been canceled'? It's just in case anyone shows up at the theater, really." I walked to the utility closet at the back of the store and pulled out the little freestanding chalkboard I occasionally put in front of the shop to highlight events or sales. One of my earlier attempts at signage humor, *High Fiber Content Inside,* still covered one side.

"Why don't you use this?" I suggested. Somehow using the chalkboard felt slightly less awful than taping a piece of paper to the theater window.

Arlene nodded, walked over to the bucket of chalk by the blackboard, and began sorting through the colors. "Just 'Today's event has been canceled'? Nothing more? I mean, shouldn't we say why?"

"Oh, I think the yellow crime scene tape pretty much says why," Jeanette said with a bittersweet smile. The attempt at a joke fell rather short.

Crime. The word dogged at my heels like Hank in search of his supper.

"I suppose you could add 'See shop for refunds,'" I said. My stomach dropped at all that pretty new income that was about to fly right back out of my bank account. Not that it compared to a loss of a life as amazing as Perle's, but I still couldn't deny this was going to hit me. Hard. I hadn't been open long enough to take a setback like this. The shop had inched its way into the black two weeks ago, and now that fiscal accomplishment was going to evaporate before we closed up this evening.

"Should we issue a press release or something?" Linda asked.

I could call my new friend Caroline. An entertainment reporter would know what to do and how to do it. But I couldn't muster the courage, even though I knew Caroline would be kind and supportive. Who wants to announce tragedy and failure to the world?

The bell over the front door rang and Mom came into the shop. "Oh, hon, I knew you'd be here." She barely slid her handbag onto the table before pulling me into a giant hug.

I'm thirty-eight, and Mom can be a colossal pain most

days, but there's something timeless about a mother's hug when you're down and out. She hadn't called to say she was coming across the river—she rarely did—but I was suddenly glad to have her here.

Mom pulled back and held me by both shoulders. "Has Frank told you anything more?"

Linda was now holding a cup of coffee out to me, complete with a healthy dose of whipped cream. I stepped from mom's embrace to take it, glad for the warmth and the sweet, comforting scent. It surprised me how much comforting I seemed to need. I felt wounded, attacked myself by the attack on Perle.

I took a deep breath. "Not much. There's been a homicide detective assigned to the case. The county morgue has her body. They'll do an autopsy, I suppose."

"Strangled with yarn, you said? Red yarn?" Linda gave a shiver. "I'm almost sorry you told me. It may be months before my stomach doesn't turn at the sight of red yarn."

I felt the same way. How dare someone tarnish yarn for me? It was a crime against the very nature of knitting. Wrong on a gazillion levels.

"There are details," I replied, only half remembering what Frank had told me, on account of my brain still operating in red-alert mode. "Things they can learn."

"DNA evidence," Arlene piped up as she started working on the board. "I watch all those crime shows. They can figure out loads of stuff from what's under fingernails, bits on their clothes, body fluids. . . ."

I interrupted her before things got too gory. "Can we not?" The thought of Perle laid out on some clinical table and being picked apart like a science project sent my stomach spinning. *Murder.* Another word that kept relentlessly banging around in my head. Murder here. At my event. No matter how many times I said the facts over and over in my mind, they still wouldn't settle as reality. I gulped coffee in the vain hope that a caffeine overdose could take my headache down a notch.

Mom planted her hands on her hips. "So, who did it? Do we know?"

Count on Mom to cut right to the chase. "No," I replied. "Well, I don't. And I don't think Frank did when we talked last."

Mom accepted a cup of coffee from Linda and sat down. "Well, who are the suspects?"

I would have preferred she found the whole thing less . . . interesting. I slowly took another sip of my coffee as I formulated a reply. It wasn't as if I hadn't been besieged by the same questions all night. "It could have been any number of people, I suppose."

"Nolan Huton comes to mind," Linda said as she gave Jeanette and Arlene coffee. If Y.A.R.N. had an unofficial barista, it was Linda. "We don't know anything about him or why he's here. And he was acting sneaky."

"We should put a chart up on the wall," suggested Mom. "Don't they do that on TV? One with the pictures of all the suspects?"

"Not on your life." I scowled. "I'm not turning this shop into a detective agency." Yes, I did feel a burning need to see Perle's murder solved, but I wasn't in a hurry to be the one to solve it.

"The big fellow. Rick," Mom offered.

"Henrik?" I asked.

"He's certainly big enough and strong enough," Mom replied.

"I don't see how it could be him," Jeanette said. "He loves her."

"*Loved* her," Arlene corrected her, reminding me we'd have to start talking about Perle in the past tense.

"That's not true. He still loves her. Love doesn't stop when the person you love passes on." Jeanette's words were tinged with grief. She'd lost her husband six months ago and told me just last week she still couldn't bring herself not to put two place mats at their kitchen table. That love hadn't gone away; it just now had nowhere to go. Except for the kitten Jeanette had adopted a week ago. Linda and I had a wager going on how long it would be before Jeanette attempted to knit kitty wear.

"Of course that's absolutely true," Mom said as she put a hand on Jeanette's shoulder. "I've loved Thomas every day of the eight years he's been gone." She had. I had grown up with parents who were happily married. It's what made my divorce extra tough to swallow. Although to be honest, Sterling's transformation into a first-class cad did make it go down a little easier.

"Many a murder has been committed in the name of love." Arlene gave the words the air of a declaration, as if they were the opening line of some tragic novel.

"Not in this case. Come on, didn't you see how utterly heartbroken the man was? It was hard to watch," Jeanette said, defending Henrik.

"I saw a man who *looked* utterly heartbroken, yes," Arlene replied. "We can't go on how things look or draw conclusions like that. No one can be held above suspicion."

I had a thought that dropped my stomach to my shoes. I'd had access to Perle and been the last person to see her alive. I'd found her body. Did that put me on the suspect list? Even two gulps of hot coffee failed to warm the ice that went down my spine at that realization. No one in Collinstown would actually think I murdered Perle, would they?

CHAPTER SEVEN

Thankfully, Gavin walked into the store a few minutes later, before my Saturday-morning shop hours could turn into a meeting of the Junior Detectives' Knitting Guild.

"You holding up okay?" he asked. His voice was a weary sort of hoarse, and his shoulders were missing their usual broad set of command. He was mayor of a town that had just had its first murder in recent memory—that can't have made for an easy night. I admired him for taking the time to worry about me, but then Gavin had always been the sort to take his responsibilities very seriously.

"You shouldn't keep the shop open if it's too much," he said with genuine, more-than-mayoral concern in his eyes. "People are going to come in." By the way he said "people," I knew he didn't mean my regular customers.

"I know." I would have liked my voice to sound less shaky. Opportunistic Perle fans I thought I could handle, but would I be hounded by reporters? I wasn't so sure that the knitting world mattered enough for the press to cover this, but murder made for a juicy headline anywhere.

"It could get messy." Gavin cast his gaze between Mom and the customers. I got the sense there was a lot he wasn't saying. "I don't want you to have to . . ." His words fell off in a vague huff of worry.

"I need to be here," I assured him. "Besides, it's not as if staying home would change anything." Few things in life were more unalterable than death. "At least here I can do something about it."

"What are you going to do about it?"

I crossed my arms over my chest. "I'm not exactly sure. I made a list, but it's just the basics. Refunds, notifying people, that sort of stuff. The rest . . . I haven't figured that out yet. But," I added, "I'll be better figuring it out here."

My answer did not appear to satisfy him. Gavin gave another uneasy glance around the room. "Can we . . . ?" He nodded toward my office door. Clearly, he had something to say that didn't warrant an audience.

My "office" is really an oversized closet with the world's smallest desk, a teetering file cabinet, a narrow bookshelf, and a dog bed for Hank. As such, it was far closer quarters than I wanted to share with a man I'd once steamed up car windows with down by the river.

I opted for the stockroom, and started walking toward the back of the shop. "Let's go back there." The space was less official and was madly cluttered, but at least it gave us more breathing room.

The stockroom door was barely shut behind us when Gavin blurted out, "The Huton kid. Frank says they can't find him. He's vanished."

That news sank in my gut with an uneasy weight.

"That's certainly suspicious," I replied. My mind recalled the silhouette of him watching my shop from a distance.

"Exactly. And if the police don't know where he is, he could be anywhere." Gavin kept looking over my shoulder as if Nolan Huton were hiding in my stock shelves. As if I'd managed to let a killer on the lam slip in behind my merino wool.

"I don't know, Gavin. He's acting strange—I'll give you that—but when you brought him into the shop, I thought the he looked more scared than anything else."

"You don't know what he could have been thinking." Gavin looked as if he'd settled on Nolan's guilt already.

"Still, wouldn't he have to be boiling up a serious rage to strangle someone like that?" I gave a small involuntary shiver at the word "strangle." It seemed like such an awful way to go.

Gavin dismissed my thinking with a doubtful frown. And an intense stare—the man had riveting eyes. They were a changeable gray, like the color of clouds on a stormy morning. "Libby," he said, lowering his voice even though the door was shut, "this Huton kid *was* angry. Scared but definitely angry. And he knows where you work."

"Everyone in Collinstown knows where the shop is," I countered. "Everyone at the event, for that matter."

"Which is why maybe you should have stayed home, where he can't find you so easily. He may think you saw important evidence. Or that Perle told you something. I don't want him to be able to get to you."

His concern set a glow in my stomach warmer than Linda's coffee. As sweet as it was, Gavin's worries coaxed my own fears out of the mental box where I'd finally managed to stuff them down. Suddenly, a Perle fan on a killing spree no longer sounded as ridiculous as I'd told myself a hundred times last night. I couldn't really discount the possibility, could I?

I fought back with the same defense I'd recited to myself as I drove here this morning. "My friends are here. Linda's here. It's a public place. Isn't that safer than being home alone?" As much as I treasure the blissful solitude of my cottage, I didn't want to stay there today. Certainly not alone after everything that had happened.

A frustrated pause stretched between us before he muttered, "I suppose." He didn't sound at all convinced.

I tried harder—whether for myself or for Gavin, I wasn't sure. "And we don't know it's Nolan anyway. Hundreds of people knew Perle was going to be here last night. It could be any of the people who bought a ticket. Or someone else entirely. I don't know that the police have any idea who they're looking for."

"Who do *you* think they ought to be looking for?"

I had spent far too much time fretting over that question. Just to keep my gaze averted from the intensity of Gavin's eyes, I began rearranging the balls of mohair-silk blend on the shelf next to me. "The way I see it, it had to be someone Perle knew. If she locked the door—and I'm guessing she did—she had to open it up to let whoever it was inside." I had to admit, the notion that Perle was killed by someone she knew just made the whole thing more tragic.

Gavin ran a thoughtful hand across his chin. "That's true."

"And the space over at the theater is too big for someone to have snuck up on her. Not only that, but you can't strangle someone from a distance."

Gavin's jaw tightened. "But you can strangle them from behind."

I imagined the sudden shock of something coming around my neck from behind, and swallowed hard. Such a terrible, violent act. "I don't think she'd let just any fan in. She seemed to really want to be alone. Who else would she have let in there with her?"

"There was that guy from the publishing house, yes?"

"Yes and no. He arrived late enough to miss the workshop, and when I saw him, he was running around town looking for her."

Gavin leaned back against one of the shelves. "A conveniently public alibi."

I finished rearranging one box and moved on to the second. A small wave of nausea rose up as I touched the balls of red yarn. "I'll admit he's lacking in scruples, but I can't think of a reason why Derek Martingale would do it. Why take out his star author like that? He seems too smart to shoot himself in the foot, even if he had some kind of beef with her."

"What about Henrik?"

He seemed the least likely choice to me. "Have you seen him? The man's in pieces. If those tears aren't real, he could be in the running for an Oscar." The man was completely, utterly undone. I wasn't sure he could fake that. "But I still don't think it's Nolan."

Gavin raised an eyebrow. "Why not?"

"Well, for one thing, I think whoever it is would be doing anything he or she could *not* to look guilty. Which would mean not disappearing into thin air and drawing attention with their absence."

"Well, he clearly had an issue with Perle. Or Henrik, or both. He had a mouth on him when I tried to get him to come into the shop yesterday afternoon. Maybe you didn't see it, but I saw an angry man. If you ask me, he was the kind of guy volatile enough to do something like that."

I didn't like sorting through murder suspects. I should have been sorting through event sales, or new yarn orders, or deciding which classes Y.A.R.N. should start offering. I groaned and let my head fall against the shelves, tired and overwhelmed.

"Libby, please, until Frank sorts this out, promise me you'll be careful." He let his hand rest on my shoulder for a second, then checked his watch and pushed out a weary breath. "I've got to go sign off on a statement from the mayor's office. I was hoping for a load of press from your event, but . . ."

"Yeah, I know." I sighed my agreement. "Not this kind."

"The town's . . . well . . . I'm doing damage control the best I can."

Gavin is so gung ho about Collinstown, it's adorable. The man was born to be our mayor, and he was very good at it. This would be a new test of his leadership. Murder isn't exactly good for tourism, and our town thrives on weekend and day trip business. I could see all the consequences of Perle's death spinning behind Gavin's eyes.

Collinstown Yarn Day indeed. I'd be taking that certificate down off the wall first thing when I got out of the stockroom.

I heard the store phone ring, and Linda's emphatically accommodating voice uttering the word "refund."

"It's started," I said, trying not to sound like the whine of a balloon deflating. "I'm going to be spending my day issuing refunds." Not even store credit—this was going to have to be a cash-back kind of deal. What should have been Y.A.R.N.'s big leap forward had been turned into a massive "never mind." There was no getting returns on the significant marketing and advertising dollars I'd spent. The shop was going to lose a whopping amount of money on this, even if we sold every bit of the Perle merchandise we'd brought in. Margo didn't have a pie dish deep enough for this one.

As wrecked as I felt, Gavin looked almost as bad. He

took Collinstown's success so very seriously. This was bigger than just my setback—I knew Gavin was weighted down by how it would affect the whole town.

Even forgetting the financial implications, someone had died. Here in our happy—okay, quirky and occasionally aggravating—little town. The wrongness of it stuck to both of us like a thick fog. "Are you going to be okay?" I felt I had to ask.

"Me? Oh, yeah, sure. I'll be fine." It was obvious neither of us believed him. He had a long day ahead of him. It made his trip here to check on me all the more endearing.

"Me, too," I said with about as much confidence. I put my hand on the stockroom door. It was time to get back out there and face the world.

"Just . . . be cautious," he implored again. "Don't take chances. Call me or Frank if you need anything, or something doesn't feel right."

It was going to be a long time before things felt "right" in my world. Still, I appreciated the sentiment. "I will. Let's just hope we find out who did this quickly so we can all get on with it."

"Get on with it" had been one of Gavin's favorite sayings for coping with anything. I adopted it when we were a couple, and it hasn't left me yet.

It seemed like excellent advice for the day.

I said, "Just get on with it" all through the endless stream of inquiries and refunds that filled the following hours. Several customers came by to check on me, to say how sorry they were about Perle's untimely demise. I appreciated their support, but none of it seemed to help me rise above the dark flood of anxiety. I was stuck in disaster mode, overflowing my emotional banks, and no amount of peaceful, lovely knitting seemed to hold back the current.

Chief Reynolds came over that afternoon to hand back the theater key to me. "We're done over there. You can start doing . . . whatever it is you need to do."

"Thanks, Frank," I said almost mechanically. I couldn't understand how I could feel so raw and so numb at the same time. I stared down at the key as it sat uncomfortably in my palm. It was a beautiful key, one of those big old-fashioned kinds with a long shaft fixed to an oversized oval top. It looked as vintage and classy as the theater itself when I used it to turn the ornate brass locks on the theater's side door.

I fingered the lighter color of the worn metal on the top. Perle had held this key. Perle had left it in the door. She had likely turned it to let in whoever had taken her life.

I was in no rush to go back into that space. At the same time, I hated the idea of all that yarn and those gorgeous needles held hostage to crime scene protocol. They were inanimate objects, unaffected by the atmosphere. Still, I felt as though they would never shake off where they'd been any more than I could shake off what I'd been through.

"How are you holding up?" Frank asked as he took off his hat.

"Okay, I guess." How are you supposed to feel when a murder has been committed at the event you'd hoped would launch your store? "Derailed" came close. "Frightened"? Take your pick of trauma adjectives—I seemed to be cascading through them by the hour.

"It can wait, you know."

"No," I replied, squaring my get-on-with-it shoulders, "it can't. I'll feel better knowing everything is back where it belongs." Of course, that couldn't really be true, but rescuing it all from the scene of the crime would have to do for now.

I heard Mom's voice in my mind even though she was just a few feet away. *Get out of your own head. Think about someone other than yourself.* I had just lost a business asset. Henrik had just lost the woman he loved. "What about Henrik? How is he?"

Frank let out an exasperated breath. "The man's a tad on the extreme side. Can't really get much out of him at the moment. The most I could do was get him to agree not to leave until we could get his full statement. But at the moment I don't even know the man's last name."

"And here I'd always thought of Norwegians as the strong, silent type."

"He's neither of those at the moment." Frank shook his head. "I don't know how to handle wild cards like him. I told the Martingale fellow and Bev to keep an eye on him until we can try again tomorrow."

I reached for my coat. It was time to get started packing things up over there. Margo had said she'd help me when we were cleared to get into the theater. "Do you know anything more? From the coroner or whoever?"

"We've confirmed the cause and time of death. Of course, that wasn't anything we didn't know before. Coroner says there were no other marks or signs of injury on her body. Preliminary toxicology shows no sign of drugs, poison, or alcohol, but the other tests can take weeks. Her prints are on the needles that were by her body, but they're only ones. There's some blood on them, so we've sent that to the lab."

Blood on knitting needles. The image struck me as beyond wrong. "So she used them, not the murderer."

Frank nodded. "Self-defense, I gather. They were pretty

big ones. Still, that doesn't tell us much without lab results, and even those may not tell us what we need to know."

It seemed to me that we should have more information by now, but I was new to all this, and I trusted that Frank was good at his job. "Okay." I nodded as I texted Margo, Ready to go over there?

Frank put his hat back on his head. "Libby, we'll sort this out. And I'm sorry your event got ruined. Marjorie likes this place. We were pulling for you. Still are." Frank's daughter, Marjorie, was a knitter. She'd made a very handsome forest green pullover for her father for his birthday last month and he came in on his day off just to show it to me.

"Anything else you need from me?"

He shook his head. "Not right now. We already got your statement. You just get on with fetching the stuff from over there. We went over the place with a fine-tooth comb, but if something turns up, or if anything useful comes to you, you know where to find me." Frank gave my elbow a squeeze and headed out the door just as Margo came across the street. She was pushing one of the large rolling carts from the store, filled with boxes. While the yarn, needles, and garments over there were a mix of what I'd ordered for the store and what Perle had brought with her for the event, everything was going to come back to my shop until we could figure out what came next.

"Any news?" she asked, turning to watch Frank take his leave.

"Nothing we didn't know already."

"Want my help?" Mom called from her seat at the table.

I know her heart was in the right place, but Mom's constant chatter and distractible nature weren't going to be useful in this situation. "No, Mom. You stay here and keep an eye on Hank. Help with the register if Linda is swamped with refund calls."

"Gotcha," Mom said with a nod. "Will do."

I closed my eyes for a fortifying moment before tightening my fingers around the key. "Okay, Linda, let's get over there."

As I pulled the shop door shut behind me, I caught sight of the dozen or so beautifully decorated trees. The spectacle of color and texture stopped me in my tracks. Mom and the Gals had done a marvelous job in Perle's honor. In Perle's *memory* now. A lead weight dropped into my stomach as I remembered, for what felt like the hundredth time, that today was Collinstown Yarn Day. Can you take back a proclamation? Pull it down like I had the certificate or return it like a pillow that clashed with your couch?

I was pondering that sad thought when Margo grabbed my elbow and muttered, "Uh-oh. Incoming."

CHAPTER EIGHT

Margo nodded up the street to where Chamber of Commerce president George Barker was barreling down the sidewalk at an irritated speed. "He looks peeved."

George, for all his salesmanship, had a terrific talent for getting peeved. And peeving other people. It made for an oddly annoying dynamic in the man. People were known to call him King George behind his back, which, as you can imagine in a colonial town like Collinstown, wasn't a nod to his leadership skills. He was the only person I'd ever met who could smile, shake your hand, and look down his nose at you all at the same time.

George loved to lead—he just had no idea how bad he was at it. As the self-described "premiere real estate broker" of Collinstown—never mind the two other real estate offices in town—George saw himself as the vision caster of local success. That wasn't in itself a bad thing, except that in George it manifested as a fiercely competitive streak.

Collinstown's success was only as valid as his success. If he felt someone was more successful than him, well, it was never pretty.

One look at the man's pumping fists and furrowed eyebrows told me George wasn't on his way over here to console me. "Should we make a run for it?" Margo whispered.

"No, he's seen us." Knowing George, if I tried to duck into the theater, he'd probably stomp on in right behind me. I put my hand to my forehead. "I'm really not up for this right now." Stopping our progress toward the door, I used the last shred of my composure to paste on a smile and say, "Hello, George."

"Vera and I go away for three nights to the Realtors' convention and you vandalize Collin Avenue?"

"What?" I said, too weary to follow George's train of thought.

He looked at me as if I were lacking in wits. "The trees. There's yarn all over our trees."

"The yarn bombing?"

I wouldn't have thought George's scowl could deepen. Clearly, the man did not appreciate the fine art of yarn bombing. "I was never in favor of Gavin singling you out for your own day."

It would be just like Gavin to leave out that the vote wasn't unanimous. I could have guessed that the one dissenting vote was George's. There seemed little point in replying even if I'd had a good comeback for that.

"And what do you do? You take that as license to take over the entire town for your event." He flung a beefy hand toward the nearest tree, one decked out with a lovely set of crocheted circles in primary colors. "They might as well be advertising billboards. We look like a circus."

"That's art, George," Margo defended me. "It's not advertising. Besides, I hardly think today is—"

George cut her off. "It's yarn, and you're a yarn shop. That makes it advertising. All the other businesses have to pay for that sort of thing, you know. How would you like it if I stuck one of my signs in your window?"

I looked down the street. Mom and the Gals had indeed bombed the tree right in front of George's office. Knowing Mom, it was deliberate.

"The town council approved it," I shot back, and then wanted to slap my own forehead for letting my temper get the best of me. Why on earth, today of all days, was I getting into it with King George?

"*They* approved Collinstown Yarn *Day*." He said it with such a sneer that I had no doubt he'd cast the dissenting vote. George could never see the beauty in something like this— to him it was only someone getting an unfair advantage over his spectacular business skills. "No one approved"—he pointed up and down the block as if the decorated branches had directly yanked profits out of his pocket—"that."

Margo stepped between us. "When did you get back into town, George?"

"An hour ago." He crossed his arms over his chest. "I practically drove off the road as I came down here and got a load of this nonsense."

I like to think of myself as having a long fuse, but George was toeing right up to the end of it.

"Then perhaps it would help you to know that Libby's celebrity guest was murdered last night."

George's mouth snapped shut. While I would like to have thought his expression was shock and horror at the loss of life and my misfortune, George was more likely calculating how a murder might put a dent in Collinstown home values.

Margo narrowed her eyes at George. "This might be the moment when you say how sorry you are that something so terrible has happened to a fellow business owner and neighbor." She didn't say "friend" because no one was actually sure George had any friends. Every human in Collinstown was a "potential customer" to George, and everyone knows that isn't the same thing at all. Well, everyone but George.

"I'm sorry for your misfortune," George said with all the bland obedience of a bickering kindergartner told to apologize.

"Thank you," I managed, despite the flurry of less gracious responses barreling through my head.

"And for the black mark now on our fair town."

He looked down his nose at me as if I'd personally brought crime to Collinstown's doorstep. Hadn't I?

"Now, if you don't mind," I said, "I'm rather busy at the moment. It's all been very difficult, as you can imagine."

I took it as an act of universal grace that George simply nodded. If he got into it any more with me at the moment, I was sure I'd say something we'd all regret.

"Thank you for your concern," Margo said, not entirely hiding the sarcasm in her voice. "See you at the next Chamber meeting."

Margo took the handle of the cart from my irritated iron grip and began pushing it across the street. I gave George one last look and followed her as George turned and stalked up the sidewalk. I wouldn't be surprised if he came down the street with a pair of scissors tomorrow, determined to "unbomb" every tree once my "Yarn Day" was over.

To my surprise, one tiny corner of my heart thought how

good it would feel to beat that man as Chamber president. If I wasn't sure he would be a spectacularly sore loser, it would almost be worth it.

"So this is vandalism, is it?" Margo snapped in George's direction. "What does that make all those Barker Realty yard signs, then? Lawn ornaments?"

Any other day I might have had a good laugh at that. Or run back up the street to ask if I couldn't put a little Y.A.R.N. blackboard sign on every customer's front lawn the way he did. Today I could only shake my head and take a deep breath. "He's just being George."

"He's jealous," Margo grumbled as we lifted the cart onto the curb in front of the theater. "King George wants his own day."

"Collinstown Grump Day?" I sneered, feeling worthy of the title myself.

Margo stopped and gave me a tight hug. "See? You're not beaten by this if you can make a joke. Even one as bad as that. You'll get through this, Libby."

I hadn't realized how much I needed someone to say that to me. "Thanks." I hugged my friend right back. George had a lot more to be jealous of than some proclamation and a bunch of decorated trees. I had Margo, Gavin, Frank, and a load of dear shop regulars who were so much more than customers. "For everything," I added, feeling a bit weepy. Friends like those I had in Collinstown were the reason I was so grateful to have come back here to start over again.

Speaking of starting over again, Margo began pushing the cart resolutely toward the theater door. "Well, let's get in there and see what needs doing."

My breath hitched as Margo pushed aside the strip of yellow tape so that I could fit the key into the ornate lock.

The click of the tumblers echoed too loudly into the quiet space. What had been an ordinary creaky door yesterday now gave an ominous groan as we pushed it open to maneuver the cart into the theater's back hallway. Unnerved by the dark, I groped across the wall next to me until I found the light switch. It snapped on, the click and resulting buzz of the overhead lights noisily invading the empty room.

Even though we had come just a few feet into the building, the whole place felt unnaturally—dare I say deathly—quiet. As if it had been hollowed out, even though the only thing missing was Perle—and whoever had sent her to her death.

For a few irrationally panicked seconds, I considered that we didn't actually know that. It wasn't impossible that the killer was still hiding in here. It was a far-fetched idea—half a dozen law enforcement personnel had just combed the place. Still, I couldn't help but wonder . . . and worry.

"You don't think . . . ?" Clearly, Margo's brain had gone down the same suspicious path.

"No," I replied with more confidence than I felt. "Couldn't be, right?"

"Right," Margo agreed halfheartedly. "Right."

We began pushing the cart down the wide aisle between the dark green velvet seats, and I confess my eyes scanned every shadow of the vacant hall.

"Okay, then, let's get this stuff counted to see if anything's missing and get it back to the store. The sooner we get out of here, the better."

The police had done a crime scene search. What we truly didn't know, however, was if any of the show stock was missing. I'd be the only person to know that, given that I was handling the transactions for Perle and she'd given me a com-

plete list of the yarn and needles she had for sale. I also had
a complete list of the garments since she'd shipped them
ahead of time and we had been discussing which of them
would be auctioned off at the end of the show.

I'd like to think no one was so low as to steal knitting
or needles from a dead woman, but there was no denying the stock in here was worth a fair amount of money. I
couldn't rule out the possibility of theft somehow being part of
the motive for murder. But what did I know? Turning amateur sleuth hadn't been a chapter in my business plan for
Y.A.R.N.

Margo stood beside me, both of us hesitating to walk
farther onto the stage, where a lone light was on.

"What's with the light?" Margo asked, pointing to the
single bulb sitting on a stand in the center of the stage.

With a shudder I remembered the tradition from my
drama class in college. "That's the ghost light. It's a theater
thing. Supposedly every theater has a ghost, and this is to
keep them away."

"Well, if it didn't before, I guess this one has a ghost
now."

I didn't find the thought at all comforting, but chose to
press on. "It's got to be here," I said as I pushed the cart
toward the side ramp that led up to the stage. "Somewhere
in here there has to be a hint as to why it happened."

Margo grabbed the front of the cart and pulled as I
pushed. "Why do you say that?"

"Perle was so insistent that she spend time here alone.
And so specific that the stock stay here before the show."

"Which is weird," Margo said as we made our way onto
the stage.

"Or just artistic. Whatever's here—or isn't here—may
have nothing to do with why she was murdered." When

Margo gave me a skeptical frown, I replied, "You're right. I don't believe that, either."

Once the cart was settled onstage we both surveyed the scene. The original setup had been rather artful—a vignette of tables, textiles, enlarged images of the needles sitting on easels, baskets of the needle sets, and a few garments. Most of the other garments were on a rack backstage to be worn in the fashion show that was to feature a few local women as well as Perle and, of course, Henrik.

"Any idea *what* we're looking for?" Margo asked as I walked to the side of the stage and threw the switch that bathed the stage in bright work lights. The banished shadows made us both feel better. Together we began piling the empty boxes from our cart onto the stage in front of each of the displays.

"Not a clue," I replied as I set an empty box down in front of a breathtaking blue and white Nordic sweater with a matching hat and mittens laid out across a bentwood rocking chair. Perle's work really was extraordinary. "I'm sort of hoping we'll know it when we see it. If we see it."

I wasn't quite ready to venture to that backstage alcove where I'd first discovered Perle's body, so I pulled out my paperwork and walked over to the first basket of smaller needles. "My gut says to start with the needles. They were the whole point of today, after all."

I handed Margo the sheet documenting all the yarn on-site. Loads more were available in my shop down the street, but we did have a limited selection on sale here in the theater. "You start with the yarn. Then we'll both tackle the garments."

We managed to work in thoughtful silence for about half an hour before the quiet of the place began to make my skin crawl. I was grateful when Margo decided to make conversation. "How'd that appointment go with your mom's new doctor on Monday?"

As distracting subjects go, this wasn't a true winner. Mom's old general practitioner had retired, and the new, younger doctor taking his place wasn't winning Mom over. Mostly because he wasn't letting her get away with half the stuff her old doctor did. Moving on to the medium-sized needles, I answered, "Better than I expected."

Margo slid several hanks of gorgeous turquoise wool into a bag and checked a line off on the stock sheet. "Meaning?"

"Meaning she told this doctor she's exercising, but I think he knows she's lying. He pressed her about it, so she shot back with a rather enthusiastic complaint about the cost of her medicines. When that didn't work, she defaulted to a rousing chorus of 'Elizabeth worries too much.'"

Margo looked at me. "You do worry."

"If you had a mom who found her cell phone in the freezer last week, you'd worry, too. I asked him if he'd take an appointment with me but without her, and he agreed. A little too easily for my peace of mind actually. Like he's got something to tell me Mom will either deny or isn't ready to hear." I wasn't sure I was ready to hear it, either.

"Maybe it's just him trying to be nice. It took me half an hour to find my reading glasses yesterday morning, and that was because they were on my head. I thought only old people did that kind of stuff. We're not old."

"No, we're overworked," I defended, thinking about my own far-too-long hunt for car keys a few days earlier. The past twenty-four hours made me feel like I had no brain cells left at all. They all fled my body with the ghastly image of Perle's lifeless corpse.

I pulled a dozen exquisite pairs of size ten needles out from their basket and slid them into their shipping box.

How she managed to get all that beautiful inlaid design on them and still keep them smooth enough for even the finest yarns was beyond me. I dearly hoped we'd still get to sell these. These deserved to be in the hands of devoted knitters, not tucked away in boxes unused.

Margo moved on to a box of bright red yarn. "Your mom told me she goes to the YMCA twice a week for aqua aerobics. Is that not true?"

I started on the next basket of needles. "Well, she does go to the Y twice a week." A singular design was worked into all the needles, but it grew in intricacy and complexity with the expanded space of the larger needles. Each size had a different ornament on the blunt end. As such, all the needles had versions of the same design, yet each size was unique. It made for a visually exquisite set. I had already put in my own personal order for two full sets: a second set for me and one for Mom's much-requested Christmas present. I also ordered several of the extra-large sizes Perle offered at an additional price. Those were even more expensive, and I didn't often knit with those really large needles, but they were a marvel to behold. Now I was glad I'd made the purchase. "As for exercise," I went on, "let's just say I doubt Dr. Gregory would classify gossiping in the hot tub as exercise. Mom's version of aqua aerobics is more of a spectator sport."

"Oh, dear," Margo said.

"It's not exactly out of character for her," I replied.

"No, something else." I turned to find Margo holding the large bag of red yarn and the stock sheet. "We're missing one hank of this color." In the moment it took her to swallow hard, I followed her thinking. Our murder weapon. It was impossible to even get my brain to grasp the concept of yarn as a murder weapon.

It hadn't hit me until just this moment. "Yarn from *my* store was used to murder someone." It came out as a sad sort of whimper.

"Yarn *stolen* from your store was used as a murder weapon. It's not like they left a twenty-dollar bill in the bag for payment. And that does not make you an accessory to murder."

My sigh seemed to well up from the bottom of my shoes. "Let's hope that's the only thing missing and we can clear all of this out of here as soon as possible."

Margo tried to make conversation again as we continued the inventory, but I just wasn't in the mood. Normally I'm grateful to talk to someone about my mounting worries over Mom, or her continual antics, but not today. I didn't like the silence much, but I couldn't muster up the energy for conversation when the thought of my yarn around Perle's neck kept pounding me down.

We were on the last of the yarn and the largest sizes of the needles when I stopped and recounted. And counted again, not trusting my stressed-out brain cells. There was no denying it.

"I expected to be missing one set of these," I said to Margo as I held up a pair of Perle's largest needles. These were great big ones, size fifty, almost the size of a broomstick. "But we're not. So either there was an extra set we missed, or the needles they found with Perle came from ones she brought and not our show stock."

"I have to say, it's going to be a long time before I look at any needle that size and don't think of it as a murder weapon. But the needles didn't kill her, did they?"

"No," I confirmed. "They think Perle used them in self-defense." Small traces of blood had been found on the tips of both needles, and Perle bore no wounds other than the marks of strangulation around her neck. "But if I had to pick any knitting accessories to use as a weapon, those would be the ones."

I fought the wave of nausea that hit me. "I hate that we're even having this conversation. Can I just say that?"

"You can absolutely say that," Margo replied. "Let's pack up and get out of here. The air is getting too thick to think."

That's exactly how the atmosphere felt—too thick to think. I was going to have to unravel the mystery of where those two extra needles came from, but I had little hope of doing it in here.

CHAPTER NINE

After Margo and I shuttled the stock back to the store and I called in our findings to Chief Reynolds, I tried to have a conversation with Mom.

I say "tried" because if there is one thing my mother is a consummate expert in, it is avoiding conversations she does not want to have.

As we sat at the store table packing up the extra yarn to go into the storage room, I ventured a casual "So, have you thought about that supplement Dr. Gregory recommended?"

"He's such a handsome fellow, that man. He's only about ten years older than you. I could set you up, maybe."

"I'm not dating your doctor. Ever." Round two: "Are you going to try it? It sounded like a good idea to me."

"I don't need vitamins for my brain. I'd love one for my knees, but I don't think they make those."

They do actually, but that wasn't the point of this discussion. I wanted to see if Mom would even consider the fact that her clarity wasn't what it used to be. I suspected Dr. Gregory had the same goal in suggesting the supplement. Mom ignored more advice than she took from her old doctor, and I was hoping this new one would have better success.

"Why not try it?" I tried to ask with ordinary curiosity. "I read that lots of people take vitamins to boost brainpower."

"Reading up on my supposed ailments, hmm?" Mom's glance had a watch-your-next-move edge to it. "Did you see how expensive that stuff is? Insurance doesn't cover vitamins, you know."

So she had looked at it. I filed that away under "Tiny Victories."

"It was easier to swallow those ridiculous prices when I knew you and Sterling were living off those fat profits. Now I just can't stand the thought of padding his pockets."

"Sterling's company doesn't make vitamins, Mom. And even if he did, wouldn't Dr. Gregory's recommendation be reason enough to try it?"

Mom deployed the irrational midconversation topic switch, of which she was a master. "It's been a dreadful, long day. Do you want to come back across the river for dinner? Or we could eat in town. Just as long as I make it home by dark. My car doesn't drive well in the dark anymore."

I didn't believe Mom's night vision issues were the fault of Toyota, but that was an argument for another day. "Thanks, but no. I barely slept and I just want to go home."

She caught the tone of my voice and pulled me into a hug. "Oh, sweetheart, I hate that this happened to your big day."

"Me, too," I replied, feeling small and young and over-whelmed.

"I raised a tough cookie. You'll get through this. Fix yourself a nice dinner and walk Hank and tuck yourself in. It's got to look better in the morning."

"Yeah," I agreed. "I think I'll walk Hank along the river before we drive back home. Maybe pick up something to eat on the way. You head on back."

"Want company on your walk?"

Walking Hank was a favorite activity of Mom's, but my brain needed space and solitude to sort things out. "No, I'm fine. Head on over the bridge before the traffic gets bad."

After a big smooch, Mom headed out the door as I grabbed my coat and Hank's leash. I didn't even have to say a word. At the sight of his leash, Hank made for the door with an enthusiasm that sprouted one of my first smiles in hours. I turned the keys to lock the shop behind me with a tiny burst of accomplishment.

It's been my experience that few problems in life cannot be made better by a twilight walk by the river with a dog.

With Hank clad in his dapper Perle sweater, his amiable waddle beside me managed to settle my spirits. I began to feel the storm of worries subside somewhat as we walked. There's something about the flow of a river, its constancy, the eternal feeling of the moving water, that soothes like nothing else. A river feels old and wise. As though it has survived centuries and always will.

The riverfront is one of the most charming things about Collinstown, in my opinion. A small cobblestone path winds its way along the side closest to town, dotted with small benches perfect for a rest or a ponder. Even a gazebo or two sit at the prettiest points.

Hank and I walk this path often, wandering past locals and tourists picnicking or painting or just taking in the view. The far bank gives a sense of scope and perspective, while the near bank surrounds you with a thousand little details— grasses and ducks and ripples of current. If I could knit scenery, this would most definitely be the scenery I'd knit.

Several neighbors, out walking with friends or dogs of their own, stopped to offer words of support. As in most small towns, it had taken milliseconds for such sensational news to spread. As far as I could tell, none of them held George's disparaging viewpoint. In fact, two shop customers pulled me into enormous hugs, spouting their confidence that this, too, would pass.

Every hundred yards or so, Hank would swivel his head around and stare at me with his great big brown eyes as if to say, "You doing okay back there?"

Was I? I couldn't be sure. The shock of the tragedy had worn off a bit, leaving in its wake an odd combination of determination to survive—both as a business owner and as a woman—and curiosity about the crime. Who would want Perle dead? Why?

Of course, the police were on the case. And I had confidence in Frank and the county team that had been called in. But I found I couldn't leave it at that. My mind kept replaying that moment at the shop from the night before when I had returned after discovering Perle's lifeless body. I kept feeling my hand clenched inside one of Perle's beautiful mittens. I made a promise last night, one I intended to keep. I would indeed do all I could to see justice done for Perle. I had to. Even though I still had no idea what that meant, or what I'd discover, the conviction to see it through seemed to be the one solid thing I could hang on to as chaos swirled around me.

After all, I was a knitter, and we knitters are great at sensing patterns. We're also a highly persistent bunch, known to methodically work our way down a complex piece of lace knitting to find that one dropped stitch that threw everything off. These were characteristics that would serve me well. If I just kept my eyes open to all details and followed where they led, I could unravel this. And I would.

I was so lost in my thoughts, I nearly walked straight into one of the riverside benches, where a young man sat. It wasn't until Hank woofed a greeting—Hank feels it his duty to say hello to everyone—that I realized with a start who the young man was.

Nolan Huton.

CHAPTER TEN

His frightened eyes darted up at me as he made a move to flee the bench.

"No, please!" I said, grabbing his arm. "Don't run. We've been looking for you."

"I didn't do it!" he shouted, yanking his arm out of my grip. For a spindly young man, Nolan was surprisingly strong.

"If that's true," I replied, "hiding isn't helping anyone believe that. Don't run."

His eyes held as much sadness as fear as he glanced all around us. We were standing on an open part of the riverfront that didn't offer many clean escapes. There wasn't really anywhere to run. Nolan must have realized it, because he fidgeted, swallowed hard, but didn't try to run.

He was a lanky sort, limbs dangling from a lean torso with spiky white-blond hair atop an angular face. He wore the trendy distressed clothes of an urban artist, accessorized with an earring, chunky rings, and a collection of leather bands gathered on each wrist. More the type to be at a music festival than booking a weekend getaway in quaint Collinstown. Perhaps that's why he'd hidden earlier; he stuck out like a sore thumb here.

I sat down, hoping that would convince him to do the same. He had good reason to look terrified—so that didn't surprise me—but the sadness did. It struck me as stemming from more than simple fan devotion. I applied an old rule of knitting problem-solving: start at the stitch you can see. "You knew her," I ventured. When he didn't deny it, I went on. "And I'm pretty sure she knew you."

"Maybe." He more gulped the word out than spoke it. He shook his hands as if they itched. "I didn't do it," he repeated.

I opted for the most obvious question. "I'm trying to figure out why you didn't come into the shop yesterday afternoon. Why did you stay outside? You had tickets for all three events."

Nolan looked away toward the river, spinning the ring on his index finger nervously with one thumb. I could tell he was deciding whether he could trust me, calculating how much to reveal. I remembered a tactic Sterling always touted, letting the silence do the work in a negotiation, so I simply sat there while Nolan fidgeted.

Hank, who never listened to Sterling, walked over and showed the young man his best wide-eyed pout. Nolan gave the tiniest of laughs as he reached out to pat Hank's head. Sometimes adorableness gets more results than strategy.

"I did want to see her, you know."

That much was clear. Nolan's thrift-store-chic wardrobe didn't cast him as a man flush with cash, and the event tickets weren't cheap. It had cost him a lot to come—so why had he?

"I don't doubt that."

We sat for a few more minutes, Hank doing a splendid job of applying animal cuteness to keep Nolan from walking away.

The session of dog petting also drew my attention to the intricate tattoo that ran down Nolan's left arm. It looked like the "sleeve" of tattoos so popular these days. As Nolan ran a hand across Hank's wide, flat head, I studied the sleeve. It wasn't so much the presence of it that startled me as it was the design.

It looked exactly like a version of the inlay work on Perle's needles. In fact, it bore a remarkable resemblance to the designs on the big size fifty ones—the kind left at the crime scene. The ones we seemed to have gained an extra pair of.

That couldn't have been just coincidence. Had Nolan brought that extra pair to the theater? And if so, how and why? Was he the person Perle let into the building?

I had to be careful about what I said next. "That's Perle's design, isn't it?" I said, nodding toward his forearm.

"No, it's not." His words were quick and sharp.

I wanted to say, "Look, you're already in enough trouble, so don't mess with me," but that wasn't going to get either of us anywhere. Instead, I opted for "It looks to me just like the design on her size fifty needles. I just packed them up a few hours ago."

"It's *my* design," he countered bitterly. "I sold it to her."

Had they had some kind of business relationship that went sour? I'd heard Perle use the phrase "my designs" more than once. Lots of artistic people gather work from multiple sources, and Perle was quick to talk about the cultural traditions that inspired her designs. But she didn't seem like the kind to use the talents of someone else to create those needles and not give them credit.

I opted not to pick at that point just yet and to try a gentler approach, given how upset he looked. "It's beautiful. You're very talented."

The compliment did manage to soften the hard edge in his shoulders. The fidgeting slowed and he slumped forward a bit, making him look even younger. He couldn't have been more than twenty-five.

"So Perle was a customer of yours? She bought your design to use on her needles?" I didn't think that required her to give him credit, but artists can be very touchy about that sort of thing. If Nolan felt she was promoting his design as hers—which seemed to be what she had done—could that have soured things between them? Enough for murder?

That seemed extreme, especially given how Hank had taken to him. Hank, like most dogs, is an excellent judge of character. Still, it had to be considered, especially given the way Nolan had been acting. All that sneaky behavior was making him the prime suspect from where I stood.

"Sorta. Not really. Well, it's complicated."

Time to uncomplicate things. I pivoted to face him directly. "Nolan, exactly how did you know Perle?"

The fidgeting returned and he shifted his weight on the bench several times before blurting out, "She's my aunt."

I didn't know how I hadn't seen the resemblance before. His eyes were the same arresting shade of blue as hers, and the set of his chin mirrored Perle's striking features. The blond hair had been bleached to a funky white, but I could see hints of the flaxen color of Perle's longer tresses. She was long and willowy to his lean and lanky, but the body types were essentially the same.

"My mom was her sister. Older sister."

Was the past tense used on Perle's account or for another reason? "Were they close?" I asked.

The sharp dark laugh he gave at that told me they weren't.

"Does she know? Your mom? Have you told her about what happened to Perle?"

"Kind of tough to do that. Mom's been gone for seven years. Car accident." His attempt to deliver the information with a neutral tone failed. I don't claim to be psychic, but even Hank could have picked up on the dark water under that bridge.

"I'm sorry. It's hard to lose a parent at any age, but I think it's especially hard when you're young." He had to have been only in his teens when his mother died. That had to be devastating at such a volatile age.

Nolan slumped back in the bench, finally shedding that I'm-gonna-run-at-any-moment air he'd been giving off. "Yeah, well, she and Aunt Perle weren't exactly close. They weren't even speaking to each other when Mom died."

A broken relationship that would never be repaired. Was there anything sadder than that?

"I'm sorry about what happened to Perle, too." I thought to ask, "How did you hear she had been . . ." I couldn't bring myself to say the word in front of him. "That it hadn't been an accident?" After all, he'd disappeared after the workshop and no one could find him. How had he heard the news? His instant I-didn't-do-it! declaration told me he surely knew.

He shrugged, but not before I noticed a bit of a flinch. "Dunno. I just heard."

No one "just hears" that their aunt was murdered. Given how hard Frank and the team had looked for him, he had been hiding. And, it seemed, lurking somewhere. A chill skittered down my spine as I thought he might have been hiding in that theater when I found Perle. Or when Margo and I were back in there earlier today.

I told myself he didn't look like a murderer. Then again, does anybody? Does anybody really know what someone else is capable of?

I watched the light start to fade from the east side of the river. I couldn't let this man slip back into the shadows. "You need to talk to the police, Nolan."

He tensed up again. "No, I don't."

"Yes, you do. You're making it far worse by hiding and not cooperating."

"I'm not hiding. I'm keeping away from the Viking idiot."

"Henrik?" Now things were getting interesting. Henrik hadn't been pleased to see Nolan show up in the back of the shop. Then again, neither had Perle. "Why do you need to steer clear of him?"

Nolan gave me an incredulous look. "Isn't it obvious?"

"Well, I admit he didn't look happy to see you, but you knew he would be here when you bought the tickets." Which brought up another point. "How did you know he would be there, Nolan? We hadn't announced it when you called and ordered your tickets."

"Aunt Perle and I had been talking. Well, e-mailing and texting mostly. She told me he was coming."

I shifted my feet as Hank settled down beside them, clearly resigned to the fact that our walk wasn't going to continue anytime soon. "But Perle didn't seem that pleased to see you, either."

"We were fighting."

"About what?"

Nolan stood up, and for a moment I thought he was going to run off. Instead, he paced the brick walk in front of the bench. "At first I thought I was going to get to design all the needles. But then she only bought the one design. She said she was going to adapt that one design to put on the rest of the needles, and she didn't need me to do that. That wasn't fair. She gave me an extra payment when she realized she could do it all from that one design, but it wasn't what I could have made from doing all the needles. I wasn't her partner anymore. I was just another vendor." He sat down again, bitterness cutting a deep edge into his words.

"So she broke your contract with her?" That didn't sound like Perle to me.

Nolan gave me a look that told me there had been no contract. Just assumptions between family members. Fertile ground for misunderstandings, to be sure.

All the revenue from the needles would have been hers. Needles that would have been in high demand and at a hefty price point. We were getting a little closer to a viable motive here.

My thoughts must have shown on my face, because Nolan pointed at me. "Yeah, I'm ticked. Really pissed off actually. But not enough to . . ." His words fell off. Evidently he couldn't bring himself to use the word "murder," either. But the needles found at Perle's feet were the large ones with the full version of his design. That seemed like too important a clue to ignore.

"Did Henrik know about this?"

"Who knows what she tells the 'Viking' idiot? I don't know what it is she sees in that jerk anyway," Nolan huffed, putting "Viking" in jabbed air quotes. He clearly didn't think much of Henrik as his aunt's muse or business partner. There was more to that, but I didn't get the impression he was ready to share it.

"I get the feeling you weren't in favor of their engagement."

Nolan's eyes grew fierce. "I can't believe she was gonna *marry* him. I thought . . ." He let his voice trail off. "Nothing."

"Henrik led us to believe they were going to announce it last night. You didn't know?"

"Of course I didn't know. I kept trying to talk her out of even considering it." Nolan tossed a hopeless hand in the air. "Not that she would have listened."

"He seems to love her very much."

Nolan cocked his head to one side. "Yeah, *looks* that way, doesn't it?" His emphasis spoke volumes.

"You don't think so?"

Nolan opened his mouth as if to launch into a laundry list of Henrik's lesser qualities, but he snapped it shut and simply said, "No."

So Perle and Henrik might have been irritated that Nolan showed at their big weekend. Fearful, perhaps, that he'd do something to ruin it if he'd already made his opinion of Henrik and the prospect of Perle marrying him known.

Nolan Huton seemed strong enough, and perhaps bitter enough, to strangle Perle Lonager. But it still didn't sit right with me. If his beef with Perle seemed to be over the needles, why use the yarn to kill her when the needles in question were right there?

"What will you do now?"

"Who wants to know?"

"The police, for one. Seriously, Nolan, you've got to go talk to them." I pulled out my phone. "At the very least, you should know I'm going to tell them what you've told me." I gave him a pointed look. "Don't you think it would sound a whole lot better coming from you?"

He shifted on the bench as if disappearing into the night was his preferred choice. Not wanting to let that happen, I pressed him. "Don't you want the person who did this to Perle to get caught? To pay? The police need to know what you know. Right now they don't know how you're connected to Perle, and they could be making all kinds of assumptions. And based on how you've been acting, they aren't ones that will work in your favor." When he still looked as if he'd vault up off the bench at any moment, I added, "You're kidding yourself if you think they won't find you eventually."

"They'll think I did it."

As far as I could see, the police were already thinking that, and I was getting exasperated at Nolan's foolishness. "So don't hand them reasons to think you did. Cooperate with them. That's a way better choice than hiding. Or running. You're making yourself look like the guilty party."

Nolan stood up, and I thought all was lost. I had no hope of keeping him here by force if he chose to turn and walk away. I'd made my case, but he didn't look like he was going to agree with me anytime soon.

Think. Fast. I opened the contacts screen on my phone. "I can have Chief Reynolds here in five minutes. Let him hear what you just told me from you, not from me. You seem like a smart guy, so act like it."

It must have been a full minute before he finally nodded his agreement. The moment he did, I hit the connect button on my phone.

"I'm sitting here on a riverside bench with Nolan Huton," I said when Frank came on the line. "Could you join us?" I didn't have a lot of confidence that I could convince Nolan to head down to the station.

"Huton?" Frank sounded impressed. "You found Huton?"

"Well, Hank found him first," I said, trying to lighten the tension of the moment. "We're just beyond the Bryson place, past the gazebo."

"I'll be there in five minutes. Maybe four."

In a flash of brilliance, I looked at Nolan and asked, "When's the last time you ate?"

He wasn't expecting that question. "Huh?"

"What do you take on your cheeseburger?"

He blinked, looked startled for a moment, and then said, "Um . . . ketchup and mayo."

I returned to my phone, victorious in my tactic to keep Nolan from dashing off while Frank was in transit. "Stop by Tom's on your way. Get my regular, and one with ketchup and mayo for Mr. Huton. Put it on my tab."

"If you've got Nolan Huton, I'll do the buying," Frank said. "See you in ten minutes."

I settled back and patted the bench beside me. "Tom's Riverside Diner makes the best cheeseburgers in Maryland and you look hungry."

There aren't too many of the male species not lured by the promise of a great cheeseburger. Many of the female species—myself included—as well. Hank looked up at me as Nolan settled himself uneasily back down on the bench. "No worries, Hank," I said. "I'll share."

I didn't do it," Nolan said the moment Frank walked up to where we were sitting.

"Nobody says you did. *Yet*," Frank replied, handing greasy brown bags from Tom's Riverside Diner to Nolan and me. The kid tore into his burger with the enthusiasm of someone who hadn't eaten since breakfast. Score one for women's intuition and persuasion tactics. "'Course, you're not helping yourself with the disappearing act you pulled."

As I bit into my own sumptuous, artery-clogging burger,

I sent Nolan a what-he-said look. "Nolan does have information I think you need to hear."

In between bites of burger and handfuls of fries, Nolan told Frank about his relationship to Perle and his disapproval of Henrik. The dark look Henrik had given Nolan in my store was starting to make a lot of sense. Still, I couldn't work out why Nolan and Perle were at such odds, even if things were dicey between them over the needles.

Especially when Frank asked, "Was she your only living relative? No grandmother? Your dad?"

"Dad and I stopped getting along just after Mom died. My sister sides too much with Dad. And Gran? Let's just say I could only take so much disapproval before I skipped town."

"How did you leave things with Perle the last time you talked?" Frank asked, digging into his own order of fries.

"We . . . fought." Nolan's tone told me it hadn't been a small fight, either. "I was ticked off that she'd taken my design and used it on all the needles. That wasn't what we had planned."

Frank gave a grunt. "Do you have that in writing?"

Nolan rolled his eyes, probably because Frank had expressed the same sentiment I had. "She was my aunt. What did I need a contract for?"

"This," I replied. "Now it's just your word with no document to back it up. Henrik could claim the designs were his and you'd have no way to disprove it."

"Don't I?" Nolan held out his arm, showing off the tattoo. "I think this makes my case just fine."

I'd spent enough time around Sterling's attorneys to know it didn't. "Not unless you've had your arm dated and notarized."

"Jeez, what's the matter with you people?" Nolan shot back. "I said I didn't do it."

"Everybody says they didn't do it," Frank said with enough exasperation that I thought Nolan was going to leave the rest of his burger untouched.

I decided on a different tactic. "What do you know about Derek Martingale? The man from Perle's publishing house."

Nolan stiffened immediately, despite saying, "Nothing."

I didn't believe that for a second, and neither did Frank. "Don't be stupid, son. Tell us what you know."

Nolan rose up off the bench, leaving the food behind. "I don't know anything."

I suspect even Hank could have seen that wasn't true. "So you don't know why Perle was so insistent all of a sudden that he be here for the event?" I asked.

"I just told you I don't know anything about that guy." He was lying. He knew something.

"Nolan . . ."

"Are we done here?" Nolan said angrily.

"You tell me," Frank nearly growled.

"Okay, I'm telling you. We're done here." He looked smart enough not to antagonize the police in his position, but clearly the kid had a temper. Now seemed a poor time to show it. Nolan gave me one last dark look before turning his back to us and stalking up the path.

"Don't be dumb enough to leave town," Frank called after him.

"Or what?" Nolan shouted into the night air without turning around. "You'll arrest me?"

"I'd like to," Frank muttered as we watched Nolan's lanky form head down the path. "Believe me, I would. Smart-ass kid."

CHAPTER ELEVEN

The shop didn't open until noon on Sunday, and I relished the peace and quiet of the morning after such a tumultuous Saturday. I'd planned on a celebratory brunch with Margo, and she tried to get me to keep the date, but I opted out. There didn't seem much worth celebrating, and I didn't want to risk a million questions, even for the very good eggs Benedict at my favorite spot.

There was only one engagement I felt like keeping, and that was with my latest knitting student. Hank gave a cheerful bark as Jillian pushed the shop door open after lunch. She wore a friendly smile and a bright purple backpack, bending over to give Hank a playful pat on the head. "Hi, Ms. Beckett."

As Gavin walked in behind her, it was so easy to see she was her father's daughter. Gavin's sandy hair was halfway between brown and blond, with just enough wave to make it look continually mussed. That look had always done me in when I was a teenager, and I had to admit it still gave the man a particular charm. Gavin moved with powerful, athletic grace, which combined with his considerable height gave him an instant air of authority. The unruly hair, however, softened his appearance enough to give him the handsome accessibility I have always thought helped him win his landslide victory in the run for mayor.

He was the opposite of King George in every possible way—and I considered that a very good thing. While he hung on to his Chamber presidency with an iron grip, George was somehow smart enough to realize he could never get elected mayor of Collinstown. Personally, I hoped Gavin stayed in office a long time. A smart and sensible politician is a rare thing this close to DC, and I was grateful to count Gavin as an ally.

Gavin's unruly waves manifested themselves as soft curls in Jillian's long hair, currently pulled back into a thick braid down her back. She had her father's gray eyes as well, but hers were large and doelike where Gavin's were intense. His eyes were still capable of being downright mesmerizing—not that I'd ever admit that to anyone.

Looking at Jillian, I could also see her mother in the girl's still-awkward teenage features. Much like Sterling, Gavin's ex-wife, Tasha, had been stunningly attractive on the outside while turning out to be far less appealing on the inside. I'll live to be a hundred and never quite figure out why some people change so dramatically—or maybe just reveal their true colors—after they say, "I do."

We'd both felt duped and burned by our marriages, but I give Gavin a lot of credit. He continually took the higher road as much as he could on account of Jillian. I'm not sure I could say the same of myself when it came to Sterling. Suffice to say, most of my current nicknames for Sterling couldn't be said in front of Jillian.

Gavin clearly wanted to speak with me. "Got a moment before she gets started?" he said, nodding toward the stockroom. It wasn't hard to guess the subject matter if it needed to be discussed out of Jillian's earshot.

"Jillian, honey, I know you want to begin right away on your dog sweater, but we're going to start you off with some simple stitches on a small project." I pointed to where I'd set out a basket with some skeins of basic yarn in a wide variety of bright colors. "Linda will get you set up with needles and some hot chocolate while I grab a word with your dad."

"Okay." She gave us a grin and plunked her backpack down on the table.

Gavin made a beeline for the stockroom while his daughter meandered over to the basket and began sorting through the colors.

"So, you found Nolan Huton." I was expecting a happier face at that observation, but Gavin's eyebrows were practically furrowed into his eyelashes. Why is it God always gives men the best eyelashes? We women crave them and pay hoards of money for magical thickening or lengthening mascaras while men just *get* them.

"Well," I said, repeating what I'd told Frank, "technically it was Hank who found him. I just kept him talking and staying in sight until I could get Frank on the scene."

"With cheeseburgers?"

I resisted planting one hand defiantly on my hip, not enjoying his dubious tone. I'd been rather proud of my persuasive tactics. "Can you think of a better way to get a starving artist to stick around?"

Gavin gestured in the direction of the river. "He's suspected of murder and you walked up to him *alone*?"

Let's just pause for a moment here. Protective male

dominance has never been my thing. Call it a trigger, or a hot button, or whatever pop-therapy term you'd like, but anytime a man even comes close to implying that I can't handle myself, I get snarky. Fast.

Just because this was Gavin, and we shared a long history, didn't get him off the hook for the look he was giving me at the moment. I had no doubt that if Frank had stumbled across Nolan, we wouldn't have learned half of what we did. Who knew I was skilled at playing "good cop" to Frank's "bad cop"?

And a very self-sufficient good cop at that. "As a matter of fact," I replied, "I did. But I had Hank with me."

Gavin looked as if Hank was flimsy protection. He's not, and I have seen that dog produce a threatening growl on the rare needed occasions, but I didn't feel like splitting that hair at the moment. "As you can see, I am quite fine. And we now have more information because of it. I didn't see any point in letting him get away."

Gavin would probably have defined "not letting him get away" as tackling Nolan to the ground. I doubt that would have gotten anybody anywhere. "I would have called Frank," he grumbled.

"Which I did."

"Right away."

I crossed my hands over my chest—something I found myself doing way too much in this man's presence lately. "Nolan wouldn't have talked to Frank if I had called him right away. Which would have meant not learning some very useful things."

"Frank mentioned some of it, yes." The begrudging admission in Gavin's voice was almost amusing.

"Well, if you want more details from me you're going to need to wait until after Jillian's lesson." *And until you get that caveman chip off your shoulder,* I added silently. "I'm fine. I don't regret it, and while your concern is appreciated"—not entirely true—"it's not your call."

"Fine." He opened the stockroom door and gestured me out into my own shop.

I walked out, feeling a bit victorious. Gavin was a dear man with a protective streak a mile wide, but I wasn't the sweet, besotted teenager I was back when we were in high school. "Thank you."

"You're welcome." Could everyone hear the hint of gritted teeth in his words, or just me? "Jillian, just walk down to my office when you're done here, okay?" One of the joys of living in a small town like Collinstown is that you can ask your thirteen-year-old daughter to walk anywhere on her own with confidence that she'll be okay. Evidently in Gavin's view, that safety did not extend to thirty-eight-year-olds confronting potential criminals.

I was puzzled by Jillian's near smirk as she watched her father walk out the door in a thinly veiled huff. It looked to me as if she rather enjoyed her father's irritation. Was that the simple defiance of teenage years, or did the girl take after her mother more than I realized?

"Dad was crazy worried about you," Jillian offered as I settled myself at the table with her, my giant mug of coffee keeping her hot cocoa company.

"This whole business has everyone a bit shaken up," I replied. I gave her a genuine smile. "Which is why it's so nice to get to do something like teach you how to knit." I nodded toward the lovely blue and lime hanks of yarn she had chosen. "Good choices."

"Thanks. What's first?"

Nothing could have been a better balm to my frazzled nerves than her enthusiasm. "We turn these skeins into balls so they're easier to work with." We have a spindle and winder that does this task quickly, but I have always preferred the traditional method most people see in old paintings—one person holding the skein while another winds the yarn into a tidy ball. As we worked, stopping occasionally to sip our drinks, Jillian and I talked about the kinds of things that are important to girls her age. She eagerly offered her opinion on school, braces, mean girls, and why algebra doesn't seem to be the least bit important.

I was especially happy to weigh in on that last one by showing her how knitters use a quadratic equation to check gauge and to adapt patterns.

"You actually use that stuff?"

"At least once a week," I replied as I snipped off the end of one ball of the gorgeous royal blue wool and began another. "There's a lot of math in knitting."

"I think I'll like knitting a whole lot more than math."

"Who knows? Maybe knitting will improve your opinion of math."

Jillian gave me a smirk. "Mrs. Fredericks sure won't. She keeps saying, 'Math is fun,' but I've never seen anyone make math less fun in my life."

"My Mrs. Fredericks," I offered, "was a Mr. Dawson. And he had the same opinion of chemistry. Which is not fun, or nearly as useful to a knitter as math."

Her giggle struck up a warm glow in my heart. I genuinely liked this girl.

Once we'd finished the ball winding, I grabbed a set of needles. "You strike me as the smart type, so I'm going to teach you a more complicated way to cast on."

"Cast on?"

I made a slipknot about two feet down the strand of yarn and slid it onto the needle in my left hand. "That's what we call it when you mount the first row of stitches on your needle."

"Gotcha," Jillian affirmed.

"This method is called the long-tail cast-on." I waved the length of yarn on the opposite end of the slipknot from the ball of yarn. "It's a bit harder to learn, but you can use it on almost every kind of project."

I demonstrated, and true to my prediction, Jillian caught on quickly. The grin she gave me as she held up her twenty-five perfectly cast on stitches made me grin myself. There's something so satisfying about giving someone—especially a young person—a sense of accomplishment.

I had hoped Gavin wouldn't feel a need to cancel this lesson. I would have understood, seeing as Gavin and I had way more on our plates as a result of Perle's murder. But looking at Jillian's fascination confirmed my belief that canceling would have been the wrong choice—most especially for me. This lesson was exactly what I needed: a peek into a future generation of knitters.

We added the second needle, and I slowly went through the basics of the knit stitch. After a few demonstrated stitches, I handed the set of needles to Jillian and she tackled her first row of knitting one fumbling stitch at a time. Halfway down the row, Jillian looked up from her work and asked, "Was it creepy? Finding that lady dead, I mean."

Kids and their directness. "It was," I replied. "I liked her very much and I'm really sorry it happened."

"Dad said it wasn't an accident."

Points to Gavin for finding a softer word than "murder" to relay what had happened.

"No, it wasn't. And I'm really sorry about that, too."

"Dad's pretty freaked out about it. He's worried tourists might stop coming."

I wasn't quite sure what to say to that. "Your dad takes his job as mayor very seriously."

She rolled her eyes. "Dad takes everything seriously."

I laughed. "I remember feeling the same way about my father at your age."

By the end of her second row, Jillian wasn't fumbling anymore. As a matter of fact, she took to knitting at lightning speed. She finished her third row and handed it to me for inspection much faster than I expected.

"Not a single dropped stitch," I admired. "You're a natural."

Jillian grinned and promptly executed another perfect row. "Dad said you captured the guy who did it."

I thought "captured" sounded more dramatic than necessary. "Not exactly. I found someone who knows things we need to know about Perle and can help us figure out what happened. We don't know if Nolan 'did it.'"

After a second I realized she knew a few too many details. "Did your dad tell you those things?"

A sheepish look crossed her face. "No. But I heard him talking to Chief Reynolds."

Somebody had been eavesdropping. "Both Chief Reynolds and I would tell you that in this country we presume people are innocent until we can prove them guilty. I'll admit Nolan's done some things that make him look suspicious, but frightened people often make bad choices. I'm just glad we got to talk to him." That was an oversimplification of presumed innocence and interrogating a person of interest in a case, but I hoped it would allow us to move on to happier subjects.

Not so. "I mean it about Dad being crazy worried about you. He was getting all worked up as he was talking to Chief Reynolds."

While it isn't hard to picture Gavin "getting all worked up," he certainly shouldn't have been doing so on my account. And I wasn't sure why Jillian thought it was so important that I know that until she leaned in and whispered, "He let it slip you guys used to date before he met Mom." She clearly enjoyed knowing that secret.

"*Way* before he met your mom," I corrected.

"But you were super serious."

"Did he say it like that?"

Jillian sat back. "No, but I could tell." For a moment Jillian looked thirteen going on thirty-three.

Gavin and I were "super serious," in that all-consuming way that only teenagers can be. I was madly in love with him back then. Gavin and I had grown up in very different directions, and that was turbulent water under a very old bridge.

Still, one look at the young girl in front of me and I could tell where this was heading. Recounting my dreamy teenage love affair with her father wasn't the way to go.

I was grateful to be able to point out, "You dropped your stitch there. And your dad and I were a long time ago. We're very different people now."

Just my luck, she picked up the wayward stitch in a jiffy. "But you're not married anymore now, either, are you?"

Leave it to a thirteen-year-old to put it so bluntly. "I think you're ready to learn how to purl." I avoided further conversation on this topic by showing her the second of knitting's two basic stitches. It required a bit more of her concentration, and for a few minutes we worked in companionable silence—me on the second of Perle's dog sweaters I was stitching up for Hank, and Jillian on the small rectangle that would become a cute little pocket while she learned knitting's basic skills.

Her cease-fire of invasive questions lasted only two rows. "So, do you have a boyfriend?" she asked. Jillian possessed her father's persistence—in spades.

I heard Linda chuckle softly from the sales counter.

"People my age do not have 'boyfriends.'" I don't know that that's entirely true, but I have never found the term appropriate. Not that I've found a decent alternative, but then again I haven't had a chance to need the term yet. Opening Y.A.R.N. consumed enough of my attention to keep me off the market. "But no," I went on, "I don't, and I'm rather fine without one at the moment."

Jillian turned her needles and started on another row. "Dad's been on a few dates. He thinks I don't know, but when he puts on one of his good shirts, it's pretty obvious."

This made me laugh hard enough to nearly spit out my coffee. Poor Gavin. I wondered if he knew just how much scrutiny he was under. And just how shamelessly his daughter was selling him out.

"I can tell when it goes badly, too." Her voice held an amusing presumption of authority.

I shouldn't have encouraged such talk, but I couldn't resist. "Oh, really?"

"Yup." She nodded. "He makes a huge breakfast the next morning and goes off on some speech about how I'm not dating until I'm eighteen."

I could picture this with incredible ease. And it would definitely take a courageous soul to date the daughter of Mayor Gavin Maddock. "Just how many huge breakfasts have you had these days?"

It was a mistake to show any curiosity. "Oh," she said, "so you'd like to know, huh?"

I set down my knitting. "Jillian, did you really come here to learn to knit? Or is something else going on?"

"Oh, no, I really want to learn. I want to make the sweater for Monty and a scarf for Dad. Plus, Mom says I need a hobby that doesn't involve me staring at a screen." She batted her enormous eyes innocently. "Why?"

I met her gaze directly. "Because I'm getting the feeling you're really here to try to set me up with your dad. And you're smart—you should know that isn't really any of your business."

"I think it's totally my business. I mean, I've got friends with totally fiendish stepmoms." She punctuated that last declaration with a dramatic eye roll.

Awkwardness aside, I was growing rather fond of Jillian's spunk—not that I'd admit to that right now. "Fiendish?" Jillian boasted an impressive vocabulary of over-the-top terms.

"Totally."

"Your dad adores you," I replied, holding her gaze with an earnest seriousness. "I can't name another man who would accompany his daughter to a knitting event just because she wanted to knit a sweater for her dog. He's not going to bring someone fiendish into your life." In the back of my mind, I considered that Gavin had already had his share of fiendishness in how Tasha conducted herself before and during their divorce. In fact, I was rather shocked to hear he was back in the dating pool already. Tasha had done him enough wrong to put him off women for a decade, if you ask me.

"I hear stories," Jillian said, sounding once again all too much like an adult. "I gotta be careful."

"I don't think you do," I assured her. There was a glimpse of the little girl whose life had been turned upside down. To hear Gavin tell it, Tasha hadn't paid much attention to Jillian at all after she opted to ditch the conventions of Maryland life to "find her true self" in the Caribbean.

I'm all for people finding their true selves—heaven knows I feel like I've done it—but not at the expense of their children. Antics like Tasha's stuck a knife in my chest after wanting kids for so long and not being able to have them. Too many people had no concept of how precious children are.

"Your dad's careful enough for both of you. You're gonna be just fine." I bumped her shoulder in a friendly way to cover the pinch I felt in my heart. We shared a surprisingly warm little moment before I opted to move this lesson along.

"You've picked this up faster than most of the adults I teach. Ready to learn how to decrease?" I showed her the end of the rectangle that narrowed down to a point so that the piece could be folded to resemble a small knitted envelope. Most people need two lessons to get the whole way through the small project, but Jillian was going to polish it off in one. "Then you can pick out a button to finish it."

"Cool," she replied, eagerness lighting sparkles in her eyes. "This is even more fun than I thought it'd be."

She might have been an unapologetic meddler, but I was defenseless against her sweet enthusiasm. "You know," I replied, "I was just thinking the same thing."

By the time our hour was over, Jillian's little pocket project was completely stitched. She beamed with pride as she chose a bright silver button and sewed it on. "Could I make another one for my cell phone out of the same yarn?"

"Sure. But it'll take algebra."

"Bring it on."

I showed Jillian how to measure her phone and calculate the stitches and rows per inch.

"Whoa," she said as she stared at the pattern we'd sketched out. "It really works. Maybe math isn't totally evil."

She made me laugh again. I'd like to think I personally redeemed algebra—and maybe even Mrs. Fredericks—that afternoon. And today I really needed a boost like that. "Only just a little bit. Someday when you have to balance a checkbook, you may find it way more evil."

"What's a checkbook?"

Ah, youth. How effortlessly they can remind you how old you are. "I expect your father is waiting for you down at the town hall. Next time we can start on a scarf for him, so be thinking about colors. You'll be ready to start on your dog sweater kit in no time if you keep this up."

"Sure thing." Her smile was so endearing as she stuffed everything into her backpack. "Thanks, Ms. Beckett."

"My pleasure, Jillian." It was.

As she trotted off down the street toward her dad's office, I took a moment to savor the feeling of a smile on my face. The last couple of days hadn't given me much to smile about, and a mountain of problems still loomed ahead of me. But I had opened up a new world of craft for one girl. That counted for something. Maybe it counted for a lot.

"No shortage of opinions in that one, huh?" Linda chuckled as we watched Jillian. "She's a lot like her father."

I thought of Jillian's less-than-subtle hints. "From what I've heard, that's better than taking after her mother." Then, with a laugh of my own, I added, "But then again, Jillian sounds a bit too much like *my* mother."

"We should keep those two away from each other," Linda offered. "If Rhonda and Jillian joined forces, Gavin wouldn't stand a chance." After a moment, she added, "Neither would you."

"There's where you're wrong. I've had years of practice evading Mom's meddling. And I doubt Gavin's any more enamored of a reunion romance than I am. Besides, Jillian just needs someone to encourage her. I don't need to be dating her dad to do that."

As I was still gazing down the street, I saw Henrik push through the front doors of the Riverside Inn. His face pinched into a scowl, he wasted no time making an angry beeline straight for my shop.

"Which stage of grief is anger?" Linda asked, backing into the shop.

"I'm not sure, but I expect we're about to find out."

CHAPTER TWELVE

"You went through her things," Henrik snapped even before he was two steps into the shop.

"Pardon?" Henrik was intimidating when he was happily doting on Perle. Angry and grieving, he was a bit
frightening. A wall of blond fury filled up my doorway.

"Her hotel room. You must have gone through her things.
Why did you do that?"

I reminded myself this angry Viking had just lost the
love of his life under horrible circumstances, and spoke as
calmly as I could. "I have not been in Perle's room since we
were in there together."

"Someone has." He began stalking around the shop as if
he'd find the culprit hiding among the worsted wool. "Someone's been through Perle's things. Her *personal* things."

I had been through her needles and our yarn from the
theater, but that wasn't the same as going through her personal items in her hotel room. "I would think that the police

would have had to search her room at the inn. What's wrong, Henrik?"

"Things are missing." His ice-blue eyes blazed in pain. "They *cannot* take her things." Henrik's gaze wandered over to the string of mittens still hung up on my shop wall, a varied display of Perle's clever designs. If I had come into the shop to discover someone had taken a pair of those, I'd have been upset as well. Neither of us was ready to bear the fallout of Perle being *gone*.

"It's Derek," Henrik said. "He was in there while she went to the theater. It has to be him. I've never trusted that man. Have the police talked to him?"

"Chief Reynolds told me they've taken a statement from him." And while we didn't have a detailed formal statement from Nolan, I was able to give a statement on what he had told me, thanks to my "cheeseburger interrogation," as Chief Reynolds put it.

Frank had also complained that every one of his efforts to get a detailed statement from Henrik had ended in emotional outbursts. Clearly, I was about to endure one of Henrik's emotional outbursts myself. He was a big, loud man—I fought the urge to batten down the shop hatches for whatever was coming.

Linda, bless her, tried to offer Henrik a cup of coffee, but he waved her away with a flailing hand. Hank, perhaps the smartest of all of us, headed off into the safety of his bed in my office. If he could have, I'm sure he would have shut the door behind him.

I tried to be grateful there were no customers in the shop at the moment and motioned Henrik toward a seat at the table. "Sit down," I said in my steadiest voice. "We're all upset, so let's do our best to be calm."

"I cannot be calm," he declared theatrically as he collapsed his big frame into a chair I actually feared wouldn't hold him. That iconic mane of blond hair tossed about as he buried his face his hands. For a moment I thought the man would burst into tears. It was unnerving, and a bit heartbreaking, to watch the suave, stoic Viking go to pieces in front of me. Again.

"I understand that," I said gently. "And I am so very sorry for your loss. But let's try to look for a solution, shall we? What exactly is missing?"

Henrik looked up. "Personal things. Her journal. Her sketchbook. Even her speech notes. She told me she spent hours on that speech. She wouldn't let me read it. I always read her speeches but she said she wanted the way she announced our engagement to be a surprise." His eyes filled with tears. "I wanted to keep that speech forever. Who would take that from me? Who would be so cruel?"

That did seem particularly heartless. And rather specific. The items didn't seem to have any value—unless one of her parasitic fans had gotten in there and had plans to sell Perle's personal effects on eBay. I'd like to think no knitter would ever stoop so low, but humanity has a way of surprising you in such assumptions.

"Could someone have taken them for practical reasons? Could Derek have taken them to protect Perle's privacy? Or perhaps the police needed them for some reason, like dusting for fingerprints?"

Henrik shook his head at that suggestion. "It's got to be Derek. He has never respected Perle's privacy. Or her artistic vision. She is—*was*"—he moaned out the correction—"just a paycheck to him."

"Derek was in her hotel room alone after you came over to the theater." I was mostly thinking out loud, trying to keep Henrik from dissolving into a total mess. "If he does have them, could you ask him to return the papers and sketchbooks? Surely he could see why you'd want them."

Henrik's chin thrust out in manly defiance. "I will not go begging that man for what ought to be mine." The guy did have a certain flair for dramatic statements.

"Isn't it illegal to take something from a crime scene?" Linda offered, setting a cup of coffee down in front of Henrik despite his earlier refusal. "Tampering with evidence or something like that?"

"If Perle wasn't"—I avoided the word "killed," thinking it might send Henrik over the edge—"found there, I'm not sure it is a crime scene." I motioned to the coffee. "Why don't you drink that while I go find Derek's card? I'll call him and ask." Maybe I could solve this one little thing for the poor man.

"I will not talk to him," he announced loudly enough for me to hear clearly from my office.

"You won't have to," I assured him as I came back out, cell phone in hand. "I'll do it."

Martingale picked up right away. "Hello, Libby."

"Hello, Derek. I'm wondering if you can solve a little riddle we're having over here." That seemed a ridiculously cheery way to put it, but I was willing to try anything to keep the drama out of this.

"What?"

"Well, Henrik is here, and he's rather upset."

"When is Henrik anything but rather upset?" That felt harsh, given the upsetting circumstances. I was glad I hadn't opted to put the phone on speaker mode.

"He seems to feel you might be in possession of Perle's speech notes and some of her journals. Personal things he'd like very much to have."

The way Henrik narrowed his eyes, I felt like I was mitigating a growling match between angry dogs. My heart went out to Perle. I could only imagine how many times she must have played peacemaker between these two.

"Of course I have them," Derek said without hesitation or remorse. "And her notes for her next book."

I nodded the affirmation, which started Henrik rising from his chair until I gave him my best oh-no-you-don't point and glare.

"I'm glad to know they're safe," I replied, trying to sound cordial to Derek and appease Henrik at the same time.

He merely deepened his scowl and stood up. "Tell that little man I'm coming to his room to get them right now."

I was losing patience with these two. "I thought you didn't want to talk to him."

"I don't," Henrik shot back. "I don't need to say one word to him to get back Perle's *private* notes." He nearly shouted the last two words, clearly wanting there to be no doubt on the other end of the line.

I resisted the urge to count to three. Or maybe three hundred. "Neither of you may get to keep them," I reminded both of them. "It's possible the police will want to see them." How much of such squabbling had Perle endured between these two? I decided I wanted the advantage of neutral ground—or at least a stronger set of hands to bust up the fight that seemed likely to break out if these two were in the same room.

I turned to Henrik while still addressing Derek on the phone. "Mr. Martingale, I wonder if you wouldn't mind bringing them down to the lobby. I'll ask Chief Reynolds to come over from the station." The semipublic space would hopefully keep them civilized, but I knew I was still going to need Frank to pull this off without Henrik breaking any of the inn's furniture.

"Are you sure that's absolutely necessary?" I wouldn't have thought you could hear that much reluctance over the phone.

As a matter of fact, I did. "I think it's best. I'll call Frank and tell him to head on over right after I hang up with you. Find one of the little salon rooms on the first floor, and the three of us will meet you there."

"You'd better tell the Viking to mind his manners," Derek muttered.

Henrik leaned over toward my phone. "Tell the little man to mind his morals."

I started to scold the pair of them, then decided it wasn't worth the effort. Instead, I left a grumbling Henrik finishing his coffee and went into the office to grab my handbag. For a moment, I looked around for a defensive weapon. A Roman shield, a referee whistle, or perhaps a pair of Perle's very large knitting needles. The terrible accuracy of that last thought left a lead weight in the pit of my stomach.

Linda gave me a cautious look as Henrik and I headed for the door. "You know where I'll be," I called with false cheer. If you ask me, a gladiator arena would have felt safer than my next hour. I silently mouthed, *Warn Bev,* to my associate and headed out the door.

At the rate Henrik's long legs ate up the sidewalk, I practically had to run in order to keep up with him as we barreled back down the street toward the Riverside Inn.

For expediency—or my own personal safety—we stopped to gather Frank from the police department building. I used to joke to Mom that Collinstown had the cutest police department on the Eastern Seaboard. The colonial brick building with white trim windows and black shutters looked more quaint than utilitarian—I doubt it would have intimidated even the most timid of criminals. While I had never actually seen the jail cells—in fact, I wasn't even sure the department had any—I would have believed they came with gingham pillows and a stoneware coffee mug. Shoplifters and the occasional drunk teenager were about the lowest of Collinstown's criminal element. It was something Gavin took particular pride in, which made his heavy mayoral response to Perle's murder understandable, if challenging.

The police department had even won the Collinstown Christmas decoration contest twice in recent years—something Margo had been striving for as long as I'd known her. Still, considering how many complimentary pies Margo sent over to the force each holiday, I doubt the rivalry was too fierce.

While the chief fielded quite a few jokes about his *"Better Homes & Gardens* police station," he never really seemed bothered by it. I suspect that had a lot to do with the source of the station's gorgeous, colorful planters and window boxes: namely police receptionist Angie Goldman. Those two had the most adorable budding senior romance in the county.

What made it all the more adorable was that neither Angie nor Frank thought anyone was wise to their affections. I'm sure they thought the subtle winks and remarks and looks were the height of discretion. In truth, you'd have to be oblivious beyond measure not to pick up on the sparks between them. I was just waiting for the day Angie would muster up the courage to come in and ask for lessons to learn how to knit up something sweet for Frank.

Mom's theory was that the station's homey appearance *was*,

in fact, the chief's own fault. To Gavin's never-ending mayoral bliss, Frank was almost too good at his job of keeping order in Collinstown. Without crime keeping her desk busy, Angie dreamed up decor and landscaping merely to pass the time.

Whether or not Mom was right, I doubt Angie had gotten much chance recently to tend to the mounds of fat marigolds that currently graced the window boxes and planters.

Frank met me at the door. "Been seeing a lot of you lately, Libby."

"You don't say." I panted, out of breath from Henrik's stalking speed.

Henrik lost no time in continuing our trek to the inn. "Let's get those papers."

"Hold on there, Emilsen," Frank said. "Let's not let this get out of hand."

Emilsen? What do you know? Henrik actually does *have a last name.* I gloated inwardly at the thought of now knowing what appeared to be a closely held secret.

Henrik did not appreciate the disclosure. "Henrik," he insisted, giving me a glare just as sharp as the ones I'd given him back in the shop. "Just Henrik."

Frank offered me a long-suffering look as we followed Henrik's quick strides toward the inn.

Derek was waiting for us in one of three little salon rooms on the first floor of the building. Not surprisingly Mr. Martingale had chosen the only one with a door that closed. Four high-backed upholstered chairs sat arranged around a low oval coffee table set with a silver bowl filled with marigolds and greenery. I hoped the refined setting would keep the conversation polite, but I had my doubts.

Derek sat stiffly in the left-side chair, recoiling a bit when Henrik planted himself boldly in the chair directly opposite on the right. Frank motioned for me to take the seat at the far side of the table while he took the seat closest to the door after latching it shut.

Before Henrik could launch into whatever accusations he had planned, Frank spoke up. "Now, Mr. Martingale, I should tell you I'm not especially pleased to know you removed something from Perle's room without telling us."

Henrik gave an irritated grunt as if to say he was no more pleased than the good chief.

"It wasn't a crime scene," Derek defended himself.

"You didn't know that at the time. I'm sure you can see why we might find Ms. Lonager's notes pertinent to her case. I'll have to ask you to surrender them."

When Derek involuntarily clutched at the fancy leather portfolio on his lap, Frank added, "We don't really want to get into the mess of a subpoena, do we?"

"*You* get them?" Henrik balked. I wanted to say, "I told you so," but chose to keep quiet.

"For the time being, yes."

Henrik looked as annoyed as Derek at that. He held out a hand toward Martingale, wagging his fingers in demand. "I want to read Perle's speech!"

Derek looked at Frank in a way that made me think he was hoping the chief would decline Henrik's request.

Henrik, of course, was having none of it. "If he's got it, I should be able to see what it says. I deserve that much."

"I see no reason why that can't happen," Frank agreed.

Derek folded his hands across his chest. "Don't bother. You won't like what you see."

"What's that supposed to mean?" Henrik challenged.

I thought Derek's smug smile was unnecessarily mean. "There's no mention of any engagement in there."

"Of course there is. We. talked about it. She was going

to announce it, and I was going to give her the ring right there." The huge man's eyes started to tear up again, and I held my breath for another scene.

"Well, I hate to say it." Derek didn't look to me like he hated to say it at all. "There's no mention of getting married in either speech."

That caught my attention. "What do you mean, 'either speech'?"

Derek opened the portfolio. "I found two speeches in Perle's things."

"Like a rough draft and a final one?" Frank asked.

"No, two different speeches."

"I don't know anything about this," Henrik said, ticked off that Derek knew something he didn't about Perle. "We spent a lot of time talking about that speech. You have to be mistaken."

"I'm not," Derek replied. "I didn't know anything about this, either." He pulled six sheets of slightly crumpled typed white paper out of the folder with the air of someone who'd rather be doing anything else. "And it's not hard to see why."

"You're going to have to explain that," Frank remarked.

"To both of us," Henrik insisted.

Derek picked up the first four sheets and spread them out to face Frank. "This speech looks exactly like what Perle and I talked about: stuff about the knitting, the cultural importance of the patterns, how she researched them and developed designs from them. A bit scholarly for my taste, but the kind of stuff her fans eat up." He shifted his gaze to Henrik. "And while Perle goes into great detail about the mittens being a traditional engagement gift, she makes no mention of an engagement between you two."

"Perhaps she felt no need to script out such a highly personal moment," Henrik argued.

If it were me, I'd go out of my way to script such a big announcement, but I kept my mouth shut on that matter. Instead, I pointed out what no one else seemed to have picked up on. "The second script is much shorter. What's that one about?"

Derek's face grew longer. "It's missing the last part." Just as Henrik was drawing a breath to say something, Derek pointedly continued. "And it's not about an engagement. It's not even about knitting. Well, not directly."

Frank was losing his patience. "How about you get to the point, Mr. Martingale?"

"This is a goodbye speech," Derek said with growing reluctance. "The whole thing reads like a farewell to her career, her books, everything."

CHAPTER THIRTEEN

G oodbye?" Henrik swore in Norwegian. Or at least I think he swore. I'm not up on my Norse profanities, but the tone was pretty clear. "That can't be true."

"I'm not happy about it, either. But that's her handwriting." Derek pointed to some edits written in blue ink over the printed words.

Henrik sat back and crossed his arms. "Perle was not calling a halt to her career. Certainly not now."

"Maybe *you* didn't know she was. I sure didn't."

I picked up the two pages and began reading. Derek was right. The thing read like a farewell. A reluctant farewell, as a matter of fact. As if something was forcing her to leave a career she clearly loved.

"So now maybe you can see why I wasn't exactly eager to have this found by just anybody?"

While Derek and Henrik traded accusing glares, I read more of the speech. The words were building to the one thing that wasn't there: a reason. "Why?" I asked. "Why would she be saying goodbye?"

Henrik looked stunned. I didn't blame him. He clearly thought he had known Perle, and he had just discovered a great big secret she'd kept from him. For a selfish second I wondered if there would have been an enormous emotional scene, had the lecture and dinner gone on as planned. Had my big event been doomed from the start?

"I don't know. You don't know. Nobody knows." Derek threw his hands up in exasperation. "Whatever it was, it was on the last pages of that second speech."

"Pages you don't have," Frank finished for him.

"Oh, I looked for them. Believe me, I looked for them. If they're somewhere, they weren't in that hotel room."

"There were no papers found on Ms. Lonager's person or at the crime scene," Reynolds cut in. "Did you find anything while you were packing up, Libby?"

"Only that there was an extra set of the largest needles in the stock. If you have one set, we should be short one set, but we're not. And that doesn't really tell us anything."

That was the last straw for Henrik. "Something's amiss with her needles? The most expensive ones? You didn't tell me that. Why is no one telling me anything?"

"Maybe if you'd stop sniveling like a baby, we could have a conversation," Derek snapped.

"I've lost my beloved!" Henrik moaned, launching out of his chair so fast, it sent the thing flying backward, and Frank had to dart out and catch it before it clattered to the floor. Henrik tried to pace the tiny room, but his size made it nearly impossible, making him turn in small frustrated circles and nearly bump up against the walls. Maybe my worry for the furnishings wasn't that far off. "You can't begin to understand that, you heartless little—"

"Let's calm down, folks," Frank commanded. "We won't solve anything by arguing."

Henrik gave up his pacing and pressed his forehead and hands against the bookcase behind me. Derek pressed his lips together as if he'd had his fill of Henrik's theatrics. Frank and I exchanged now-what? glances.

"Mr. Martingale," Frank began in the tone of a man attempting to hold his temper in check. I wasn't far behind. These two bickering men were getting on my nerves, and fast. "Had you left those papers where they should have stayed, or at least brought them to me, we might have been able to get usable prints off them. We'll still try, but I don't have much hope." He fixed Derek with a serious look. "Is there anything else you've got that I don't know about? I'd *strongly advise* you not to hold anything else back."

"Other than her outline for the next book, no." Despite Frank's warning, I wasn't sure I believed the man's denial. There was always too much of a shifty, what's-in-it-for-me look in his eyes.

"Henrik," Frank said, using the single name with barely hidden annoyance, "do you know anything that can shed light on this situation?"

Henrik turned and simply leaned up against the bookcase. His drama was exasperating, but I couldn't help but feel for him, as I could see the grief that filled his features. This new information clearly deepened his pain. He ran frantic hands through his white-blond hair. "She would never leave her career. Not without telling me. And not like this."

Frank looked at each man in turn. "And neither of you has any idea what might be on the missing pages?"

Both men shook their heads.

A single unwelcome thought settled in my brain like an

ominous black crow on a windowsill. "What if whatever it was is why she was killed?"

"How is that even possible?" Derek asked.

"Well," I said carefully, "doesn't it make sense that whoever killed her took those pages to hide what's on them? Perle must have known she was making some huge declaration that had to be kept secret until the last minute. That's the reason for the two different speeches. The first version is a decoy."

The chief ran a hand down his face in thought. "Maybe those pages weren't taken. If Perle went to the trouble of making a decoy speech, she might have taken the trouble to hide those missing pages."

The idea made sense. "She did insist on going over to the theater alone right before the dinner. But I went over everything that was left. I didn't find any pages, and neither did you."

"And they were missing from the hotel room, not the theater," Derek said. "Unless she felt she had to take them out of the building so that prying eyes didn't see them." I wished he hadn't given Henrik the look he had while saying that last bit.

"How dare you cast suspicion on Perle!" Henrik shouted. "She is the victim here. She has been killed. How can you even think to imply hiding and sneaking and things like that? It is you we should all be worried about investigating."

Frank held up two hands in the calm-down gesture he'd been making all afternoon. "No one is disparaging Ms. Lonager's memory. But she has left us clues that tell us she had something to hide. Or at least something she felt she had to keep from someone."

Henrik and Derek traded glares as if each felt the other was the "someone" Perle was hiding things from.

Henrik jutted his chiseled jaw out in defiance. "I refuse to believe that."

Frank puffed out his cheeks and blew out a breath. We were done here—this meeting wasn't going to provide anything further except a mismatched fistfight if it went on any longer.

"Gentlemen," the chief commanded with a tone of finality, "let's leave it at this for now." He carefully picked up the sheets of paper. "I'll need to keep these, and I'll need two things from the both of you." He stood up and waited until each of the fuming men met his eyes. "One," Frank said, holding up a finger, "keep it civil between you while we work this out."

The nods Derek and Henrik gave were so begrudging they were almost comical.

"Two, don't leave town. We've had enough disappearing acts with the Huton fellow. I don't need the same foolishness from the two of you."

"I've made arrangements to attend a publishing conference in DC tomorrow. You're not going to keep me from that, are you? It's an hour away."

"Make sure we know where you are and how to contact you," Frank relented.

"Perle has died and you're going to a conference?" Henrik accused.

"Some of us have jobs that still need doing," Derek shot back.

Frank picked up the papers. "That will be all, gentlemen."

Curt nods and dark looks ensued as we made our way out of the small room. The four of us had almost squeezed out the door without incident when Henrik turned back to Chief Reynolds and said, "I bet the boy knows."

"Nolan?" I asked. I had had the same thought. It was possible Nolan either knew what was on the missing pages or had them himself.

"If you're looking for someone acting suspicious," Henrik continued, "he's been stalking Perle for months. I've asked him to keep his distance, but clearly he can't."

Derek's jaw dropped. "Why is this the first I'm hearing about this? Someone's been stalking Perle and neither of you told me?"

Henrik narrowed his eyes. "What would you have done? Issued a press release?"

"I've had just about enough of your—"

Henrik silenced Derek with a raised fist that made Frank growl loudly. I didn't give Derek good odds if those two fell to fighting.

I decided to drop the only bomb I had. "We know Nolan Huton is Perle's nephew." It did manage to stop both men in their tracks. "I'm not so sure all of this was a publishing-related problem."

The look Derek tried to quickly hide told me volumes. After all, Nolan's reaction had also hinted that there was something between those two.

"Yes, we've talked to Nolan," Frank confirmed. "I admit he did keep his distance at first, but the young man was pretty forthcoming with us when we finally did get to talk to him."

"His late mother and Perle were estranged," I continued. "He was attempting to patch things up with Perle—or so he says." I raised an eyebrow at Frank, wondering if it was my place to reveal investigation details like this.

"Patch things up?" Henrik nearly shouted. "He was trying to steal from her."

Frank shut the door again and sank back into one of the

chairs. This meeting wasn't going to end anytime soon. "Care to tell me more about that?" He looked up at Derek. "You can go if you like, Mr. Martingale."

Derek returned to his seat. "Are you kidding me? I'm not going anywhere until I hear this."

Frank retrieved a notepad and pen from his shirt pocket. "What was it Nolan was trying to steal?"

Henrik sat back down as well. "The needles. She bought the design concept from him, but that wasn't enough for him. He wanted the whole line to be a partnership between them. Riding on Auntie's coattails. Oh, he couched it in terms of 'helping her,' but I could see what he was really doing. He was angling to steal the whole line right out from under her." After a dramatic pause, he added, "Such a shame that Perle didn't have people around her she could really trust."

"I was just thinking the same thing," Derek replied.

Sure, that sounded a bit extreme, but then I remembered that Nolan had that design tattooed on his forearm. That's not your garden-variety level of commitment to an idea. I could see him being ambitious enough to steal a business, but to murder his aunt? Three days ago I would have called the notion far-fetched. This whole experience was teaching me not to assume anything about anybody.

"The speech was announcing the line of needles," Derek added. "If she was going to roll it out without giving any credit to him . . ."

"Then why leave the first speech behind? Why not take both?" Frank asked. "This doesn't add up yet. We're missing something."

"Pages of a speech, to be exact," I said. "Or someone who knows what's in them."

"We're going to need to get Nolan in here." Frank looked

at Derek and Henrik. "Stay civil, stay in town, and steer clear of Huton. The kid spooks easily, and I don't need either of you driving him back into hiding."

"Why hide if you're not guilty?" Henrik nearly growled. "He did it, I tell you. He took my Perle from me." The drama ratcheted up again from our bereaved Viking. He pointed a finger at Frank. "You'd better hope I stay away from him, because I can't be held responsible for what I might do if I see him."

Frank, never one to be intimidated, pointed right back. "You *can* be held responsible, and you will. So I suggest you get ahold of yourself." When Derek looked smug, Frank added, "The both of you."

It was ten minutes to closing by the time I made it back up the street to the shop. And here I was sure today couldn't be longer or more taxing than yesterday. Linda and I closed up Y.A.R.N. and I retreated home to the solace of a Gruyère-and-mushroom quiche, a glass of excellent white wine, and a quiet evening of getting started on a new shawl I was test-knitting for the shop's first series of classes.

Knitting makes for excellent thinking time. The repetition of stitches both frees your mind and quiets the crazy thinking. I get my best ideas—and do my best problem-solving—with yarn and needles in my hands.

Tonight as I worked, I pondered where and why someone like Pearl would hide a set of speech notes. Despite hours of knitting, when my bed began to call, I was still no closer to a theory.

"Time to let it simmer for a while," I said to Hank as he parked himself in my lap. Usually I get annoyed when he decides to invade my lap while I'm knitting, but tonight I was grateful for the close canine contact. The weight of his chubby bulldog jowls always feels like a hug against my legs. I let him out once more, and then we both went to bed early. I slept decently for the first time since this whole thing unraveled.

Good thing. Monday morning showed me how much I'd needed it.

A good bit before seven a.m., I woke to the sound of an incoming text. Bleary-eyed, I reached for the device and swiped the screen to see a one-word text from Gavin. Sorry.

I could almost laugh. Clearly, Jillian had attempted her full-throttle matchmaking on him as well. I found it sweet that he was apologizing for her meddling.

. . . Until a photo came in just after the text.

I bolted upright and gasped at the shot of one of Collin Avenue's trees. I recognized it instantly as the one just south of my shop; each tree had been so distinctively decorated that walking down the avenue was like taking in an art show—not the "circus" George had called it.

But no more. This tree had been savagely "unbombed." The now-naked tree stood amid bits of yarn strewn about like shrapnel around the roots. Collinstown Yarn Day had clearly been called to a brutal halt.

Wide-awake now without the benefit of a single drop of coffee, I hit the button to dial Gavin.

"All of them?" I asked the moment the call connected even though I knew the answer.

"Afraid so. Well, all but the one in front of your shop that was there before."

I thought of Mom and her Gals and all the gleeful hard work they'd put into yarn-bombing those trees. The joy it had given me—and I'm sure other people as well—to walk amid all the creativity and color. Why was the world suddenly brimming over with senseless violence? It was *yarn*, for Pete's sake.

That was it. I would not stand by while yarn was being weaponized. Against Perle, against Collinstown.

It took all of two seconds to know whom to blame. Only one man hated my yarn-bombed trees enough to shear them clean under the dark of night: George.

"I mean it, Gavin. Frank's going to have a second murder on his hands when I find George," I growled into the phone, not caring that it was an insensitive wording choice. I used to think of myself as having a long fuse. Not anymore.

"It's not George."

I plunged my arms into the sleeves of my bathrobe and stomped to the kitchen. "Of course it's George. He gave me an earful Saturday about how I shouldn't be allowed 'free advertising.' He called those beautiful trees vandalism. He stood there and griped how Collinstown Yarn Day gave me an unfair business advantage." I was amazed how fast I went from peaceful sleep to full-blown agitation. "It has to be him. Who else would do something so . . . so . . ." I searched for a suitably evil adjective as I reached into my fridge for the coffee creamer.

Thanks to the miracles of modern appliance technology, the pot had already started brewing ten minutes ago. I hit the speakerphone button, set the phone down on the counter, and began the time-honored caffeine-impatient ritual of slipping my mug under the still-dripping coffeemaker while pouring the rest from the glass pot. Some days you just can't wait for the luxury of a complete brewing cycle, and today was one of them. "Really, who else would it be?" I snapped to the phone sitting on my counter, not caring that I'd already just asked that question.

Gavin gave a weary sigh. "I don't know, but it's not George."

I frowned at the phone, unconvinced. "You can't know that."

"Well, not a hundred percent, but I happened to be on the avenue when George drove up, and the man practically veered up onto the sidewalk in surprise. So unless he has supreme acting skills, I don't think it was him."

I actually wouldn't have put it past George to have supreme acting skills, but I did trust Gavin's take on this. I leaned against the counter, suddenly a bit wobbly with the idea of someone *else* doing that kind of violence against knitting. It felt like violence against *me*, and I didn't have much of a shield to fend it off after everything that had happened. George, I could handle. But someone else? An *unknown* someone else? I tried to say something, but a sudden surge of fear had a choke hold on my throat.

"I already called Frank," Gavin said.

I couldn't respond. While that was clearly the right thing to do, it confirmed the act as a *crime*. George might have thought the decorating of the trees was vandalism, but this met my definition. Or destruction of property or whatever slashing wonderful knitting off defenseless trees was. Getting Frank involved heightened my sense of being victimized.

"Libby," Gavin said softly.

Curse him. I always fell to pieces when he said my name like that. Falling to pieces was not an option. I swallowed a blistering gulp of coffee, hoping it would loosen my throat, but it only added burning to the tightness.

"Oh, my God!" I heard Margo's shocked gasp from somewhere near Gavin as he stood on the sidewalk. Of course, as a baker, she'd have been at work for hours by this

time. She must have come out to unlock the bakery front
door just then, as she usually entered through the back so
early in the morning. "Who did this to Libby's trees?"

They weren't my trees, of course; they belonged to the
whole town. But wasn't that exactly George's point? That
I'd been given unfair chance to make them my trees? Even
if for one silly, wonderful weekend?

"How dare George—," Margo started, sounding just
as capable of Chamber of Commerce presidenticide as I
just had.

"It's not George," Gavin cut in again.

"Of course it's George. Who else would it be?" Margo
and I have often been accused of thinking alike, and I could
hear Gavin's exasperated sigh at the echoed reply. "I don't
know who did this, but I'm pretty sure it's not George."

Now, on top of figuring out who had killed Perle and
why, I was going to have to figure out who was out to harm
Y.A.R.N. Could both be the same person? I fought the wave
of panic flushing through my system with another enormous gulp of coffee. Hank, hearing the distress in my voice,
walked over and put his head against my shin as if he could
hold me upright.

"Do you need me to come over there?" Gavin asked.

A quick glance at my reflection in the microwave door
glass had me blurting out, "Oh, God, no." The circles under
my eyes were nearly purple and my hair stuck out in all
directions like a dirty blond bird's nest. *Think, Libby, think.*
I pictured the row of trees down either side of the avenue.
"There was a tree in front of the bank, wasn't there?"

I could hear Gavin walking down the block to get a view
of the bank. "Yes, there was."

"Isn't there one of those security surveillance cameras
aimed at the front of the bank building?" I reached into a

kitchen cabinet for a bottle of Tylenol. The sun wasn't even fully up, and already a headache was blooming behind my eyebrows.

"Good thinking. There's a streetlight not ten feet away."

"So there's a good chance it picked up whoever did this." I suddenly felt like I hadn't slept a wink. I took the phone off speaker, and held it back up to my ear. The slim device felt as if it weighed ten pounds and the coffee roiled in my empty stomach. "Worth a try, don't you think?"

"Absolutely. Listen, Libby, are you sure you don't need me over there? Check out the house, make sure nothing's out of order by you?"

Despite any shreds of female vanity, I knew that if I saw Gavin right now, I'd probably fall sobbing into his arms. That was definitely not a good idea. "I'm fine." Realizing he'd see through that in a minute, I amended it to, "Well, not exactly fine. More like actively coping."

Hank sat down in front of me, cocking his head in a you-don't-look-one-bit-fine-to-me canine stare of disbelief.

Of course I wasn't fine. Not even close. But having Gavin come over here and play protector wouldn't solve anything. "Just tell Frank to do whatever he has to in order to see that footage. I'll be there as soon as I can."

"On it," Gavin said.

I said goodbye, clicked off the call, and dumped a scoop of kibble into Hank's bowl. "Eat up," I called as I padded toward the stairs and a quick shower. "We're heading to work early today."

CHAPTER FOURTEEN

I put the keys in the shop front door not twenty minutes later. Mom was ten minutes behind me.

"Who?" she shouted to the bare tree just north of the shop. She stared the tree down as if it could point a branch and identify the culprit. "Who'd do this?"

I hadn't called her. In fact, I'd hoped to prevent her knowing about this until we'd identified who had done it, but this was Collinstown. I suspected George's wife, Vera, had probably been on the phone to Mom before George even turned off his car engine.

Public scandal aside, Mom had even more right than I to take this personally—she and her Gals and their friends had worked hard on those trees. She'd told me people had stopped her in the grocery store to tell her how beautiful they found them. While I technically had permission only for a day, I had secretly hoped those decorations could stay up for at least a week, maybe even the whole month. I loved how they looked. All those brilliant colors.

I had worked hard to get my annoyance under control by the time I'd arrived to open the shop. Mom's outrage wasn't helping. "We don't know who did this, Mom. At least not yet. Frank's trying to get the bank's camera footage to see if there's anything from last night. But . . ." If that idea didn't work, how would we ever know who had done this?

She looked at me, catching the despair in my voice in the way that only mothers can. Without another word, she pulled me into a fierce hug—in the chest-crushing way that only mothers can hug. For a moment I was twelve again, sulking home from school smarting from something some bully had said, needing my mom.

"I'm so sorry about all of this." She tightened her grip. "This was supposed to be your big moment."

Given that someone had died, I didn't really feel justified in my disappointment. I was going to take a hit here. But I was still alive and breathing, and I'd lost only an opportunity, not a loved one. The thought made me hug Mom back just as tight.

"So," she said as she pulled away and smoothed down my hair as if I were indeed twelve again, "Gavin took good care of you, did he?"

And *poof*, that lovely moment between us vanished. "Mom," I moaned. I might have even given her an eye roll worthy of a twelve-year-old.

"What? Vera told me he was there calling you just after George pulled up. If I was going to get awful news like this, I'd want it from someone who cared about me."

I pulled the shop door open and motioned for us both to go inside. "Yes, he's a good friend to have," I sighed, trying to hide my exasperation at the tired subject.

Mom waggled an eyebrow as she walked into the shop. "He could be more. Maybe he should be more."

"Have you been talking to Jillian?"

Mom looked guilty. "We bumped into each other at the library. Lovely girl. I should offer to teach her to knit. What could be sweeter?"

"I *am* teaching her, Mom," I reminded her gently. "Could I maybe teach you to keep your nose out of my social life?" I turned on the coffeemaker and reached for the grounds and my largest mug. I'm not normally into my fourth mug by the time the shop opens, but these days hardly classified as normal.

"You deserve someone better than Sterling."

Now this was a sore subject. Mom had never been especially keen on Sterling, or his highbrow family. Of course, to my own rebellious nature, that just made Sterling more attractive. We'd met when I was a rep for his company, and he'd swept me off my feet. I had loved the man, and he had loved me. In an egocentric, Sterling kind of way. And he'd had the kind of financial resources that made it very easy to go along with his plans and views on things.

It wasn't until a few years into our marriage, when I began to have plans and views that didn't line up so easily with his, that I discovered Sterling's total inability to compromise. I'd been blind to how my life had become Sterling adjacent rather than anything of my own.

Well, that and some tiny-waisted sales associate named Heidi. 'Nuff said.

To her credit, Mom was trying not to fall into *I told you so*s. She wasn't really succeeding.

"Yes," I agreed as I scooped in the grounds, adding an extra scoop for good measure. "I deserve someone better than Sterling. Any breathing woman deserves better than Sterling. But it's not Gavin, and it's not now." I sounded more certain than I felt about that, but I wasn't about to give Mom's meddling any encouragement.

"Jillian adores you. She *wants* you to date her father, you know."

I began turning all the shop lights on and booted up the sales counter computer. "She only thinks she does. I think Jillian just needs another female to pay attention to her. To hear Gavin tell it, Tasha doesn't seem to be able to find the time for much more than a weekly video chat from whatever tropical island she's currently lounging around on."

Mom's pinched face emitted a snort of disapproval as she shook her head.

"That kind of inattention can be hard at her age," I continued. "Gavin's trying, but I'm sure she sees what's happening."

"Of course she does," Mom agreed. "Every tiny detail of life becomes a huge drama at her age. She's lonely for a female she can trust and admire. That's why I told her to ask you."

I stopped what I was doing. "Ask me what? I'm already teaching her to knit, remember?" Was Mom more confused than I thought?

"Not that." Mom settled herself in at the table, pulling out an intricate Fair Isle cap she'd been working on. "It's the fall concert dress she's worried about now." She began stitching with what I could only call deliberate innocence. "Kind of last-minute. And that's way out of Gavin's league, don't you think?"

Just how much had Mom and Jillian been talking? I walked over to the table. My worry over the trees fell by the wayside to worry over what it was Mom was cooking up with Jillian. The possibilities were endless . . . and unsettling. "Ask me *what*, Mom?"

"I just told her I was sure you'd be happy to take her to the mall and help her find a dress for the fall choral concert. It's next Wednesday—or maybe it's this Wednesday—and she's in a bit of a panic about it."

"Wait. What? Wednesday? As in the day after tomorrow?"

"Oh, come now. You have a great eye for color, and you and I both know Gavin will just botch it." She looked up from her knitting to give me her "wise" look. "These things are so important to a girl her age. You were just the same way."

"You told her I'd help her with that. Without asking me."

"Won't you?"

How do mothers learn to throw guilt around like that with just a look and a question? "Well, I'll have to now, won't I?" I actually might have found time to help Jillian, had she asked of her own accord, but it chafed me to be backed into it by Mom's ulterior motives. "I'm kind of swamped here, if you hadn't noticed. Murder? Vandalized trees? Promotional nightmare?"

"The mall's open until nine every night. You have more than a week. Well, not if it's this week. Still, two whole days should be enough." Mom eyed a stitch, undid it, and then reworked it as if we were discussing which pie to order from Margo's. "If Gavin has any sense, he'll take you to dinner when you attend anyway, so at least you'll get a nice meal out of it."

"I'm *going* to the concert?" I balked.

"Well, you have to see how the dress works out, don't you? Besides, when was the last time you had a good meal?

You don't come over for dinner hardly at all anymore, and I doubt you're cooking up a storm for one over at your house." I was very proud of the ten pounds I'd lost recently, and somehow Mom managed to make it look like a sign of my failing social life.

"I had a very nice quiche last night, thank you very much," I shot back.

"From Margo's," Mom said with infuriating certainty.

Maternal intuition can be a real drag sometimes. "It still counts. It had four different vegetables."

In a fit of highly regrettable timing, Gavin came through the shop door seconds later. "Frank got the video from the bank. And get this—Nolan's disappeared again."

"Nolan . . ." Mom furrowed her brow to recall where she'd heard that name. "Is he that strange young man?" I'd been trying not to give her blow-by-blow updates on how things were going with the case. Her eyes widened. "Is he the murderer?"

"We don't know who killed Perle," Gavin said to Mom. He turned his gaze to me. "But according to Frank, the bank video did catch at least parts of someone cutting the yarn off the trees. The guy looks very much like he could be Nolan."

I set down my coffee mug. Nolan would have been the last person I'd think of to do this. He was an artistic soul. He'd know what a travesty it was to destroy someone's art. "Frank told him not to leave. What possible motive could Nolan have to cut the yarn off the trees?"

"Guilt," Mom pronounced as if this signed Nolan's confession. "Rage. Emotional instability. Take your pick."

"I only found him by pure happenstance last time. If he's half as smart as he looks, he could be in Pennsylvania by now." Hank had many gifts, but I doubted playing blood-hound and sniffing out Nolan Huton could be one of them.

"You can't see the face on the video," Gavin admitted. "We don't know if it was Nolan. But the age and build pretty much mean it can't be Henrik or Derek. Or George, for that matter."

I got an idea. "The tattoo! Nolan has a very distinctive tattoo on one forearm. We'd have to be able to see his hands if he was cutting yarn off the tree in front of the bank, wouldn't we?"

"Would you recognize it?" Gavin asked.

"Anywhere," I replied, grabbing my coat. "It was the design on Perle's largest needles. Call Frank and ask him if I can see the video." I could shut down the shop, but instead I turned to Mom, glad to have a task that would keep her from coming with me. "Linda should be here in about an hour. Can you watch the shop until then?" If we lost a sale because Mom couldn't work the register or the credit card machine, I'd be okay with that. "Hank, you, too."

Mom nodded cheerfully, all too happy to see Gavin and me heading off somewhere together—even if it was to the bank to nail a yarn-shredding terrorist.

Frank hadn't gotten clearance to remove a copy of the video from the bank yet, so Gavin and I made our way down the street in the other direction, toward the Collins-town branch of a major bank chain. After half a block, Gavin put a hand on my arm.

"Listen, Libby. I know this isn't really the time, but Jil-lian's got this thing on Wednesday and she somehow got it in her mind to . . ."

So it *was* this week. "I already know about the dress," I

replied, trying to give Gavin an understanding look. "And for what it's worth, Jillian didn't just *get it* in her mind. Mom planted it there."

That halted Gavin's hurried stride. "Rhonda came up with that?" He looked horrified as he connected the dots of what they were up to. Clearly, it disturbed him as much as it did me to know Mom was in on this little matchmaking scheme. Neither one of us was eager to be tag-teamed by those two.

I grimaced in sympathy. "I think it was a joint venture."

Gavin shook his head as he resumed walking. "I'm so ticked at Tasha for dropping the ball on this."

"Maybe it's harder than it looks to dress shop from your cabana on the beach." Why was I defending Tasha all of a sudden?

"Well, don't feel obligated. You don't have to help." His face changed from annoyed to sheepish. "I mean, this is way out of my skill set, but I wouldn't want you to feel backed into anything just because my ex is being a first-class . . ." His words trailed off in exasperation. I knew Gavin. He'd try mightily to provide the whole dress-shopping experience. And that was exactly why he'd fail miserably. This required a delicate balance of attention to detail and cool faux casualness. The thirteen-year-old version of "Oh, this old thing?" when hours had been spent to select the perfect outfit. I liked Jillian too much to put either of them through that.

And to be honest, despite the last-minute time frame, I found I didn't really mind. The whole prospect actually felt like a pleasant diversion from the torments of Perle's death. I might never get the chance to do this with a daughter of my own. And I wasn't so long in the tooth that I couldn't remember how important things like the perfect dress were to someone Jillian's age. "Relax. I'll do it. Gladly."

He looked enormously relieved. "I'll buy you dinner before the concert to say thanks."

I smirked—only inwardly, of course. For all Mom's bouts of confusion, sometimes the woman could be downright clairvoyant.

"You're gonna have to come," he admitted. "Jillian says so."

"Oh, I figured that," I lied. Mom would have such a field day learning how right she had been. She might have lost a lot of facts and timetable skills, but that woman's human intuition could have been bottled and sold to the FBI.

We'd reached the bank, and Gavin stepped in front of me to open the bank door. He was the kind of man who still felt compelled to open a door for a woman—those little touches of chivalry are mighty rare these days.

Frank met us in the hallway with the branch manager I recognized from my endless rounds of loan application meetings. "Hello, Libby," he said. "Sorry to hear about what's happened. Both this and . . . before." I'd spent so much time in the last few days watching people verbally dance their way around terms like "death" and "murder" that I hardly even flinched at it now.

"Well, let's hope this can help," Frank said as the four of us walked down a hallway toward the branch's offices.

"If it is Nolan, can you send out some kind of call to bring him in? An APB or something?" I asked as we crowded into a small security office. A wall of monitors flickered alongside shelves of blinking machines while two tall filing cabinets vied for space next to a desk and chair. I didn't envy the person who had to spend their workday crammed into this tiny closet of an office.

"We have to have something solid to do that," Frank replied. "But if you can identify the distinguishing tattoo, that ought to be enough. We just have to hope it shows up."

"It's a pretty big, pretty bold tattoo," I said as Gavin tried to fit his tall frame next to me in the little office. My mind shot back to a junior high game of sardines in the church basement. "Why wouldn't it show?"

"These cameras can only do so much. It was dark. The lights are over the door, not the tree. It's not up close."

The manager angled his way into the chair and pushed a few buttons on a keyboard. Some of the monitors shifted to displaying shots of an empty sidewalk, the bank entrance, a trash can, and the lower half of a tree, all under the muted glow of a streetlamp. I knew the tree in the far corner of the screen bore a vibrant wrap of white, purple, and yellow yarn, even though the black-and-white footage did it little justice.

"Fast-forward to the time where he shows up," Chief Reynolds requested.

Suspense dashed down my spine, and I found myself holding a breath. I was about to watch a crime being committed. Even if the crime was against a tree, and maybe not even a real crime, depending upon whom you asked.

The manager squinted at a readout as he pushed more buttons to fast-forward the video through the hours. "Right about . . . here," he said when the time stamp read 1:47 A.M.

After a second or two of darkness, a slim figure in a gray hoodie—why is it always a gray hoodie in these things?—appeared. The person looked like a man to me, although I suppose there was no way of knowing the gender for sure. He walked into the frame with his back to us and looked around nervously. I actually gasped when he removed a large knife from a backpack and then began hacking away at the yarn on the tree.

It looked so much like he was stabbing the yarn that I physically recoiled at the sight. My heart ached at the way yarn and violence were colliding in my world lately. *How?* my brain kept yelling. *How can you do that? Why?*

I wanted to look away, but I knew I couldn't. I had to watch, and carefully at that, to catch the little clue that would tell us if this was Nolan. In all honesty, I think I was looking for proof that it wasn't Nolan. It might just have been my optimism talking, but I felt an artistic connection to the young man. I didn't want to believe that someone who created art would be capable of what we were watching.

I don't know if it looked as ugly to the men in the room, but it looked shockingly ugly to me. Angry hands yanked the knife up and down the yarn, pulling it off in great hunks that fell to the ground. It had all the markings of an attack rather than any kind of prank.

A minute or so into the video, I got my answer. "There," I said as an arm came barely into view under the light of the streetlamp. "Right there." As the man in the video reached up to catch his knife on the top few inches of the knitting, his jacket sleeve slid down to reveal some very familiar tattoo designs.

The manager hit a few keys to freeze the video with a relatively clear shot.

I knew that tattoo. I knew those designs.

A ball of ice formed in my stomach as I pulled out my cell phone to show the photograph I had taken of the large needles in my own set at home. I held up the phone next to the monitor. The tattoo was the dark opposite of the white mother-of-pearl inlay work on Perle's needle. Like a photo negative, but unmistakably the same design.

"It's Nolan," I said, feeling the words rasp in my throat. "That's Nolan's tattoo."

Gavin swore softly behind me.

Frank gave a gruff snort. "I'd say this is a pretty clear indication our boy is capable of violence. And he's running. He's our man."

I looked at Frank. "I can't believe it. He's . . . well, I . . . I wanted it not to be him."

Frank put his hand on my arm. "I've been at this long enough to know most of us have no idea what people are capable of."

I'd spent the time since my divorce on the lookout for the best of what people could do. It stung to be staring at the worst of what they could do. A wave of disappointed nausea hit me. All the stripped trees would look like bare skeletons to me now, even though I'd seen them without their colorful adornments for years before this weekend. I felt like I would be shutting my eyes the whole walk back from the bank, wondering when quaint little Collin Avenue would stop looking like a crime scene to me. And what about the theater? Would I ever be able to look at that stage and not see Perle's lifeless form slumped behind the curtains? I swallowed hard.

Frank caught on to my distress. "I'm sorry you had to see this," he said. "But you've given us crucial information." He looked at Gavin. "I doubt either of us would have matched that tattoo to the needle design."

"Or even thought to look for it," Gavin added. "That was some sharp thinking, Libby."

I knew they were trying to make me feel better, but it wasn't working. "What now?"

Frank thanked the manager and we all began squeezing out of the small office. "Now we get on the system and put out a call for Nolan. I doubt he's in town, and he's probably smart enough not to go home. If he's in the county—if he's on the Eastern Seaboard—it's only a matter of time until we find him."

"And charge him with Perle's murder?" I asked.

"Not yet. We'll bring him in on destruction of public property. But as far as the homicide is concerned, he's got motive, we have the weapon, and he hasn't given us an alibi that removes him from having opportunity. That's probable cause, but it's not enough to arrest him for Perle's murder just yet. However," he went on with a pointed look at Gavin and me, "the guys that look like the culprit at this point usually are."

"No last-minute surprise confessions or deductions?" Gavin's joke fell short. There was no lightening the moment.

"Don't work like that in real life," Frank said wearily. "And we don't want it to. Nice, boring crimes and misdemeanors, thank you. I'll leave drama to the DC guys."

Big-city crimes here in little Collinstown. I could almost feel the distress radiate off Gavin.

"Nolan killed his aunt. Nolan slashed our trees." Even as I said the words, they wouldn't form into solid thoughts. I was developing an unwelcome collection of mental images I'd have given anything to erase. I didn't like what I saw when I closed my eyes lately, and that was no way to live. "Can I go now?" I was eager to put distance between me and those ugly images.

"Of course," Frank replied. "I'll need a formal statement about the tattoo from you at some point, but it doesn't have to be now. Right now we'll put our efforts into finding Huton."

Gavin took my arm and we started heading back up the hallway. "And we'll all rest easier when we know who was behind all this nasty business."

I gave Gavin a lot of credit for never coming right out and saying that murder was bad for tourism, but I knew he was thinking it. George was probably shouting it to anyone who would listen—and likely some who wouldn't.

Did George blame me? Did anyone else? Half of me knew it made no sense to feel guilty about what had happened in my dear little town. I hadn't brought it. I'd set out to put Y.A.R.N. and Collinstown on the map. I'd brought Perle, but the murder—the murder*er*—had followed her here.

The doubtful half of me easily swallowed the idea that I had put a giant black mark on our community. It was only by some freak bit of good fortune that we hadn't had a pack of nosy reporters show up with television cameras.

Yet. Maybe I should have called Caroline and asked her how to defend myself.

I almost did shut my eyes once we were back out on the street. I stared at the bare tree for a second or two, feeling the odd urge to apologize to it for the trauma. With horror I noticed a knife mark slashed into the bark. At that point I did shut my eyes for a second, trying to block out the image of Nolan's hand at the hilt of that menacing knife.

And shot my eyes wide open again.

I spun on my heels and went back into the bank, not waiting for Gavin to open the door for me.

"Frank," I called as I dashed down the hall to where Frank was still talking with the bank manager in the little security room. "Get him to turn that video back on."

"Why?"

"Just turn it back on. To the point where we can see the tattoo," I said. "I need to see something."

Frank and the manager both looked puzzled for a second before going through the process of turning the monitors back on and scrolling back through the images until the tattooed arm was visible reaching up toward the knitting, knife in hand.

I stared, searched my memory, and stared again.

"That's not Nolan," I pronounced.

"You said that's his tattoo," Frank replied. "You were certain."

I bounced my gaze between Gavin and Frank. "It *is* Nolan's tattoo. But that's not Nolan."

When all three men continued to give me blank stares, I went on. "Nolan's tattoo is on his left forearm. We were sitting side by side, him on my right, and the designs were only on the arm next to me. His left arm." I pointed to the video. "Those are on his right arm in the video. Nolan's right arm doesn't have those designs on it."

"You're sure?" Frank asked.

"Absolutely certain." The full reality of that fact hit me. "Someone wanted us to think that was Nolan."

CHAPTER FIFTEEN

No one was more surprised than me when Nolan Huton burst into the shop Tuesday, shouting, "It wasn't me!"

My discovery in the bank on Monday had sent Frank into action, pulling out every stop to locate our prime suspect and bring him in. I figured someone with Nolan's talent for disappearing would be long gone despite the police's best efforts. I had gone, with the uneasy prospect that it might be weeks if not months before Perle's memory would rest in peace.

"Nolan?!" The set of beaded stitch markers I'd been holding clattered to the floor, the little rings scattering like marbles.

"You believe me, right? You said you know I didn't do that to your trees. Or Aunt Perle." He ducked farther into the shop, and for a moment, I worried he would ask me to hide him.

I wasn't itching to harbor a fugitive from justice. Nor did

I want either Henrik or Derek around to display their short tempers, should they hear Nolan was here. Frank had advised Gavin and me to keep mum, but I doubted we could keep a lid on things for long. Everyone saw the unbombed trees, and everyone was speculating about who'd done it.

. . . Which we still didn't know. Neither Frank nor Gavin nor I had any idea who had impersonated Nolan as he vandalized the Collin Avenue trees. My discovery might have cleared Nolan of the tree crime, but it did not squelch Frank's determination to find the young man and question him further about the murder.

"Thanks for your e-mail," Nolan said. I had sent him an e-mail yesterday at the address I had for him on the shop ticket records. I told him what had happened and implored him to come back and cooperate. I figured I'd be lucky to get an e-mail back, not a surprise visit.

I bent down to pick up the scattered markers. "Where have you been? Hiding was the wrong move—I thought we covered that already."

"If the police know it wasn't me who did that to the trees, why are they still looking for me?" He ran a hand through his pale spiky hair. "I'm gonna need a lawyer, aren't I?"

"What you're going to need," I said as calmly as I could as I straightened up, "is to stop disappearing like this. It makes you look like you have something to hide." I wanted to ask, "Do you?" but instead I tried to hold the young man's eyes. "You're in a fair amount of trouble here. You strike me as smart enough to see that."

Nolan set down his backpack and paced around the shop. He was quite different from Henrik—that large man stormed around my shop like a bull, whereas Nolan darted around my shop like a trendy cornered mouse.

His sporadic movements slowed at the wall of Perle's mittens that were still on display. I hadn't been able to bring myself to take them down.

This time I wasn't leaving it to cheeseburgers to keep Nolan here. I reached for my phone and placed myself between Nolan and the door. "I'm going to call Chief Reynolds and we're going to walk over to the police station." I kept my words steady and level. "You have got to start cooperating with the police if you want any hope of getting out of this." I reminded myself he was still under suspicion for Perle's murder, even if he hadn't been the man who defaced the trees.

Linda opted for the hospitality tactic as I dialed my phone. She calmly picked up a mug and began pouring Nolan a cup of coffee as I talked to Frank. "We've got some granola bars in the back," she offered. "Are you hungry?"

He shook his head, but readily accepted the coffee. When I got off the phone with a stunned Chief Reynolds, Nolan burst out, "It's Henrik they should be hauling in. If anyone had motive, it's him."

"Yes, well, Henrik is not vanishing into thin air every other day." As Nolan took an enormous gulp of coffee, it occurred to me that I ought to ask, "Why are you convinced Henrik did it?"

"Because *he* was trying to steal her needle business, not me. I was trying to help Aunt Perle's business—not that she wanted my help much. But the Viking idiot? He wanted it for himself."

This was news to me. "How do you know that?"

"Because he was trying to convince me to do designs for *him*."

That made no sense. "What?"

"Henrik knew Aunt Perle was talking to me about the design concept." He held up his arm. "This one."

"I know that."

"Yeah, well, long before she started working on the whole line, Henrik sends me this sneaky e-mail. Says he wants to 'surprise' Perle"—he made angry air quotes with his fingers—"by creating the whole line and getting it to market for her. Offers me a lot of money if I'll do designs for all the needles but keep it quiet. How dumb does he think I am? Who steals their girl's idea like that? The whole point was that these were Danish designs, and he's not even Danish. I'll bet he doesn't even realize Norway and Denmark are different countries," he muttered before narrowing his eyes at me. "Mark of a guy in 'true love,' huh?" More angry air quotes.

Perhaps we should have been making our way to the police station by then, but I decided to get the whole story out of Nolan now while he was willing to spill it. I poured my own cup of coffee and sat down across from Nolan. "Are you saying Henrik was working with you behind Perle's back?"

"*Trying* to work with me," he corrected sharply. "Or thought he was working with me. I was trying to string the guy along until I had enough information to prove it to Perle. Only she got her own designs out faster than either of us expected." He paused to give me a smug look. "A really good design concept will make that speed possible, you know."

I tried to ignore the jab. "Why didn't you just tell your aunt what Henrik had done? Didn't you think she'd believe you?"

"Come on. She has—had—a massive blind spot where he was concerned, if you know what I mean." He drained the last of his coffee, and I poured him more. "Although maybe not, when you consider the letter."

This was getting more interesting with every passing minute. "What letter?"

"She gave me a letter I was supposed to get to Martingale. A sort of plan B, I guess."

I stared at him in surprise. "And you haven't? Why on earth not?"

"Because he's as much of jerk as Henrik."

I was just about to dig into the subject of whatever was between Nolan and Derek when the young man's eyes darted around the store and he lowered his voice. "And because of what's in it."

"What's in it?"

"She told me it hands over her business to me—well, the needle part, at least. I'm not exactly sure about the other parts. I sure hope they don't go to Henrik." He cocked his head at me. "So, if you were me, would you give that to someone like Derek Martingale under the circumstances?"

He had a point, sort of. That letter documented a pretty handy motive for murder on his part. "You could have given it to the police and not to Derek. Witholding evidence makes you look bad. You've got to stop digging your own grave here."

It occurred to me at just that moment that I might have a blind spot of my own. The facts were lining up rather heavily against Nolan. Just because I felt a small artistic connection with him didn't mean he wasn't guilty. He could, in fact, be Perle's killer, and I couldn't ignore that. I stood up. "When Chief Reynolds gets here I want your word that you'll tell him everything you know. No more secrets."

His eyes widened. "You want me to confess?"

His question surprised me. "I want you to tell the truth. *Did* you kill Perle?"

"No!" he shouted back. "It was Henrik. I'm sure of it."

Not wanting to get into a shouting match of accusations, I tried a different tactic. "Was it also Henrik who hired someone to slash the yarn off our trees disguised as you?"

Nolan's laugh was sharp and dark. "Of course. It's a stupid move, but the idiot Viking is dumb enough to try something like that, isn't he?"

I didn't know about that, but quite frankly I hadn't come up with any ideas about who would have pulled that stunt. But it was a dramatic move, which meant I wouldn't put it past Henrik.

Frank pushed through the door only a minute or two later, not bothering to hold his frustration in check. He frowned at Nolan and made a sound that was something close to a growl. Nolan wilted slightly at the chief's glower, but I pulled Frank into the shop and sat him down at the table opposite Nolan.

"Son," he said, "you've got to stop this disappearing or I'll be forced to show you part of the station you haven't seen yet."

So, what do you know? We *did* have cells. For a ridiculous second I wondered if they had real iron bars like in the movies. I decided now wasn't the time to ask.

"Nolan came in of his own accord," I pointed out as I joined them at the table, even though the words "came in" sounded too much like some spy thriller. "And he's got a lot to say."

Frank pulled out his notepad, clicked his pen, and hovered it above a new page. "Well, then, you'd better start talking."

"I didn't do it," Nolan said with a hint of desperation. He'd realized, I hoped, just how close he was to the end of

Frank's patience. "Not the yarn-bomb thing or what happened to Aunt Perle."

Hoping to speed matters along, I jumped in. "Tell Chief Reynolds what you just told me about Henrik."

Frank gave me a look I suspect loosely translated to "Why do you keep finding things out without me?" before nodding toward Nolan.

"He was scheming to take Aunt Perle's needle business right out from underneath her," Nolan offered.

That caught Frank's attention. "And you know this because . . . ?"

"Because he thought he was scheming with me. I was pretending, of course, leading him along until I had enough stuff to prove it to Aunt Perle. She was so sure he loved her." Nolan's bitter laugh told me just what he thought of that idea.

"Go on," Frank cued him.

"Right after I sold the design concept to Aunt Perle, before she decided to design the rest of the line herself rather than make me a partner and let me do it . . ." Nolan seemed to realize how bitter that sounded, so he exhaled and calmed his tone. "Right after that, I got a call from Henrik. Which I thought was weird."

Frank made a few notes. "Because . . ."

"The needles were Perle's idea. Not his."

Frank whirled his hand in a keep-going gesture.

"He laid out this whole idea to do the line himself. Made it out like it would be a surprise, like it was this big favor to put together the line and get it to market without her help. It got weird when he kept going on about how I couldn't say anything to her or anyone else. That didn't seem legit to me, so I just sort of went along with things until I could figure out what he was up to."

"So you strung him along?" Frank's annoyance was replaced with a fierce curiosity now.

"Until I thought I had enough to convince her." Nolan swallowed hard. "But I shouldn't have waited, should I?"

The young man fidgeted with the stack of leather and steel bracelets on his right wrist. I realized none of them looked as if he ever took them off, and they certainly hadn't been on his right wrist in the video. "When Henrik told me he was going to propose at the dinner thing, I figured I had to tell her."

"He told you he was going to propose?" I asked.

"Yeah, he just sort of changed his story. He started talking like the needle line was going to be an engagement gift to her, which made no sense because she was already announcing the needle line. What was he going to do, produce a competing line or something?"

"Or go back on his story and make sure you stayed quiet about what he had been planning," I added, remembering the dark look Henrik gave Nolan when he first saw him.

"Well, yeah. That's why I showed up, why I bought all the tickets. I couldn't think of another way to get to Perle before the dinner thing. Before she said yes to him. But he was always around her. I finally got a chance when she went over to the theater. That's when she gave me the letter."

Nolan had been in the theater that afternoon? That was a new twist.

"So it was you she opened the theater door for." Frank had always theorized that she'd unlocked the door for someone she knew. I was waiting for him to pounce on the fact that Nolan had just placed himself at the scene of the crime, but Frank did not continue.

"It was the only chance I had to tell her everything. Only,

go figure—she already knew. She'd worked out what he was doing. She wasn't going to say yes." This case was taking more twists and backtracks than turning a sock heel—which is nothing but twists and turns if you're not yet a knitter (notice I said *yet*).

"Or," Frank said very deliberately, "none of this is true and she was going to say yes, and you killed her. You just admitted you were alone with her at the crime scene during the time she died."

"No!" Nolan protested. "I went to talk to her, that's all. It was the only time I could find when *he* wasn't right beside her. I didn't kill her. I swear it. I mean, I was mad at her and worried about her, but"—he wrung his hands—"I didn't."

I have never seen someone express such obvious doubt by the simple act of setting down a pen. Frank was really good at this. "Can you prove your story?"

Nolan huffed. "It's not like I wore a wire."

Frank grimaced. "Why does everyone think we live in *Law and Order* episodes?" He leaned in toward Nolan with fierce eyes. "E-mails between you and Henrik? Text or voice messages? Drawings or papers you gave him or he gave you?"

Shaking his head, Nolan replied, "Henrik's a dork about lots of other things, but evidently he's smart about keeping his hands clean. We did everything over the phone. No e-mails, no text. No paper trail."

"But if we get phone records, they will show calls between the two of you?"

Nolan straightened. "Yeah, they will."

Frank pushed his notepad across the table to Nolan. "Write down your cell number and provider here."

When Nolan hesitated, Frank added, "Relax. We're not

going to read your texts to your girlfriend or see what movies you downloaded. Just numbers you called and who called you."

"*Boy*friend," Nolan corrected defiantly. "And you'd better not be reading his texts or anyone else's."

Frank wasn't an especially cosmopolitan guy, but I gave him points for not stumbling over Nolan's revelation. "Tell him about the letter," I nudged.

Reluctantly, Nolan pulled a business-sized envelope from his backpack. It was crumpled in the corners and had a smudge of something blue on the back, but elegant and artful handwriting addressed the piece to Derek Martingale at Gibson House Publishing. "Aunt Perle gave this to me to keep if something went weird at the dinner. She was all tense about everything. I definitely got the sense she was going to drop some big bomb there. And I asked her about it, but she just denied it. Wouldn't tell me anything."

"Why didn't you show this to me before?" Frank asked.

"Because of what's in it."

Frank looked at the sealed envelope. "She told you what this letter says."

Nolan's face drew itself into tight, angular lines. I couldn't blame him. He knew the contents of that letter didn't reflect well on his claims of innocence in Perle's murder.

"She told me it leaves the needle line—and I think the book royalties—to me if anything happens to her."

Frank sat back in his chair. "Well, that does complicate things. For you. From where I sit, you had both motive and opportunity."

Nolan stood up, nearly shaking as he alternated between stuffing his hands into his pockets and raking them through his hair. "I didn't do it, I swear to you. I wouldn't. I mean, yeah, Perle and I had our moments, and I was mad that she

went ahead and designed all the needles without me, but"—
he turned and looked at Frank—"not enough to strangle
her."

"And you've shown this letter to no one before now?"
Frank pressed. To me it looked as if the envelope was still
sealed, but I suppose that could have been faked.

"Come on, would you? Doesn't exactly help my case,
does it?"

"Nor does disappearing," I interjected. "Twice."

Nolan slumped back down into his chair. "I get it, okay?"

Frank looked at both sides of the envelope one more
time before producing a small jackknife from his pocket
and sliding the tip under the envelope flap.

"You can do that?" Nolan protested. Honestly, I was surprised the young man hadn't opened it already, given the
situation. Funny how Nolan felt it was okay to disappear
during a homicide investigation but not to peer at mail that
wasn't his. "It's addressed to the publisher guy."

"It's not US mail, and it's pertinent to the case. So yes,"
Frank said pointedly as he pulled out the contents of the
envelope, "I can."

We fell silent as Frank scanned the single sheet of paper
filled with elegant script. It didn't look like much of a legal
bequest to me, but I have no idea about such things.

"See what I mean?" Nolan said nervously as Frank
moved his eyes down the page. "That says I benefit if something happens to her."

Frank finished and looked up. "No, it doesn't."

Shock flashed across Nolan's face. "She lied to me? I
follow her instructions and save the letter for Derek and
she's leaving it all to the stupid Viking? Why'd I even
bother?"

"She's not leaving anything to anyone. This letter is not

a bequest. It's a demand that Gibson House Publishing stop all production on her next book, *Norwegian Wedding Knits*."

That wasn't at all what Perle had told Nolan. Had she made him believe the letter benefited him to ensure he did turn it over to Derek? How much scheming was going on between these people?

"The goodbye of her second speech," I finally said, catching Frank's eye.

Frank slid the paper back into the envelope. "Seems it's time to have another conversation with Mr. Martingale. I'll give him until that conference of his is over, but you can bet I'll be waiting for him upon his return."

Frank glared at Nolan. "Are you going to wise up? Or do I need to show you to what Angie calls our special guest accommodations?"

Nolan pulled out his phone. "I'll have an Airbnb within the hour."

CHAPTER SIXTEEN

I would have liked to see how things played out after that, but I had a crucial after-school appointment to keep with a certain young lady at our local mall.

Ah, the mall. Few places are more crazily unique than a mall with a thirteen-year-old girl. It's a whole world to a teenage girl—one we adult people have nearly forgotten. As Jillian and I walked the terrazzo halls of a shopping mall two towns over, I was reminded how huge everything is to someone her age. Not in size, but in scope.

She'd chosen her current outfit carefully—jeans with those absurd deliberate rips I still don't understand, a striped sweater in colors that did wonders for her eyes, boots, and a little brown leather cross-body bag for her ever-present phone and such. Everything matched well—but not perfectly. Any woman can recognize "chosen to look thrown together"—not that I'd ever admit it to her. We chatted amiably, but often her eyes would scan the retail landscape for schoolmates. I wasn't so old that I didn't remember those days when a trip to the mall was as much about *being seen* as about buying something.

Given the last-minute nature of our mission, I'd come with a shopping strategy in mind. I quickly abandoned it when Jillian laid out her own: shop her four favorite stores, pick one or two possibilities from each, then circle back for her winning choice. Her smart system wasn't far off my own, clever girl. My only addition—a welcome one at that—was a pause for snacks at the food court as we considered her finalists.

Slurping on a brightly colored smoothie as I sipped a latte, Jillian pulled out her phone. We had, of course, taken photos of each preferred dress. "So, I've got five that I like," she proclaimed.

Remembering how much I hated my mother's weighing in on any such consideration, I steered clear of voicing any preference. I simply smiled and said, "You really do have a great eye for line and color. All the ones you picked looked great on you."

She didn't reply, but her cheeks did turn pink a bit at the compliment.

"So, is any one standing out to you at the moment?" I dared to ask.

Jillian started to answer, but was interrupted by yet another text. Her phone had been going off nearly nonstop throughout our visit. She tapped a reply with fingers flying at an impressive speed, then swiped back to the photos. It made me wonder if kids today even know that there was an era when people did only one thing at a time. They multitask like we breathe.

She returned to the shot of a peacock blue velvet dress with satin touches. "This one."

I debated the wisdom of letting her know it was my favorite as well. Instead, I opted for "Why?"

It didn't surprise me that she had a ready answer. "The color will stand out, and like you said, it looks good on me. It's pretty but it's not all ruffly. And the sleeves only go halfway, so I won't be hot up onstage, 'cuz it gets hot up there with the stage lights on."

I caught a slip of hesitation in her voice. She'd said over and over again, in true middle school angst, that her dress had to be perfect. "But . . . ?"

The phone went off again. She scanned the text, rolled her eyes in oversized exasperation, and moaned, "Katy Davis is such a drama llama," before tapping back a reply.

I amused myself by wondering what Henrik would say if I referred to him as a "drama llama." I suspect his response would put a mere eye roll to shame. Actually, if you combined Henrik, Derek, and Nolan, I felt surrounded by a whole herd of drama llamas.

Jillian met my gaze with analytical eyes. "The price is right up to what Dad told me I could spend." Gavin, in his usual highly efficient way, had presented Jillian with a prepaid credit card for the amount he was willing to spend on this little adventure. I thought it was clever, if calculating, and perhaps a tad overcontrolling, given how little time we had. Men don't seem to understand that sometimes *the* outfit for a big occasion doesn't pay much mind to your budget.

"But you've got enough to get that dress," I assured her.

She slumped back in her chair. "Yeah, but it's gonna need a blue headband. They had one I saw on the way out of the store." She set the phone down and rested her chin in one hand. Not exactly drama llama, but definitely pouty. "It wouldn't be perfect without the headband."

My heart went out to Jillian. This wasn't just a dress for

a concert. This was something that needed to go right after a summer of a whole lot going wrong for her. Her mother was the kind of beautiful, flawlessly dressed woman who made most of us feel understyled. It was tough to have that kind of mom while you were still bumbling through all the awkwardness of middle school. And then imagine that icon of style leaving you in the dust while she traded up for a new, more luxurious life. Jillian needed to feel pretty. Any woman could understand that.

I paused and took a sip of my coffee before I casually suggested, "You know, I could spring for the headband as my contribution to the cause." Truly, I very much wanted to. While a large purchase to her, it was an easy one for me. And who doesn't want to be part of making *the* dress *the perfect outfit*? After all that had gone wildly off course in the past few days, I craved the chance to put something perfectly right. Especially for her.

Her eyes went wide. "Seriously?"

The glow of being in on something so fun warmed me down to my hand-knit socks. "Sure. I'm with you on this one—it needs to be perfect."

"Dad would never get that."

"Your dad tries hard." I felt compelled to defend Gavin. "But he's a guy, and guys don't always understand stuff like this. You did a good job here. You could have looked at dresses that were way over your budget—"

"Like that red one," she interjected with yearning eyes.

That red one was not only far out of her price range; it wasn't a dress that belonged on any thirteen-year-old any-where. It made me want to stomp up to the cashier in the so-called junior department and shout, "What's the matter with you people?"

I fought an eye roll of my own. "The blue one is definitely a good choice, Jillian. And I had fun. Your dad will be happy."

She polished off a piece of the gargantuan cinnamon bun we were sharing. "He'll be happy he didn't have to come. That's for sure." Her phone went off again.

"Everything okay?" I normally wouldn't have asked, but Jillian looked genuinely worried as she tapped out a reply this time. Gavin had admitted to a bit of concern over one of Jillian's friends, and I wondered if Katy was the one he felt was veering toward being a bad influence.

"Katy's really freaking out."

"She can't find a dress?"

"Actually, it's Jake who's freaking out. He's her brother. The one going to college after Christmas."

Gavin's concern wasn't unfounded. Katy's father had spun through half a dozen jobs, and her mother always seemed in the midst of some enormous crisis—usually of her own making. Drama llamas indeed. If I remembered correctly, Jake was a tall, lanky fellow who had managed to land a much-needed basketball scholarship to the state college. "Jake?" I asked.

Jillian leaned in, eager to tell someone the juicy secret. "Katy says some guy paid Jake a whole bunch of money to do something bad Sunday night and now Jake's flipping out about it. He's telling Katy he has to go hide out in New Jersey for a month 'cuz he's gonna be arrested any minute."

That sounded like a Davisesque drama. And it wouldn't be the first time Jake had gotten himself into trouble. Accepting a big wad of cash to do something bad—would the kid ever learn . . . ?

In a burst of insight, my brain connected the dots. Jake

was tall and lanky. Shrouded in a gray hoodie, he could easily pass for Nolan Huton on a dark night. Trying hard to tamp down the wild curiosity clanging in my brain, I asked, "Did Katy say what it was that Jake got all that money to do?"

My sudden interest stumped her. "No. Just that Jake thinks he could get arrested for it if anyone found out."

I leaned in close to Jillian. "I need you to do me a favor."

"Okay," she said slowly, unsure of where this was going.

"It's gonna sound weird, but it's important."

"Okay," she repeated, looking a little alarmed.

"I need you to ask Katy if Jake was paid to cut the yarn off the Collin Avenue trees."

Jillian pulled back in reluctance. "Wait—what? You're serious?"

"I am," I replied. "And it could be really important and helpful, believe it or not, if it was Jake. Tell Katy I absolutely won't be mad if it was him. In fact, I'd be grateful."

She hesitated. Understandable since I was essentially asking that Katy snitch on her older brother.

"I'm not mad at Jake," I assured her. It wasn't exactly true. I was deeply hurt and disturbed at what had been done, but I wasn't mad at a teenager for giving in to the lure of a huge wad of cash waved in front of his face. No, I saved my outrage for whoever had been waving that wad of cash. And right now Jake could be our means of finding out who that was.

"Please," I said, pleading with Jillian. "It's really important. And if it wasn't that, I don't need to know whatever it was that Jake did. But if it was the trees, I need to talk to Jake about whoever gave him the money."

After an agonizing stretch of time, Jillian nodded and typed in the question.

Seconds later, Jillian turned her phone to show me the one-word reply: YES.

Today was turning out to be a twisty-turny sock heel of a day.

There were two dozen shop tasks that had been left undone in the chaos of Nolan's appearance and Jillian's shopping excursion. I was running on snacks and caffeine. Hank was long overdue for a walk. And now I was about to spend my dinner hour convincing a teenage boy to come clean about his crime-for-hire experience.

I was grateful Jillian's perfect dress had been the one thing to go as planned.

I was also beyond thankful when Margo met me in front of the shop, holding a bakery box. I had called her after I brought Jillian and the Perfect Outfit home. I filled Margo in on the events of the day and asked if she could whip up a dozen fresh chocolate chip cookies. If you need to persuade a teenage boy on short notice, it pays to have a friend who can whip up a dozen cookies in the time it takes to drive home from the mall.

"You're turning into a regular private investigator," Margo said with a wry smile as I accepted the box and set it on the passenger seat.

"It wasn't the side hustle I had in mind," I sighed. The days when I could just sit in the shop and stitch and help customers almost felt like a vacation compared to the past week. "Thanks for these."

Margo leaned in through the open window. "Shouldn't Frank be doing this? Or that detective guy from the county?"

"I thought about calling Frank. But Jake's had enough run-ins with him that I think I might get further on my own." I tapped the box. "Or on my own armed with these. After all, the food tactic worked to get information out of Nolan, so maybe it'll work with his stunt double."

Margo laughed and waved me off as I put the car in gear. "Keep me posted. And congrats on the dress, by the way. Sounds like you hit it out of the park."

"I did," I agreed, still feeling the glow of that success. "And I got a break in the case as a bonus." It almost made up for my anxiety over the job ahead. I had no idea if I could convince Jake to tell me who had hired him. It was possible, I supposed, that he didn't even know.

"'Break in the case,'" Margo said with one hand on her hip. "Listen to you. You're a natural at this."

"Let's hope so."

My pulse felt as if it were shouting in my ears as I drove to the park basketball court where I'd arranged to meet Jake. He could back out so easily, opting not to show. Then again, he knew that I knew he'd cut the yarn, so I hoped that my role as his shot at leniency would work in my favor. And yet I couldn't guarantee that Frank would go easy on him for helping me. Frank had been as grumpy as I'd ever seen him with Nolan earlier today, so I doubted he was inclined to let it slide. The trees were public property, so it wasn't as if I could help Jake by deciding not to press charges. Legally, Jake hadn't done anything to my shop— even though it felt to me like he had.

The truth was, whether Frank treated Jake's act as vandalism was out of my hands. Then again, I had no doubt George had done his best to convince people that what Mom and the Gals had done to the trees in the first place was vandalism. Is unvandalizing vandalism a crime? When had my life become so ridiculously complicated?

Relief flooded my chest when I pulled up to find a lanky

teen I recognized as Jake Davis nervously shooting rapid-fire baskets at one end of the asphalt court. The color was draining out of the sky, but it hadn't started to get too cold. I got out of the car, making sure the box of cookies was in easy view, and settled myself on the small set of bleachers beside the court.

The metal net clanged with the last of Jake's shots, and he palmed the ball as he took slow steps toward me with wary eyes. His hair was a bit darker than Nolan's stark white, but the build was slender enough to match Nolan's. Jake was more athlete to Nolan's artist, but it wasn't hard to imagine they could easily pass for each other in the dark.

"Cookies?" I offered, suddenly finding my tactic silly. I opened the box, hoping the irresistible scent of warm chocolate chip cookies would keep Jake on the bench long enough for me to learn what I needed to know.

"Yeah, sure," he said, sitting a good distance from me on the same bench.

I slid the box over to him—but not before taking one myself. Of course, I told myself it was to establish a connection, to foster communication. Only a total fool passes up a warm, freshly baked chocolate chip cookie in a stressful situation such as this. I might have brought him a hand-knit cap, but somehow I didn't think it would have had the same appeal. Or stopped the growling in my stomach. A latte and half a mall cinnamon bun made for a skimpy day's nourishment.

"Thanks for showing up."

Jake merely nodded, not quite meeting my eyes. Still, I chose to view his selection of two cookies as a sign we were getting somewhere.

"I'm not mad at you," I reassured him. The poor kid looked so stressed and desperate, I found that I really couldn't be angry with him for what he'd done. Jake was a pawn in some larger conflict I didn't fully understand yet. Yes, he'd made a stupid choice, but can you really hold stupidity against a teenager? I made dozens of idiotic choices in high school for less incentive than a thick roll of cash. Most of us could say the same.

He leaned his elbows on his gangly knees. "It was a stupid, weird ask. If it weren't for the two hundred bucks, I probably would have said no."

Two hundred dollars to go cut up some yarn in the middle of the night—certainly my idea of a questionable gig. "Jake, believe it or not, this isn't about what you did. It's about who asked you to do it."

He turned to look at me. "I'm not dumb enough to ask the guy's name."

I was hoping maybe he was. But at least now I knew I was looking for a male. "Okay, then how did he find you?"

Jake turned the ball over and over in his hands. "Here. Sunday afternoon. He walked up to me, flashed the cash, and asked if I wanted to make a quick two hundred. Told me what to do, when to do it, and to wear a gray hoodie. And the sleeve. That was the weirdest part."

It took me a moment to work out what he was talking about. "The tattoo? Or what was supposed to look like the tattoo?" I had genuinely wondered how they'd managed to pull that off.

To my surprise, Jake reached into the pocket of his sweatshirt and pulled out what looked like a flesh-colored compression sock. It had the design I'd spotted in the video, and at one end was something similar to a leather bracelet to hide the seam. To be honest, it seemed crudely and hastily made—as if someone used a black marker on the sock to make the design. After all, it didn't have to look convincing up close, only on a grainy video. It was clever and re-sourceful, in a creepy kind of way.

"Is it okay if I keep this?" I asked. *Evidence,* my newly sleuth-focused brain said.

He shrugged. "Yuh." He polished off the second cookie and reached for a third. I won't lie and say I wasn't relieved to feel free to choose a second myself. Sweet, gooey, and still just a bit warm—cookies should never come any other way.

We sat for a minute in silence until I carefully asked, "Jake, did it occur to you that this man was using you to frame someone else?"

"It was two hundred bucks." He was starting to tense up. He gobbled down the cookie and began bouncing the ball on the asphalt at his feet. I wasn't sure how much longer I could keep him talking.

While part of me wanted to launch into a speech about how "easy money" is never easy, I thought better of it. "If you don't know his name, do you think you could you de-scribe him to me?"

Jake stopped dribbling the basketball and thought a mo-ment. "Shorter than me."

Jake stood well over six feet. That didn't really narrow things down much. "Hair?"

"Dark. One of those slick cuts that's supposed to look mussed up. A hair gel user, if you ask me. Fancy clothes. Oh, and glasses. The brown-speckle kind."

"Tortoiseshell?" I asked.

"Yeah, I think that's what they call it."

I couldn't believe what I was hearing. Then again, what about all this made any sense? "Fancy watch," I went on, "leather jacket, sounds like maybe he's from New York?"

"'Bout covers it," Jake said. "You know the guy?"

I wouldn't claim to know Derek Martingale well. But I'd bet a ball of vicuña—which clocks in at three hundred dollars a skein, mind you—I now knew what he'd done. "It's complicated," I replied. "But you've helped a lot. And I mean it—I'm not mad at you."

"Do I have to give the money back?"

That was a good question. He had been paid to do a job, and he had done it. Only the job was vandalism of public property. Or was it merely undecoration of public property? "I think that'll be for Chief Reynolds to decide."

Jake looked shocked. "You didn't tell me he'd have to know."

I did omit that little detail on purpose. "I think it will help a lot that you've cooperated, but yes, the chief has to know. We think the man who paid you to do this is involved in a much more serious crime."

"The dead lady."

I winced at the idea of beautiful, brilliant Perle Lonager being reduced to "the dead lady." "Yes," I replied with a sigh. "The woman who was murdered at the theater on Friday night."

Jake began bouncing the ball again. "I don't have to . . . go with you now, do I?" He looked concerned I might be considering a citizen's arrest.

I was considering no such thing. "No." Then, thinking of Nolan's mistake, I added, "Just don't disappear. We may need to talk to you again."

His eyes scanned the park. "Okay, then. I . . . um . . . I gotta go."

"Thank you, Jake. Keep the cookies."

"Yeah." He scooped up the box with one hand while still dribbling the ball with the other as he stood up. It was an oddly impressive feat. Jake looked back over his shoulder twice at me before disappearing around the fence at the far end of the park.

I sat there for a few minutes, trying to wrap my head around what I'd just learned. Derek Martingale tried to frame Nolan Huton. But why? To what end? To make him look more guilty and therefore the prime suspect for Perle's murder? To scare me? And how was Derek involved in all of this?

I had no idea. But Derek had more than a few questions to answer. From me and most likely from Chief Reynolds.

CHAPTER SEVENTEEN

"Derek? The guy from the publisher?" Margo's eyes were as large and round as one of her shortbread cookies when I brought her up to speed.

We were sitting at the shop table sharing take-out Chinese and slices of Boston cream pie after Y.A.R.N. had closed. Derek hadn't yet returned from DC—if that was really where he was—and he wasn't returning calls. Frank was threatening to send his two biggest officers to go fetch Derek if he didn't show soon.

Since Margo's husband, Carl, was playing poker with his brother, and I was too wound up to go home alone, we opted for this offbeat version of "girls' night in." Well, "girls' and dog's night in" if you counted Hank.

"Anybody got a guess as to why?" she asked over her carton of moo shu pork.

"I can't work it out," I replied, dipping into my Kung Pao chicken. "Even if his goal was to stop Perle from walking away from her book deal, murdering her makes no sense. Nor does framing Nolan."

"Except that it worked," Margo said as she waved a chopstick at me. "You all thought it was Nolan in that video and it made him that much more suspicious. I mean, if you hadn't worked it out about the tattoo being on the wrong arm, would you have believed Nolan if he denied it was him?"

Margo had a point. "Probably not. And we'd be even less likely to believe him denying anything about Perle. I'm not sure I believe everything he's telling us now. All his disappearing hasn't done much for his credibility." I fished out a piece of chicken and fed it to Hank. Spicy food is a favorite of his—next to Margo's sweets, of course. He gobbled it up and proceeded to loudly lick his chops for the next few minutes as if that might entice me to give him more. Hank's a first-class mooch. Then again, I'm an easy mark.

"So Perle was planning to ditch her publisher. Her whole career, for that matter." Margo reached for more rice. "Sad, when you think about it. She had a ton of talent."

"The whole thing is just so sad. It's like getting a front-row seat to the dark underbelly of people." I sat back, feeling the weight of the very long day. "I got into the business because crafting brings out the best in people. I don't want to see the worst of people. And lately, I feel like that's all I've seen."

"Well, at least we haven't seen any more outbursts from Henrik today. What's he doing anyway? Still in town?"

"He told me he's not leaving until Perle's murder is solved. I'm trying not to seek him out, honestly." I sighed. "He's a bit much, you know?"

"Did I tell you he came into the shop asking if I had any Danish Dream Cake left over?" She gave a small laugh.

"Of course I do. I have tons left over and it doesn't keep. I did have to listen to a long speech and a lot of mournful wails. I do feel sorry for him, but he's kind of a lot to take."

I had forgotten about all the desserts Margo had made for the event. And what about the dinner at the inn that hadn't happened? I had no idea—and hadn't thought to ask—if any of the event guests had actually eaten. After all, the food had to have practically been in the ovens when we discovered Perle was missing. Bev had been terribly apologetic and supportive, not yet bothering me with details, but was I on the hook for all those dinners while having to refund ticket prices? How many of my friends and neighbors had lost money on my dream event?

I felt helpless to squelch the guilt that I had let myself, the shop, and the whole town down. I'm sure George would have heartily endorsed that theory.

"Hey," Margo said, catching my sudden quiet, "it's Frank's job to settle this, not yours. This isn't your fault. None of it. And it's not on you to fix it."

My attempt at a smile must not have been very convincing, because Margo straightened up and said, "Tell me about Jillian. You said the knitting lesson went great. And let's hear about the perfect dress you found."

Now that did make me smile. I recalled Jillian's excited eyes and rows of quickly perfected stitches. "You should see how that girl took to knitting."

"She had the best teacher I know," Margo boasted. "And the dress?"

I felt my smile broaden. Margo was right. I'd let all the dark complications overshadow some very positive things that had happened lately. A dear friend is always good to refocus you when your thinking gets out of whack.

"Honestly, it couldn't have gone better." I recalled Jillian twirling like a princess before the dressing room mirror. "Jillian got the most beautiful peacock blue dress. It made me happy just to see her look so happy and confident."

Margo grinned herself. "I'll bet. No fights over price or her wanting something too old for her?"

I thought of the racy red dress. "I didn't think girls her age could be that sensible, honestly. She stayed right within the budget Gavin set for her. I only helped a little."

Margo caught that. "A little?"

"She wanted a headband to go with the dress." I felt myself flush. "I might have funded that purchase. And a pair of earrings. But I did draw the line at a manicure."

Margo laughed and drowned her dish in more soy sauce. "Well, aren't you sensible?"

Actually, had Jillian not dropped the bomb about Jake Davis, I might have sprung for whatever the nonmother equivalent of a mother-daughter manicure was at the mall salon. That, and I didn't know Gavin's position on nail polish.

"The concert's tomorrow? Rhonda said you were going."

I tucked in the flaps on my box and reached for two fortune cookies—one for me and one for Hank. Given the recent course of events, I was actually a bit nervous about cracking mine open. The odds of bad news felt too great. "Mom said I was going to have dinner with Gavin at the Blue Moon even before Gavin asked." I grimaced. "Does it make sense that she's more annoying because she's so right?"

"I've never gotten the impression Rhonda cares about making sense." Margo raised one eyebrow. "She's paired you and Gavin off. You know that, don't you?"

I groaned. "Mom doesn't leave much to the imagination. About anything. If she was as blatantly honest with her doctor as she is with me, we wouldn't have half the problems we're having these days."

"So Gavin is taking you to dinner before the concert. And at the Blue Moon."

I gave Margo a glare. "Why do I get the feeling you knew that even before I knew that? The Blue Moon is Jillian's favorite," I reasoned.

"It's also *yours*," Margo seemed too pleased to point out.

"A lot of people like good Alfredo. I'm not unique."

"There's where you're wrong. You're as unique as they come, Libby Beckett, and don't you ever forget it."

Rather than take on that declaration, I tore open the wrapper and cracked the crispy cookie to pull out the slip of paper. "'Good gifts come inside challenging wrappings,'" I read out loud.

"That's rather apropos, don't you think?" Margo asked as she reached for her own cookie.

"That could have been Hank's cookie, you know."

Margo fixed me with a no-nonsense stare. "But it's not. That one's all yours. Hank's would have been 'Good things come in smelly garbage cans.'"

"Very funny," I murmured as I opened what Margo had declared Hank's cookie. "'You will find what you seek.'"

Margo plucked her slip from the cookie and tossed the cookie to Hank. He caught it midair, and chomped loudly and happily on the goody. "Well, look at that—it came true already." She shifted her gaze to me. "We can only hope the same for yours."

"Please tell me you're not jumping on the Gavin-and-Libby bandwagon. I need someone on my side of this mess."

"I am on your side," she replied. "I just am open to the idea that your side might very well be the Gavin-and-Libby side. Look at how much you like Jillian. That's got to count for something."

"I like your Boston cream pie, too, but that doesn't mean eating it is good for me."

Margo began collecting the containers, the napkins, and the twelve extra packets of soy sauce Madam Soo's seemed to send with every order. "Let's talk about the important subject, then."

I rested my chin in my hand. "I'm tired of talking about murder. I'm not even touching this thing with Martingale, because I'm just too exhausted to get involved with another complication. I've knit lacework shawls with less aggravation."

As she was tucking the containers into the small fridge below the coffeemaker, Margo said, "That's not the important subject I had in mind." She shut the fridge door with a resolute thud. "What are you wearing to tomorrow night's date with Gavin?"

Y.A.R.N. was starting to look like it stood for "You Attract Relentless Nagging." I put every ounce of decisiveness my weary soul had into the words "It's not a date."

"A handsome man buying you dinner is a date." The singsong way Margo said it harkened back to a schoolyard guess-who-likes-you announcement.

I held my ground. "A man buying me *and his daughter* dinner is not a date. It's a thank-you."

Margo's persistent nature was showing up. "Cards are for thank-yous. Dinners at the Blue Moon are dates." She gave me a look. "Besides, what would be so awful about you taking up—again—with Gavin? He's handsome, he's single, his daughter adores you, and he isn't under suspicion of murdering anyone."

"I'm not ready!" I blurted so loudly, Hank stood up and growled at the door. Startled myself, I tried to gather my

thoughts and explain. "It would be unbelievably complicated with Gavin. Complicated is the last thing in the world
I want right now." I looked across the street at the bare tree
in front of Margo's shop, stark and lonely on the sidewalk
in the small bit of gray daylight left. "I'm worried this
whole thing'll send the shop under."

I hadn't dared to give voice to that fear until just this
moment. My whole self was invested in this place. I didn't
know who I would be if it went under. I honestly couldn't
say I'd recover—and that terrified me. It's why I suspect the
cutting of the yarn off the trees felt like such a personal
wound. Why the murder of Perle—a woman I hadn't even
met before four days ago—pained me deeply.

Margo's face melted with the compassion of a long, deep
friendship. "Oh, hon," she said, "the shop isn't you. Even if
it folded tomorrow—which it won't—it wouldn't change
who you are. You're the shop, but it's not you."

Tears stung my eyes. "I'm going to pretend that whatever you just said made sense." Still, I knew what she was
trying to tell me. I'd fought too hard for the sense of self-
worth I'd cobbled together after Sterling. Nothing could
take that away from me if I didn't let it. And I could choose
not to let it, even in the midst of this dreadful mess. There
were a lot of reasons why I wasn't ready for things to
deepen—make that redeepen—between Gavin and me.
Y.A.R.N.'s success wasn't tied to him or to anyone. It was a
business venture, not a judgment on my life.

I thought of a dozen things to say to Margo, but in the
end I just sniffed and gave her a huge hug.

"Just ease up a tiny bit on the Gavin thing, okay?" I said
after we pulled apart, both of us wiping our eyes.

"He could be so good for you . . . ," she started, then

made a show of snapping her mouth shut when I narrowed my eyes at her. Both her hands went up in surrender.

I found my coat and keys, unwilling to admit that maybe I was just the tiniest bit lonesome at the thought of going home to a dark house alone. I consoled myself with a big snuggle of Hank's gorgeous furry face. I had loyal companionship. It just came on four legs instead of two.

I was in the shop early Wednesday morning, holed up in my office braving a first look at the financial losses from the event. Just before opening, I heard a knock on the shop door and ducked out of my office to see Frank.

"Got a minute?" The serious look on his face told me he was not here to discuss urgent needlework.

"Of course." We walked inside toward the center table. I grabbed my mug off the counter and nodded at the tray of mugs by the coffeemaker, but he shook his head.

"I had a late-night conversation with Martingale."

I could only imagine. "How late?"

"So late it was early this morning. I wasn't feeling especially accommodating. Sometimes you get more out of a surprise middle-of-the-night door pound than you do out of a nice procedural 'Come on down to the station.'"

"And?"

"When I informed him what Davis told us, our man lawyered up in a New York minute."

"I suppose we could have expected that. Did he say anything?"

"Oh, I got an earful of 'You'll be hearing from my attorney.'"

I could easily picture Derek making that declaration.

"Did he say why he did it? Did he admit to doing anything at all?"

"Of course not. But he told me what I needed to hear."

"What was that?"

Frank stuffed his hands in his pockets. "People run to their lawyers for two reasons: guilt or fear. Or both. He's a case of both. He knows we can nail him for paying Davis, so he needs legal advice to keep the damage to a minimum. That's as good as a confession to me. I can wait to tick the legal boxes now that he's as good as tipped his hand."

"Do you think he's our killer?"

"I think he knows way more than he's telling us," Frank said with a grunt. "'Course, I've thought that all along. The trick will be to get out of him what he knows."

A thought occurred to me. "Can he confess to hiring Jake without telling us why?"

"Good legal counsel makes a lot of annoying things possible. But I have my guesses as to why. He wasn't pointing us toward the kid just because he doesn't like tattoos."

"Derek was diverting our suspicions away from himself. A red herring, to use the literary term."

"A rather ineffective one at that," Frank replied. "Just because Nolan hacks down some yarn doesn't mean he killed Perle."

I used Margo's argument. "But if I hadn't figured out about the tattoo, we'd have totally assumed it was Nolan. All the denying he did in the face of the bank video would have made us less likely to believe any denying he's done about Perle. Derek has a cunning streak a mile wide."

The chief offered me the first smile I'd seen in a while from him. "For a yarn lady, you make a pretty good detective."

"I think I'd rather leave all that to you." I took a sip of coffee. "What's next?"

Frank pressed his lips together. "We keep working while we wait for Mr. Martingale's high-priced New York lawyer to find the time to take the train down. With any luck, we'll catch a break that'll let me charge him with murder while he has his lawyer handy." He sighed. "I'd like to wrap this thing up as fast as possible."

"You and me both."

Brightening, Frank nodded toward the shopwindows. "Nice comeback, by the way. George'll be furious, but that'll be part of the fun."

"What are you talking about?"

"You didn't put Rhonda up to it?"

Those are never soothing words to hear. "What did Mom do now?"

Frank pulled me over to the window, where I nearly fell over in surprise, delight, and shock.

Mom, the Gals, and it seemed a small posse of other women were spread out across the avenue rebombing the trees. And Mom herself was doing the one smack-dab in front of George's office.

I stared at Frank, then at the granny SWAT team currently wrapping yarn around Collin Avenue trees, then at Frank again.

He merely tipped his hat and grinned.

CHAPTER EIGHTEEN

Wednesday night's dinner was lovely. Two hours before the concert, Gavin, Jillian, and I sat around a table at the Blue Moon enjoying some very good pasta. Neither Mom nor Margo would ever know I'd changed dresses four times before deciding on a simple navy dress with a spectacular sky blue silk lace shawl. Not that they hadn't inquired. Mom gave her opinion yesterday, and Margo called three times this afternoon to ask me what I was wearing since I hadn't ever answered the question over dinner last night.

This is not a date dress, I assured myself as I twirled my fork around some exquisitely caloric Alfredo with shrimp. *This is a nice dinner dress.*

Gavin had spruced up for the occasion as well—although both of us were going far out of our way not to notice or comment on each other's appearance. He seemed to have the same ambivalence about what tonight was as I did.

We both compensated by slathering Jillian with compliments on her outfit. It wasn't hard to do—she looked perfectly lovely. All the praise made her smile and blush in a way that made my heart glow.

"I get dessert, right?" she asked her dad as she polished off a dish of four-cheese macaroni.

"You'd better," I teased, "because I know I want some." The Blue Moon's tiramisu is the stuff of legend, and I was feeling my first light mood in days. No way was I going to pass up dessert tonight.

"Are you sure you can sing after cheesecake?" Gavin joked. I hadn't seen that playful gleam in his eyes in a long time. For all his seriousness, the man could be downright charismatic.

Jillian punctuated her "Dad . . ." with what I could only call a loving eye roll. Only a thirteen-year-old could stretch "Dad" out to three groaning syllables and get away with it. She had Gavin wrapped around her finger, and I suspect she knew it.

Without our ever discussing it, a silent pact of sorts had grown between Gavin and me not to talk about the murder or the trees or any of that unpleasantness. By dessert and coffee, however, Jillian dared to venture a question. "So, Jake's not gonna get in trouble, is he? I mean, he helped you, right?"

Gavin's lips pressed together. It was clear this whole business with Jake hadn't improved his impression of the Davis family. Nor of Jillian's friendship with Katy, drama llama or otherwise. "Oh, no," he countered quickly. "Jake is still in trouble."

"He's not going to be arrested," I amended. "And he won't have to hide out in New Jersey. Still, it was a bad choice to take Mr. Martingale's money. He's lucky Chief Reynolds was willing to take his cooperation into account."

"So Martingale has admitted to putting him up to it?"

Gavin asked. "Paying Jake to vandalize the trees? Framing Nolan for something he didn't do?" I figured his emphatically criminal wording was for Jillian's benefit.

"Why did he pay Jake to do that?" Jillian asked.

"Well, that's just it. He won't tell us. At least not yet."

Surprise widened Jillian's eyes. "Doesn't he have to?"

I didn't want to get into the technicalities of legal representation with her; neither, I suspect, did Gavin. I think we both hoped this evening would be an escape from all that.

"Mr. Martingale doesn't have to speak to Chief Reynolds again until his lawyer gets here from New York."

"Well, sure, but it's not *that* far away, is it?" Jillian questioned. "Diane's dad goes to New York City all the time."

I sank a fork into the spongy, chocolaty square in front of me. "I suspect Mr. Martingale's attorney is taking his time getting here."

Jillian nodded. "Delay tactic, huh?"

"It's not working," I replied. "Chief Reynolds tells me the fact that Mr. Martingale won't cooperate makes him that much more likely to be guilty." I hoped that gave a sufficient always-cooperate-with-law-enforcement message.

Jillian nodded. "Seems to me it was a pretty dumb move on the guy's part. Hiring Jake and now acting the way he's doing."

"Mr. Martingale is not as smart as he looks," Gavin pointed out.

I had to agree this was one of those "teachable moments" they talk about in parenting magazines. I turned to Jillian. "Mr. Martingale thought he was diverting our suspicions, because we were all ready to believe the worst of Nolan. The way he'd acted earlier had ruined his credibility. I think that's why dads worry about all the little things. They can add up when you need them most."

"Don't worry," Jillian groaned. "I already got the whole reputation speech from Dad."

Gavin tried to steal a bit of Jillian's cheesecake, but Jillian swatted his hand away, ordering him with a pointed finger back to the spumoni he'd ordered. "Thanks to Libby's eagle eye, Martingale's scheme backfired," Gavin went on. "I don't know that I'd trust anything he or Huton says now." He looked at Jillian. "Their actions mark both of them as untrustworthy even if they are telling the truth. Which I don't think they are."

"You guys, enough with the lectures already," Jillian moaned.

I was ready to agree. "I'm sure Chief Reynolds has it all under control." I brightened my tone. "Let's not spend any more of a nice evening talking about this."

When we'd dropped Jillian off in the school music room and gone to wait out in the auditorium lobby, Gavin proved he wasn't quite done. "I can't believe how complicated this whole mess has become. With everything that we know—and don't know—now, who do you think killed Perle?"

"I honestly don't know," I admitted. "I can make a case for Derek, Nolan, or Henrik. And we don't even know for sure that it *is* one of them." I still felt a chill zing down my spine at the thought of someone else out there gloating over the murder. The unsolved case hovered over my head and made me feel threatened. I hated the thought of going through more weeks being wary of shadows and looking behind me all the time.

Gavin shrugged. "It's got to be one of them. I doubt the mob put a hit out on Perle Lonager."

"I feel like I'd know if we could just find the last part of that speech." I wrung my hands in frustration. "That's got to be the key. She wouldn't have gone to such lengths to hide it unless there was some damaging information in whatever she was going to say."

"But what? Derek already knew she was looking to stop writing books."

I looked at Gavin. "But it was more than that. That second speech read like a goodbye to *everything*. I can't think of anything that would make me leave knitting altogether. What could be that huge?"

"Maybe we should go back to the theater tomorrow and look again. Or the hotel room, if Bev hasn't booked it out."

I shook my head. "Bev says she won't until the murder's solved. She's too creeped out to let another guest in there. And Henrik's right next door anyway. She says he's rather . . . loud."

Gavin's eyebrows rose. "You don't think Henrik's got that last part, do you? And he's hiding it because there's something about him in there?"

I sighed. "As far as we know, he was never in the theater. She made it pretty clear she wanted to be left alone in there."

"But she wasn't left alone. Nolan went to see her. What did Derek know about Nolan that he won't tell us?" Gavin's grim question had to be the last word, as the lights dimmed in the auditorium and the concert began.

The concert was wonderful. Nothing can remind you that there's hope for the world than a bunch of singing children. Their joyful faces, coupled with the massive pride and encouragement oozing from the parents all around us—Gavin included—filled my heart.

I felt a long-missing smile spread across my face as Gavin and I headed over to the fundraising concession stand during the concert's intermission. Even though we'd already had dessert, that man knew me well enough to purchase a butterscotch square along with my cup of coffee.

"It'd be wrong not to support the music boosters," he said as he selected a gooey brownie for himself.

"Of course," I agreed. Who couldn't admire a man ready to justify a second course of dessert? "I'm so glad I came. This is a much-needed dose of everything that's still right with the world."

His smile warmed and deepened. "Jillian looked beautiful tonight. I owe you big-time for that."

"It was my pleasure. Truly." I meant it. Tonight really had been a counterbalance to all the wrong in my world.

"And happy," Gavin went on after a sizable bite of brownie. "You have no idea the market value of a thirteen-year-old's smile. They're rare."

"I think you've been doing a great job with her, you know." I knew how hard he had struggled to keep things going well with Jillian since Tasha left.

Gavin shifted his weight, grateful for but uncomfortable with the compliment. "I was pretty ticked when Tasha didn't even seem willing to help a little bit. Not that she could have done much from her beach cabana, but a little effort would have been nice. I was pretty sure tonight would be a disaster."

I sipped my coffee. "Am I allowed to say Jillian was the prettiest girl up there?"

Gavin's grin was 100 percent proud papa. "To me, at least."

"And to me" came a startling voice from behind us. Gavin and I spun around to find Mom and Barb standing in the lobby. "After all, it was my idea."

I had said thank you to Mom for her rebombing stunt a million times today. I had also fended off just as many inquiries regarding tonight. There are only so many ways you can say, "I love you for what you just did," and "Please mind your own business," in the same breath. Of course, she'd not mentioned she was coming.

I tried not to make "What are you doing here?" sound like an accusation. I'm pretty sure I failed.

"Jillian invited me." Mom held up her cell phone. "We text."

I couldn't get Mom to figure out how to send an e-mail. Or order her medicines online. The woman couldn't even set the clock on her microwave. How on earth had Jillian managed to get her *texting*?

"And Barb's granddaughter is in the choir, too," Mom said to what must have been my popping eyes. "Why didn't you ever show me how easy this texting stuff is? I can just talk into my phone and it types. Did you know I can send you pictures? With the right doodad my face can even time-talk to your face."

Face-palm emojis danced in front of my eyes as my coffee went sour in my stomach. A more noble woman would have been delighted someone had found a way to explain the wonders of technology to my Luddite mother. Given the surprise appearance, I wasn't feeling especially noble at the moment.

Mom leaned in. "I heard about that business with Jake Davis. That New York publishing guy really paid him to do that to your trees?"

"To our yarn bombing?" Barb chimed in, sounding equally wounded.

"Jillian told me," Mom explained. She turned to Gavin. "These are tough topics for someone her age. Make sure you talk to her about all this. Children can get the wrong message so easily."

I swear I could hear Gavin's teeth grind over this unsolicited advice. I sank mine into the butterscotch bar to keep them from doing the same.

"Have they arrested him? That horrible publishing person?"

I tried to put a shushing hand up to my mom, but she went right on.

"I haven't liked him since he was so terrible outside your shop the night Perle died. I said to myself right then, I said, 'He probably did it.'"

Two people around us turned and stared at Mom's pronouncement. The last thing I needed was Mom sparking a gossip bonfire. I leaned in with all the seriousness I could muster short of putting my hand over her mouth. "Can we *please* not do this here?"

All I wanted was to go back into the auditorium and lose myself in the beautiful music and Jillian's blue velvet happiness. Now I wasn't sure that was possible.

"Did you two have a lovely special dinner?" Mom asked. As grateful as I was for the change of subject, I knew this one was just as dangerous.

Mom cast a knowing glance back and forth between Gavin and me. "That was my idea, too, you know."

"I don't think so," Gavin said patiently. I could tell the man was tamping down his last stomped-on nerve. Mom could do that to people.

"Well, technically, I suppose I never got the chance to suggest it to you, but I did know you'd make the offer. Any real gentleman would."

I applied the closest thing to the Eye of Death, go-away-now look I'd attempt in polite company. "Enjoy the second half of the concert, Mom."

"Oh, I will. But you'd best tell Frank he needs to solve

this murder business and soon. It's all anyone can talk about." Mom gave my hand a squeeze. "You two have a wonderful evening. Jillian looks absolutely wonderful— well done, Libby."

"Thank you, Mom."

Mom leaned in toward Gavin and winked. *Winked.* "Blue Moon. Good call."

"How did you know we went to the Blue Moon?" Gavin asked.

Mom just held up her cell phone and waved it with a triumphant somebody-texted-me gleam in her eye.

I tried to ignore the images of Jillian giving Mom a play-by-play via text over dinner. And here I thought she was just talking to her friends. When Gavin asked her to put her phone away, I never dreamed he was saving our own privacy in doing so.

"The walls have ears," I said as we sat back in our seats. Only now I felt Mom's watchful eyes burning into the back of my head from somewhere behind me in the audience.

"So does the teenager," Gavin said with an air of defeat. "How am I going to get her through high school at this rate?"

I dared to put a hand briefly on top of his. "Look, you care. And you try. Hard. This whole business right now is more about Mom's filterless meddling than it is about Jillian's." If Mom had ever had a filter, it seemed to have evaporated in front of my eyes.

He looked utterly unconvinced. "You're just saying that to make me feel better."

"Yeah," I admitted with a reluctant smile, "I am."

CHAPTER NINETEEN

Leaving Nolan's and Derek's trails of secrets in the capable hands of Chief Reynolds, Gavin and I made a pact as we ended the choir concert evening. We would focus on Perle. More precisely, on the search for what we hoped Perle had left behind.

Which was how I found myself blowing a smear of dusty theater cobwebs off my arm Thursday morning. "We've been over this place twice," I grumbled, "and nothing."

We had scoured the theater stage, backstage, and even the dressing rooms and lobby in search of Perle's missing speech page or pages. Nothing turned up but some trash, a magazine from 1972, and a dead mouse. This wasn't the outcome I was hoping for. I could have sworn the ghost light was mocking us, standing luminous guard over the scene as if it really were Perle's ghost.

Gavin stood beside the fixture at the moment, turning a

slow, bewildered circle in the pool of light. "It's got to be here somewhere."

Despite our failure to "crack the case wide open"—my inner monologue really was starting to sound like a detective novel—I couldn't classify the morning as a total waste. The conversation that flowed between Gavin and me as we hunted around the space had been remarkably deep.

I heard some things that made me want to smack Tasha for the way she had discarded—sorry, but there isn't another word for it—her role as a wife and mother. I admit my own inability to have children produces some bitterness on the subject, but it seemed Tasha was giving Sterling a run for his money in the lousy-ex department. And that was saying something.

Gavin had spoken openly of his worry over doing right by Jillian. It warmed my heart and softened my irritation at his mile-wide protective streak. Who can blame a man for wanting the things and people he cares about to be safe?

Of course, he also let slip how much he worried over what he called "a high-visibility murder" and its impact on Collinstown. Perle hadn't been much of a celebrity—it was more accurate to say she had been highly regarded by a small but passionate group of knitters—but she hadn't been a nobody, either. A call with Caroline had heightened my fears that the dramatic circumstances, and Henrik's tendency for theatrics, might entice the wrong kind of reporter. I was grateful she'd offered to help if things got heated, but so far we'd kept off the press radar. No one would ever forgive me if Collinstown ended up as a *Frontline* episode.

I couldn't fault Gavin for being protective of it, even if his comments did make me feel a bit as if I'd brought harm to his beloved hometown. The town was a form of family for him. And it was my beloved hometown, too.

I came to stand next to him in the center of the stage, blew out an exasperated breath, and threw my hands up in defeat. "Well, I've got to get back to the shop. All this playing detective has left too much undone back at Y.A.R.N." Linda was putting in loads of extra hours to help, and I didn't want to take advantage of her kindness. Life—even retail life—had to find a way to go on.

Gavin shook his head in commiseration. "Trust me, you don't want to see the pile of untouched paperwork back at the mayor's office." I could hear the reluctance in his voice when he admitted, "I've had two newspapers ask me for a comment. Local ones. I've put off calling them back."

I gulped. Would press interest stay small and local, or were things about to get much worse?

Solve this, every part of me inwardly shouted. "If I get a free moment, maybe I'll go through the stock from the show one more time. I might have missed something there." I was grasping at straws—I knew that—but I could not shake the conviction that the key to this case was in the missing final part of that speech. One more page? Three? A set of note cards? I didn't even know what I was looking for. By the time Nolan and Derek agreed to cooperate, I'd be setting out Easter yarn. I absolutely did not want to spend my Christmas holiday with an unsolved murder hanging over my head.

"Jillian has another lesson with you this afternoon, right?"

There was at least one bright spot in my day. "I'm looking forward to it."

We each said a quick, friendly goodbye—one of those where you aren't quite sure if a hug is the right thing to do, so you don't—and headed off to untangle the knots of our respective professions.

Linda and I were knee-deep again in the boxes and bags brought back from the theater when Henrik walked into the shop. Truth be told, I'd been grateful for his distance—and his quiet—since our last meeting at the inn. I knew he hadn't left town. Frank had told him not to, and besides, Henrik insisted on waiting here for the county coroner's office to release Perle's body.

Bev said she hadn't seen him leave his room at the inn much, either. I felt bad for his grief, but not bad enough to risk a visit to check in on him.

He barged into the shop with his usual bombastic "charm," frowning at the items strewn at our feet. "What are you doing with Perle's stock?"

"The yarn is actually my stock," I pointed out as gently as I could. *People in grief lash out,* I reminded myself. *Try to be nice.* "I'm just going through it one more time." I thought it a kindness to leave out the fact that I was looking for murder clues.

He took a few more strides into the shop. The man really was enormous. "When can I take the needles back?"

I kept my be-nice voice intact. You wouldn't think there could be a knitting emergency, but I have talked more than one customer down off the ledge of a terrible mistake they were sure was somehow my fault. *I advised you not to buy the mohair lace weight. Yes, it's pretty, but I warned you it's not for beginners.* "I suppose when we figure out who they belong to now." I kept my words calm and even.

To no avail. Henrik furrowed his eyebrows into one blond line of exasperation. "Me, of course." He looked annoyed there was even a question about that.

"Don't you think we ought to check with whoever is handling Perle's legal affairs?"

"Me," he declared.

I don't know if Washington is a common-law-marriage or community-property state, but I did know he and Perle had not been legally married yet. "I was thinking more in terms of her attorney," I said with such polite efficiency that Mary Poppins would have admired it. "I'm sure she had a will, yes?"

Henrik backpedaled his anger into frustration. "I don't know." He nearly mumbled the admission. "We never discussed it."

Perle wouldn't have been the first person her age to ignore estate planning, but if she'd had a conversation about it with Nolan, she must have been at least thinking about such things. It occurred to me I'd not yet heard any talk of her family. "Are her mother and father still alive? They must be devastated to lose her like this."

"Perle and her sister started life in a Danish orphanage. That sister was all the family she had before me. I'm sure Nolan told you she died several years back. They were no longer close, but it still hit her hard."

"That might explain why she reached out to Nolan," I offered.

"She did not reach out to him," he shot back quickly. "He hunted her down. Years of distance and then he decides to eye a ride on Auntie's coattails. The nerve." He picked up one of the needles from the boxes stacked on the table. The irony that it was one of the large ones, with the same design as Nolan's tattoo, was not lost on me.

"Maybe he just wanted the only family he had left, too," I suggested.

"He has a father and a sister and an expensive boy-friend," Henrik spit out. "The only thing that boy is lonely for is cash." He fixed me with a glare as if I were the only thing standing in the way of his taking Perle and the needles and heading back to Washington state, never to darken the East Coast again. "This is her art. This was who she was. This is who I lost." His voice constricted as he tightened his grip on the needle. "Why are you keeping these things from me?"

I ventured a step toward him. "We're just going to have to sort this out the best we can. I'm not trying to cause you any more pain, Henrik."

His face hardened at my statement. Henrik broadened his stance, puffing himself up as if his sheer height would bend me to his wishes. "When can I have the needles?"

It wasn't a question. The Viking swagger and charm that had won over knitters' hearts were long gone from the man today.

This is a man who thought he'd be celebrating his engagement this week, I reminded myself. "I'll have to get back to you on that" was the only reply I could come up with that wouldn't start an argument.

"Make sure you do," he ground out, slamming the needle down on the table, then storming out.

"No more Mr. Nice Viking," Linda said after him as she walked over to the table. "Oh, no."

"What?"

"He broke the needle." She held up the needle to show the mother-of-pearl ornament on the end had broken free of the shaft.

I didn't need an angry man breaking stock. "Great. I suppose I was going to have to get in touch with Perle's manufacturer anyway." I picked up both pieces. The ornament had a peg on it that fit into the tube of the needle, and Henrik's slam had knocked the glue loose. "Think we can just glue it back together ourselves?" I peered into the hollow tube of the needle, then tried fitting the ornament back on.

And got an idea.

I dashed to my office and picked up the first piece of paper I could find. Coming back to the table, I rolled it up and slid in into the hollow of the tube.

It fit perfectly.

Linda and I exchanged glances. "You think?"

"We've looked everywhere else. I'm going over to the station and see if they'll let me look at the needles that were found by Perle's body."

Once I explained my theory, and the fact that I was interested only in the blunt ends, not the bloody points, Frank agreed to give me access to the evidence bag holding the two needles. Of course, he had me wear latex gloves and supervised my handling. None of that diluted the eerie sense that I was holding the last things Perle had held.

"Be careful not to go near the pointed ends," Frank warned. They were, in fact, wrapped in some sort of protective film to cover the smears of blood still on the tips from where Perle had used them to defend herself against her killer.

"Don't you have the results back from testing these?" It seemed so crucial to the case that I couldn't understand the delay.

"We're waiting on them," Frank replied, frustration pinching his features. "These stupid crime shows. Everyone thinks police work happens on a sixty-minute time clock these days. It doesn't happen like that in real life. I've got colleagues in DC waiting two years on rape kit analyses.

The county crime lab is moving as fast as they can. If I push them any more, I'll just tick them off."

I looked again at the beautiful—and gruesomely stained—needles. This might just be the artist in me talking, but I felt as if I was holding a metaphor. Henrik was overly dramatic, but he hadn't been wrong in what he'd said. This was Perle's art; this was her. In fact, you could even say it was her family, since Nolan claimed this was his design. Although these days I wasn't sure I could take what anyone said at face value.

I slid both needles from the bag and laid them on the table. Being careful to keep clear of the point, I grasped the upper part of one large needle in one hand and the beautiful mother-of-pearl ornament at the top in the other.

I gave a small gasp as it twisted with only a little effort. If it had been glued tight, it wasn't anymore. I twisted a little bit more and pulled. Like a cork, the ornament popped off the end of the needle.

Frank and I looked at each other in surprise.

I peered inside the hollow of the needle. And there it was. A sheet of paper rolled up and tucked inside. I turned the tube toward Frank so he could see what I saw.

The chief let out a slow whistle. "Well, I'll be. You were right."

"Honestly," I replied, "I would have never even dreamed to look here if Henrik hadn't knocked the end off the needle in the shop." It was a brilliant hiding place. Worthy of all of Perle's creativity and resourcefulness.

"But there were dozens of needles in those boxes. How would she know which ones held the pages?" Frank wondered. "They all look the same."

"Not really." I pointed to the inlay work. "Being hand-made, the needles are all a little bit different. Perle could tell them apart. And there aren't that many of these larger ones. Perle would have had enough time to find which set had her speech inside."

Frank nodded in admiration, finding Perle's plan as ingenious as I did. "She could have easily slipped this set in with the other stock you had while she was at the store."

"So we took them to the theater for her. And she headed over to the theater at the last minute to retrieve them. We'd never know she'd used the theater to hide them because we wouldn't count until after the show. That's why we weren't missing needles even though you had these. We didn't realize she'd added a set."

"It could be she didn't pick these up to defend herself, but that she had them in her hands when the killer attacked. Let's see what's worth all that trouble." Frank looked on as I tapped the needle gently until the edge of the paper fell out from its hiding place. With a careful touch, I grabbed the edge, slid the roll the rest of the way out, and delicately unfurled it on the table.

Perle's speech was on lined paper and all handwritten, unlike the other, typed pages. Multiple words had been scratched out and replaced as if she'd gone over it many times. Evidently Perle hadn't even trusted this to be in her computer. Frank peered over my shoulder as we both read.

It was indeed a goodbye, and a strongly stated one at that. I couldn't remember the exact wording of where Derek's pages left off, but this seemed to be a continuation. She apologized profusely to the Norwegian community, condemning her *stolen right to celebrate the art of their knitting heritage*. She alluded to a sense of her own integrity slipping, and I immediately thought of how things between her and Nolan had gone sour. She had some strong words for the publishing industry—Perle was certainly burning her bridges there—and vowed never to produce another book.

"No wonder she was so nervous before the dinner," I remarked. "I would have been terrified to give a speech like this."

"Look there," Frank said, and gestured at the bottom of the page. "She does leave the needle business to Nolan. And as of now, not after her death." Her speech didn't say why, but I had I feeling it was an atonement of sorts.

"She doesn't leave anything to Henrik," I pointed out. I recalled the man's angry eyes demanding Perle's needles. "That's not going to go down easy."

"Well, no. And I think we can safely assume she wasn't going to accept his proposal. She doesn't even mention him anywhere on this page."

I hadn't realized that, but it was true. Although to me it surely read as if she had been leading up to talking about him. This page stopped midsentence. "A page in each needle," I said, reaching for the second needle. "She really was taking no chances."

Frank grunted. "There must be something on that last page worth going to all this trouble to hide."

"And hide from whom?" I grasped the ornament of the other needle, not surprised to find it twisted off as easily as the first.

An empty needle greeted my inspection. No page, just a hollow tube.

If the final page of the speech had been in that second needle, it wasn't there now.

Frank's grunt turned into a growl. "You've got to be kidding me."

I sat down, deflated. "Whatever bomb Perle had been planning to drop at that dinner, we still don't know what it was."

Frank slumped down beside me. Another failure to "crack the case wide open." Once we'd opened the first needle, I thought this discovery would solve everything. Far from it.

Disappointed, I groped for any silver lining I could find. "Well, this backs up Nolan's story. So maybe what he says about Henrik is true as well."

"But," Frank refuted, "we don't know that Nolan ever saw this. Remember, he always maintained the business went to him upon her death. He didn't know she planned to give it to him now. So he still has motive. And he may have the other page."

I hadn't thought of it that way. "For that matter, I suppose so does Derek. This speech is downright mean. She doesn't spare any words for what she thinks of him and Gibson House." There was no way *Norwegian Wedding Knits* would ever go to press after a tirade like this, even without the cease and desist letter she'd given to Nolan.

"And she wanted the world to know it," Frank added. "She's done with whatever partnership she had with the company. But did you notice she doesn't really say why?"

I frowned at Frank. "It must be on the other page."

And we still had no idea where that page was.

CHAPTER TWENTY

I left Frank to deal with that, knowing I had a knitting student to attend to.

Jillian held up a finished row half an hour later as we sat in the shop for her lesson. "Did I do that right?"

Young minds are indeed great sponges, and Jillian had absorbed a stunning set of knitting skills in our short time together. She'd whizzed through a simple scarf for Gavin's upcoming fortieth birthday, and was starting work on the dog sweater she'd gotten on that fateful night of Perle's workshop. Monty was going to be the best-dressed dog in Collinstown at this point—next to Hank, of course.

"This is way more fun than my algebra homework."

I could only laugh. Spending an hour in this young woman's company was the high spot of my day. "But it can't replace it. Algebra is important."

"Even if I'm going to be an actor?"

I raised my eyebrows at that. Jillian had a beautiful singing voice—a talent that clearly must have come from her mother, because Gavin couldn't carry a tune in a bucket—but this was the first I'd heard of her desire to be onstage. "Does your father know you want to be an actor?"

"Actually," she said with great importance, "I want to be a Broadway star." She checked the instructions, switched colors, and kept stitching with ease despite the complicated pattern. Most new knitters I knew would have had to tackle a project like this in complete silence, but Jillian could chat and stitch as if she'd been doing it her whole life.

"Nothing wrong with aiming high," I remarked as I turned the row on my own work. "But I suspect your dad will want you to have a backup plan. Something other than waiting tables."

Jillian eyed her work. "Maybe I could be a famous knitter like Perle Lonager was. I could have a blog. Or a YouTube channel. Or my own cable TV show."

It still bothered me that we referred to Perle in the past tense. I cast a glance at the row of *Selbu* mittens still hanging on the shop wall. It was easy to imagine Jillian devising such patterns by the time she was Perle's age if not well before. And she wouldn't be the first knitter to whip up a strong social media presence—but she might be the youngest. "I have no doubt you could be YouTube's first teenage knitting star."

Jillian laughed. "Dad would think that's crazy. He doesn't go on YouTube, ever." She gave me a conspiratorial smile. "You could get him to be a lot cooler, you know. I mean, do something about those shirts. For reals." *Eye roll.*

Gavin was no clotheshorse, granted, but I thought he dressed fine. Then again, what do I know? I haven't read a nonknitting fashion magazine in ages. I chose not to reply.

She took that as agreement. "He'd listen to you," she went on. "I heard him telling the office lady at his work how smart he thinks you are. I told him girls like it when you think they're smart."

I could only imagine that conversation. "What'd he say to that?"

"He told me to mind my own business and stop listening in to adults' conversations." Jillian fixed me with a direct look as she switched colors again, making short work of the zigzag pattern that gave the dog sweater such panache. "He also told me not to believe everything I hear from Grandma Rhonda."

I dropped a stitch. Mom had Jillian calling her *what*? "*Grandma* Rhonda?" I questioned, not hiding my shock well at all. Clearly the take-it-down-a-notch conversation I'd had with my mother hadn't had any effect whatsoever. I retrieved the errant stitch. "Don't you already have two grandmothers?"

I immediately regretted the question. "Grandmère doesn't pay any more attention to me than Mom does."

The title caught me by surprise as much as the one Jillian had given Mom. "I didn't know Tasha's mother was French."

"She isn't. She just likes the fancy name." Another eye roll. "It's stupid, but I got used to it." Jillian finished a row and turned her work. With one or two more skills, this girl wasn't going to need any more lessons from me, and I admit that saddened me. I genuinely liked Jillian even despite her turning into Mom's junior meddling partner.

"Rhonda makes a way better grandma," she added. "And she said since I seem to be short one, and she's short any grandkids, I could adopt her."

My surprise must have shown on my face, because she

put her work down and looked at me with worried eyes. "You're not mad or anything, are you?"

I was irritated, a bit stunned, and maybe a touch hurt, but I certainly would never tell any of that to Jillian. "Mom's got a big heart. Why not?" I leaned in toward her. "Sometimes she pays way too much attention to me. Maybe you could deflect a bit and we'll both win." Some part of me was sure I'd regret putting my stamp of approval on "Grandma Rhonda," but I'd lived long enough to know Mom could be an unstoppable force when she got something in her mind.

I replayed the image of Mom's smug smile as she waved her smartphone at me in the school lobby. "And come on, you got her to text—how on earth did you do that?"

Jillian simply shrugged as if it had been a piece of cake. "Exactly how often do you two text?" I tried to sound like it was the coolest thing ever.

Jillian grinned. "Almost every day."

I could have scraped my jaw up off the table. This was a woman who often forgot to turn her phone on or charge it, or left it in places it didn't belong . . . like her freezer. I had never, ever received a text from my mother. One time she tried to answer a text from me and ended up dialing 911. After Frank had sent a squad car to her house and given us all a good scare, he told me never to text her again. Of course Mom just smiled, thanked the officers for their excellent service, and laughed, saying she'd never learn how to do "that newfangled stuff." How had she caught on now?

The minute Jillian had finished her lesson and walked off down the street to the mayor's office, I pulled out my phone. Defying Frank's order—I figured it was defunct now anyway—I texted Mom. You're texting with Jillian? Every day??? I decided I was allowed multiple question marks, given the circumstances.

Her immediate reply made me whack my hand against my forehead (which has its own emoji): Aren't you?

"That's it?" I couldn't believe what Frank had just told me. "That's all you know? It's been a whole week since Perle died."

I got so excited when the chief told me he was stopping by the shop Friday morning with news from the lab. We were finally going to hear the test results that had come back from the blood smears on Perle's needles. We'd know the identity of the attacker Perle was fending off.

No, we wouldn't. I didn't get the revelation I was expecting. Not by a long shot.

"Forensics isn't magic, Libby. This is actually pretty quick—the guys rushed it as a favor to me."

Disappointment pressed against my chest. "It's just . . ." I didn't have a coherent way to end that sentence.

Frank shrugged as he brushed some of the chilly October rain off his coat. The day had been the kind of dreary harbinger of winter that seeps right up through the soles of your shoes. A foggy-waterfront brand of dank that made nearly every knitter yearn for something thick and cozy on their needles. I had a lush and sparkly chunky red wool cowl on mine, testing it out as a good holiday gift for my upcoming shop newsletter.

Frank frowned at me as I set down the project. "We do know it's not Ms. Lonager's blood, which means it's from her assailant."

"Didn't we already know that?"

"We *suspected* that. Now we have proof. This type of thing works best in matching samples."

"So can't we just match the sample to ones from our suspects?"

Frank scrubbed his hand across his chin. "I can't just walk up to people and say, 'Open up and say *ah* so I can swab your cheek.' Not without a warrant, and those are a royal pain to get. Even then a sharp lawyer can poke holes in the data long enough to drag this out eight ways till New Year's." He gave me a hard look. "The tech is peering into a microscope, not a crystal ball." He pointed to the paper he'd set on the table. "This report can help a conviction, but it can't make one. We need more to go on."

I never dreamed we'd be a week out without knowing who killed Perle. The longer this case went unsolved, the longer it snagged at my impatience like a burr on a sweater. That test had to tell us *something* useful. "Well, what do we know now that we didn't know before?"

"We know it's a male," Frank replied.

I fought the urge to throw my hands up in exasperation. "That doesn't help much. Anything else?"

"We can make some basic guesses, rule things out, narrow things down." Frank reached into his shirt pocket and pulled out a second piece of paper. "There are a few interesting things in here." He unfolded the sheet and set it down on the table between us. "Like ethnicity. It takes a specialty lab to really nail that stuff down, but I asked the guys to give me their best guess until those results can come back."

"And what'd they say?"

"They're relatively sure our killer isn't of Asian or African descent."

I stared at the reports. Either page might as well have been in Greek for all the sense I could make of them. "I don't see how that helps. None of our suspects has that ethnic background—that we know about, of course."

Frank pointed to the photo of Henrik and Perle that I'd taken out of the shopwindow; it now sat on a shelf under all those *Selbu* mittens. "But we know a whole lot about the ethnic background of one of them. So I asked them to make a guess specifically about someone of Nordic descent."

Now it was getting interesting. "And?"

"According to my guy, there's very little, if any, evidence of Nordic ethnicity in the blood on those needles."

"So that definitely points away from Henrik. And Nolan has to be at least half Danish if his mother is Perle's sister, right? So are we left with Derek?" I never liked the man, but was he our killer?

"Well, now, you're assuming Nolan's mother *is* Perle's sister. He could be lying, or he could be adopted. You gotta be careful what you assume with things like this."

My head was swimming in everything I couldn't assume. "Can those specialty guys pin it down to New York or Ohio?" It was the saddest joke I'd made in ages.

Frank replied with a long-suffering look. "Ethnicity, not residency. My guy says the specialty lab may need a better sample to get as specific as we'd like. Not to mention it could take several weeks. And we'll need warrants." He pursed his lips. "Unless Derek or Nolan volunteers to be swabbed, we need to find another way."

I stared in the direction of the inn as if I could see our suspects from here. Of course, I didn't know where Nolan's Airbnb was. He could have been sleeping on a houseboat down the river for all I knew. "Derek didn't have a solid alibi," I wondered out loud, trying to think like a detective and not assume anything. "We don't actually know what plane he was on or when it landed. He *told* us he was frantically running around looking for Perle at the time of her murder, but nobody saw him. By the time he came to Bev and me, she was already dead."

Frank nodded. "We don't have solid alibis for any of them. But if you ask me what my gut says, my money's on Martingale."

"Are you going to arrest him?" My craving to see justice done for Pearl had become nearly a physical ache, a rock that sat continually in my stomach.

Frank shook his head. "Not on gut, and we don't have enough to make a conviction stick, given how much legal weight he's likely to throw at us. Not yet. What we do have is another point in the right direction." He fixed me with a direct look. "We'll solve this, Libby. I promise. Try to be patient."

When I moaned my obvious impatience, Frank tried to distract me by nodding toward the cowl on the table. "Whatcha got there?"

In all the time I'd known Frank, he'd never asked me about my knitting. I knew he was trying to be nice, but somehow his coddling just made me feel worse.

I picked up the length of sparkly red knitting. "I was trying to knit with this to make me feel better. You know, red. Christmas and all. I don't want to connect that color with death for the rest of my life."

He looked as if he found my reasoning a bit loopy. "Is it working?"

I gave him a direct look of my own. "No."

CHAPTER TWENTY-ONE

The red yarn followed me home that night—in my knitting bag, and my dreams. I tossed and turned, unable to get a vision of Derek wrapping red yarn around Perle's neck out of my brain. The strength and rage required to do something like that made my blood run cold. I felt a bit better for knowing that we now had more reason to think Henrik and Nolan hadn't been our killer. I wanted to hang on to the peace of mind I felt realizing that love and family still seemed to count for something in this world.

What would happen to those two? Nolan could make something of himself with Perle's needle business, but that hardly seemed enough to live on. Still, Nolan was young and creative, so I wanted to believe that his rocky start in life would give way to a brighter future.

But what about Henrik? What kind of career would he have without Perle? That alone seemed to rule out him killing her, not to mention his deep devotion to her. I couldn't see how someone angry enough to strangle could show the grief and sorrow Henrik displayed on a near-constant basis. What would he do from here?

Of course, this is exactly the kind of thinking that makes sleep impossible. I surrendered to insomnia, sending mental sympathies to Caroline. She'd mentioned more than once how knitting had been something soothing to do when sleep eluded her. My sleepless nights were making me crazy— how did she handle them so well?

I headed down to the kitchen, made myself a cup of tea, and opened up my laptop. I envied how Hank settled in at my feet. He looked up as the cuckoo clock in my living room announced one a.m., but then lowered his head and was snoring within minutes. The adorable beast could sleep anywhere, anytime.

"Let's do a little looking," I declared to my snoring companion. I figured I might as well give in to my curiosity about all three of the men who had turned my event, shop, and life upside down.

A search for Derek Martingale brought up the usual professional details. Middle name of James, residing in Manhattan, Ivy League education, steady rise up the ranks at a handful of New York publishing houses, one evidently failed engagement, and a sailboat on Long Island that seemed way beyond his means. It was easy to see how Derek pushed hard for success. Still, a knitting book? Wouldn't someone with Martingale's ambitions be hanging his hopes on a bigger star than Perle Lonager? Perle cutting ties with him didn't seem worth killing her over. But given how closemouthed Derek had been, and his display of sneaky tactics, it wasn't hard to believe there was more to the story than what we knew. And even though I was convinced there was something going on between Derek and Nolan, I had no idea what it was.

I had much more success getting information on Nolan, thanks to his loads of social media postings. I found a pair of interesting-looking art shows and lots of shots of him with the handsome, dark-haired "expensive boyfriend" Henrik had mentioned. An art blog started two years ago had a dozen postings, but none of them was recent.

The most interesting things I found were some social media shots of him getting the tattoo on his arm. Judging by the timeline, he'd gotten it just before Perle had begun to build her needle line. He clearly felt that was going to be his big break. A way to convince his aunt of his commitment, maybe? Presumptuous but not out of character, from what I'd seen. I tried to imagine what it would be like for him to be told he wasn't going to be an integral part of Perle's new venture, just a hired designer. Would that rejection have been enough to fuel murder?

The hardest search was for Henrik. Oh, there were lots of professional shots of Henrik from Perle's books, media appearances, and such. Looking for evidence of who he had been before his connection with Perle, I came up surprisingly empty.

Frustrated and bored, I picked up a knitting project to stitch on while clicking around. A black-and-white shadow-knit scarf fit my dark mood. Shadow knitting uses a clever mix of stitches so that it looks different from different angles. This one looked like simple stripes when viewed straight on, but the combination of raised and flat stitches showed off a clever series of diamonds when you looked at it from off to one side. That's why it's also called illusion knitting. Fascinating but not especially soothing. I ended up tossing it onto the desk after a row or two.

"I'm not getting anywhere," I moaned to Hank. I typed in Nolan's favorite dig at Henrik—*stupid Viking*—just to amuse myself.

An expected amount of silliness—comedy sketches, cartoons, and other things—came up. There was even a handful of shots of Henrik, which I'm sure would have annoyed the man to no end. I followed that trail for a few minutes until it led to *Ice and Fire*, an obscure historical drama script about Vikings that had been filmed in Denmark and picked up by a cable channel. One of the shots showed a gorgeous costume straight out of a Wagner opera. In the background was a woman knitting. "Wait a minute." I zoomed in on the image, peering with tired eyes. "Is that . . . ?"

Perle. It was. At least I was relatively sure it was Perle. The photo was grainy but she was such a stunning woman. And knitting—who else could it be? Perle had mentioned in one of our conversations that she had cut her design teeth in the costume world. Looking at some of the costumes for *Ice and Fire*, I convinced myself I could see Perle's style.

Wide-awake now, I took a huge chance and texted Caroline. You up by any chance?

Unfortunately, came back the quick reply. Sorry you are. What's up?

I rang her cell phone and quickly explained the situation, asking for her help in finding anything out about Henrik and *Ice and Fire*.

I couldn't help but think of Mom's "It's like it was meant to be" as Caroline's entertainment journalism background proved a treasure trove of resources. An hour later my e-mail dinged with a link to an audition list citing an actor named Henrik Emilsen.

Bingo! Henrik had been an actor. That made loads of sense, given his dramatic personality. Not a particularly successful one, admittedly, but perhaps with all the visibility he'd gained from his work with Perle, he could return to the stage with more success. Caroline sent me other links as well. One was to a few over-the-top headshots, including one with a beard worthy of Tolkien, but the winner led to a series of casting call videos on an *Ice and Fire* fan site. Look at screen test 216, Caroline said in the e-mail.

It proved to be a very short bit of unimpressive video. The camera certainly loved Henrik's face and physique, but I found myself unsurprised that he'd evidently not been cast. Not leading-man material. Perhaps he'd been cast as an extra.

For the next two hours Caroline and I traded findings of photographs, articles, and various Internet rabbit holes of Henrik's pre-Perle existence. I was just about to call it quits when I came across a photograph of a community theater production.

The image stopped me cold. It was Henrik. It had to be. I have always been good with faces, and even the years that had passed couldn't hide the fact that I was staring at Henrik Emilsen onstage.

Only I wasn't.

The caption cited the man in the photograph as Harold Emery of Victory Gap, Tennessee.

Harold was a dead ringer for Henrik. Same build, same hair, same eye color, same swagger in his stance. I nudged Hank awake. "Does Henrik have an evil twin?"

I shared my finding with Caroline, and we began scouring the Internet and her entertainment sources for information about Harold Emery from Victory Gap, Tennessee. There wasn't much, but everything we found about Harold's life and acting career evaporated the same year as information about Henrik began.

My cell phone rang. I picked up to hear Caroline's voice saying, "It's almost as if . . ."

The same thought froze me in my chair. I stared at the screen, then down at the knitting on my desk. The *illusion* knitting. My brain reeled from the very idea. "As if one transformed into the other."

"Henrik is Harry Emery," Caroline said. "Or very well could be. Was that the secret Perle was trying to protect?"

I swallowed hard. "Or was that the secret Perle was trying to reveal?"

The *illusion* of Henrik began coming together in my mind. Perle had met Harry when he was Henrik. The whole over-the-top Viking persona made sense. He'd become Henrik in order to land a part in this series, and when he didn't, he went for another option: becoming Perle's Viking. And we all knew how he excelled at that.

"Henrik isn't Norwegian," I said, barely believing my own words. "He's an ordinary guy from Tennessee *acting* like he's Norwegian."

I thanked Caroline for her incredible help and stared in thought at the blackness outside my kitchen window.

From what I knew about Perle, that was a big enough deception to unravel her. After all, she had invested so much of herself in the authenticity of her work. As a person of Danish descent, she probably didn't consider herself as having the birthright to become known for the Norwegian *Selbu* designs that had brought her success. Henrik became her passport to authenticity. No wonder she had seemed poised to make a big deal of their impending marriage.

. . . Until she learned she wasn't getting ready to marry into a Norwegian heritage. She would have been marrying into a lie.

I couldn't see her accepting that on any terms. Her goodbye suddenly made sense. She didn't feel worthy of the career she loved anymore. The tie-in with her own rumored engagement would have been a disaster—*Norwegian Wedding Knits* would have rubbed salt in the wound. The focus she'd placed on her Danish needles had seemed out of balance to me, but now I could easily see she had felt her future had to lie there.

Had Perle decided my event was the best place for her to admit everything? She hadn't struck me as the kind of person who could hold up a deceit like that, even for profit. Which meant Henrik would have gone down with the revelation.

I had no idea how she'd learned the truth, but I couldn't believe Henrik—Harold—would have told her.

My heart squeezed tight at the thought. To know the person you thought you loved had lied to you on such a deep level. Was there a worse wound than that? For someone with the values Perle held so dear? Sterling had been a rat on any number of levels, but none so heart-wrenching as the lie I now believed Henrik lived. For so many years. Acting to create a business venture and pretending it was love—she must have felt so used by the man who'd professed to care about her.

It was all too fantastic to be true—and yet it explained everything. Including why the DNA test of the blood on the needles seemed to exonerate him. It could rule out Norwegian blood—but only because Henrik wasn't Norwegian. He never had been.

I stood up and began pacing the room. My discovery seemed too enormous to keep quiet about. Margo and Gavin were good friends, but not good enough for me to wake them up at three thirty a.m. with my news.

I paced the living room for another twenty minutes,

Hank following curiously at my heels. He seemed to appreciate my astonishment, but that was rather beside the point at the moment.

I had no idea what to do with what I'd just learned. My pulse thudded in my ears and I felt my stomach hollow out with the chilling realization. Henrik wasn't really Henrik. I couldn't prove any of it yet, but somehow I absolutely knew I'd uncovered the truth. I wasn't too fond of Derek, but he'd never struck me as brutal enough to kill. If I found that final speech page, I would stake my shop that the truth of Henrik being Harold would be on that sheet of paper.

Of course, we hadn't found the page. And might never find it. We'd have to think of a way to force Henrik to take a DNA test—which according to Frank required a court order and a lot of messy legalities—or get our Viking to fess up to his lie.

How to do either?

"I solved it!" I shouted at Hank, who merely stared back and licked his jowls as if to say, "What took you so long?"

I'd solved the crime. I just couldn't do anything about it yet.

O ne of the great blessings of having a baker friend is knowing you can call at five thirty in the morning and not wake her. Margo was already at work when she listened to my discovery and what I was positive it proved.

"You've got to be right," she said over the phone. "I can't think of anyone else who would have gone down that road and found what you did. It's genius."

I wished for the first colors of sunrise to push their way into the clouds over the Chester River. Sunrises, by definition, are almost always beautiful, but I think the ones we get here in Collinstown are the most beautiful anywhere. The still-dark sky lacked those beautiful tones this morning. "I've just got to figure out how to prove it."

"Maybe you don't." I could hear the whir of Margo's enormous standing mixer going off in the background. "Maybe you only have to use that information to pressure Henrik—Harold—into confessing." She gave a small chuckle. "I just can't think of that guy as a Harold—can you?"

Henrik must be quite a good actor. He'd created a character he so deeply embodied that I couldn't see the man as Harold, either.

"Find a way to trigger that short fuse of his, and maybe you can trick him into spilling the truth."

It could work. "If this secret is so precious to Henrik that he'd kill to keep it, maybe the idea that I know will be enough to make him crack. He sure seems an emotional kind of guy."

My own words struck me. *Seems emotional.* Had all of the grieving-lover act been a performance? It explained how the man had displayed his grief so publicly, time and time again. It wasn't inconsolable sorrow; it was calculated deceit. Had he ever loved Perle at all?

"When are you going to call Frank?" Margo asked.

I wanted to call him now. In fact, I'd called Margo just to keep myself from rousing Frank and Gavin out of bed. Frank because this was most definitely police business. And Gavin because this felt a bit dangerous and I wanted moral support a bit sturdier than Margo's spatula. "I figured six thirty." I surprised myself by actually yawning. Then again, I was working on three hours of sleep at the most.

Margo laughed. "I bet you could ring Frank right now,

and once you told him what you had, he wouldn't mind a bit."

"I'm not so sure," I countered. "Pulling Frank out of bed for a hunch?"

"This is no hunch. You're right. I know it, and you know it." In my mind's eye, I could see Margo pointing at me with her rubber spatula. "You solved this. Perle will have justice done because you didn't give up on her. I'm proud of you."

A lump rose in my throat. I did want to make sure Perle rested in peace, with her murderer brought to justice. But that the murderer was the man who professed to love her?

"I'll still wait a bit," I told Margo. "Even if I do wake Frank, I suppose he has to wait until a decent hour to go . . ." I realized I wasn't quite sure what Frank would do with the information I was about to give him. "Haul Henrik in for questioning, I guess."

"I don't think he has to wait for anything. Who knows? Didn't Frank say there's an advantage to surprising the guy out of a deep sleep? Or at least having most of the inn guests asleep if Henrik decides to make a scene."

"Oh, I think there's no question of Henrik making a scene."

Margo's voice lowered. "This could get ugly. What if he denies everything and Frank doesn't have enough to keep him in custody? Henrik doesn't strike me as a reasonable man. Are you gonna be okay?"

Actually, I wasn't sure. "I don't know," I admitted. "I've never accused anyone of murder before. As you say, Frank could bring Henrik in and not have enough evidence to keep him." A harrowing thought turned my stomach to ice. "What if it takes days? Or never happens?" I doubted I could live with this knowledge for days or years while Henrik walked around Collinstown playing the devastated lover. The thought of him coming into the shop. Touching my yarn. After he'd done such a terrible thing with Perle's yarn.

There was only one real solution to all of this: the last page of Perle's speech. Perle, if she'd learned what I thought she had learned, could corroborate my story from beyond the grave. That would give Frank what he needed. "Margo, can you get away from the shop?"

"For you, girl, absolutely. Collinstown can live without strawberry rhubarb pie for a few hours. Why?"

I've had Margo's strawberry rhubarb. That was a sizable sacrifice to ask Collinstown to make. "We've got to go back to the theater. Or the shop. We've got to find that missing speech page. Now. If I'm right, it states exactly what I've learned. Perle figured out Henrik was a fake and he killed her to cover it up."

I printed out what I'd found on the Internet, threw on some clothes, and tried to ignore Hank's clear annoyance at being left out of the action as I dumped extra kibble into his bowl.

"With any luck," I said as I patted his head, "I'll be back by lunch. And Henrik will be behind bars."

It took some determination not to speed through town as I steered down Collin Avenue toward the theater. We were so close to solving this. I had to believe that one last page was destined to show up and lock my theory down tight. It had been a long time since I'd prayed so hard for anything, but I figured the Almighty valued justice for Perle as much as—if not more than—I did.

As it turned out, I hadn't needed to worry about waking

Frank up. His police car sat outside the inn, lights throwing streaks of red and blue across the empty block. An irrational jolt of fear that Henrik had killed again sucked the air out of my lungs. A killer was loose on Collinstown streets. Of course, since Perle's death a killer *had already* been loose on Collinstown's streets. Only now that I knew who that killer was, the threat loomed all the more drastic and dangerous.

I pulled over and parked my car behind Frank's just as I saw Margo coming down the street from the pie shop. Both of us turned to see Frank leading someone out of the inn in handcuffs.

Only it wasn't Henrik. It was Derek Martingale.

CHAPTER TWENTY-TWO

"What's going on?" I shouted, alarm pitching my voice high as I rushed toward Frank.

The chief looked as surprised to see me as I was to see him. "Awfully early for you, Libby, isn't it?"

"Why are you arresting Martingale?" I hated how my words sounded accusatory, as if Frank was doing the wrong thing. Then again, based on what I had just learned, I was pretty sure he was.

"The station got a call from the night desk clerk that our friend Martingale here was caught sneaking out the back entrance. With his bags. Without the courtesy of checking out or paying his bill." He pushed Derek none too gently toward the squad car. "We don't take kindly to folks stiffing the locals here. Especially ones who attack our trees and our celebrity guests."

"I told you I'm innocent!" Derek shouted as he was inserted into the backseat.

I pressed the chief. "Are you arresting him for Perle's murder?"

"Nothing I'd like to do more," Frank replied, looking supremely irritated. "And the tree stunt. But I'm tickled to have theft of services to nail you on right now." He grunted. "And I used to think Collinstown was the kind of place where we didn't have to run deposits on credit cards. 'My company will take care of it,' huh? Was it your company's plan to sneak out before dawn, Martingale, or just yours?"

I grabbed Frank's elbow as he was heading for the driver's seat. "Wait, Frank. I don't think he did it." When that brought a stunned look from him, I added, "Well, not the murder, at least."

"Why?"

"It's too long to go into here. Can I follow you to the station?"

Frank bounced a stare back and forth between Derek and me, scratched his chin, and relented. "All right, then. You can fill me in while I let Martingale sweat it out in the interrogation room a bit. I don't like his kind. Smug. Hides behind lawyers. Thinks the world turns on his whim." He gave Derek a look that made the man gulp. While he could be gentle as an old dog, you never wanted to get on the bad side of Chief Frank Reynolds. "Meet me in my office in ten minutes."

Margo and I watched the squad car head off with Derek and the chief inside.

I put one hand to my forehead and sighed. "I haven't had this much excitement before breakfast since I was in college."

"If he's not guilty, why is he acting so guilty?" Margo asked. "And weren't we just saying the same thing about Nolan?"

"And the one who has been acting least guilty of all is the one I think killed Perle." I blinked at Margo. "Straight out of a crime show, isn't it?"

She managed a bewildered smirk. "I've never seen a crime show with yarn and Vikings."

"Forgive me if I don't want to be on the cutting edge of that trend." I pulled my keys out of my coat pocket. "We'll have to save our search for later. Who knows? Maybe we'll get something out of Derek that will make it so we don't need that last speech page."

Margo winked. "Like that last speech page. What if he has it?"

I had thought about that. He seemed devious enough to have hidden it and lied about having it. Although if that page said what I thought it said, I couldn't see the point in his having done so.

I was about to get into my car when I turned to Margo. "Do me a big favor?"

"Anything."

"Go wake Bev if she's not up already. Tell her if Henrik tries to check out, we need her and the staff to do anything they can to keep him from leaving."

Margo turned toward the far side of the inn. Bev lived in what was the old mansion's coach house in the back of the property. "On it. Keep me posted. Today's going to be an interesting day."

I couldn't have agreed more.

The chief folded his hands across his stomach and sat back in his office chair. I'd just given him the full explanation of everything I had found.

"I think you may be right. You've got a nose for this, Libby. Calling in your friend's showbiz resources was a great move. You'd have made a solid detective."

It felt odd to be proud of discovering something so awful. "So we've got him?"

Frank rubbed his eyes with his hands and sighed, making me realize he probably hadn't had much more sleep than I'd had in the past few nights. "It's evidence that Henrik—Harry, whoever—isn't what he says he is."

"But . . . ?" I didn't like the unconvinced tone of his voice.

"It's not evidence that he killed Perle."

"It gives him a motive. And a history of deception. Those are good reasons to suspect him, yes? And all the theatrics? Doesn't it make sense?"

Frank shook his head. "If we can verify it. But it'll take time. He either legally changed his name or the Henrik Emilsen ID is fake. Have your friend send over anything else she's found. I'll get my records guys on it right away. Margo's right, though. If we can corner him with a pile of bad news, he does strike me as the kind who would crack under enough pressure."

Frank stood up. "Here's what we're going to do. I'm going to let Martingale post bail and head back to the inn."

When I looked shocked, he went on. "We'll give him about twenty minutes to think he's off the hook, and then you and I will pay him a visit in his hotel room. I want to see what his reaction is to your discovery. If he thinks he can get himself off the hook by nailing Henrik, he may come up with all kinds of useful information."

* * *

Twenty minutes never seemed longer in my life. "Are you sure this will work?" I asked for the third time as we walked the short distance from the police station to the inn. Frank had answered, "Yes," the first two times, then simply didn't answer this time. I followed him into the lobby, ping-ponging between nervous and determined. This was going to be over soon. I could feel it.

Frank surprised me by asking Bev to have room service follow us up with coffee for three. "Sometimes nice freaks 'em out," he said as he gave the hotel room door a knock. "Collinstown Police, Mr. Martingale. Open up." He looked at me and said, "Now do just like I said."

I nodded. Frank had given me specific instructions. I felt like Henrik, acting some part in a real-life drama. I'd never been one for the stage, and I wasn't very happy to be acting now.

Derek looked shocked to see us again so quickly. He yanked the door open while still tapping away on his cell phone with anxious fingers.

"You know my attorney is already on his way here," he said without inviting us in. "We both know I don't have to talk to you until he arrives."

Frank was unfazed, as if Derek hadn't spoken at all. "Thought you could use this. It's mighty early." He motioned to the poor nervous bellboy, who made short work of setting the coffee down and exiting. "You absolutely have the right to have legal counsel present," he said so calmly, we could have been talking about the weather. Me, my pulse was drumming against my ribs. "But I was hoping we could have a civilized conversation and put this whole misunderstanding behind us."

Derek looked up for a second, eyebrows raised at Frank's startling change in attitude.

Frank poured himself a cup of the coffee and sat on the room's sofa. "Bev does make a good cup of coffee."

I sat beside Frank on the couch while Derek continued to stand. After a tense moment, Derek poured himself a cup of coffee and I did the same.

He remained standing, making no reply. Frank let the silence go on so long, I thought I was going to crawl out of my skin. I wasn't used to high-stakes interrogations.

Eventually, Derek pocketed his phone and sat down at the desk chair. Then, as if he'd been waiting until the last gulp of coffee had been drunk, Frank said, "Before we get into the specifics of your shifty exit, Ms. Beckett here has a question I'd very much like you to answer."

I took a deep breath and phrased my question exactly as Frank had instructed. "How long have you known Henrik isn't Norwegian at all?"

My respect for Frank tripled as I watched the curveball of a question knock Derek off-balance. The man startled, eyes wide, jaw muscles clenching. Frank had warned me to look for the difference between startled and surprised— and sure enough, I could see it.

After a long, squirmy pause, Derek sat back and said, "Since early on."

Now it was my turn to be stunned. Derek knew? Had known for a while? My stomach turned at the number of people who seemed totally at home piling layers of deception onto poor Perle. If Perle had somehow found out what Derek knew, the bitter words of her speech made sense. "And you said nothing?" I didn't see the point in hiding my revulsion at what he'd done.

"I didn't think it was my business." He was trying to

seem apathetic about the whole thing, but I wasn't buying it. Frank's grunt beside me told me the chief wasn't buying it, either.

"Or maybe you thought it was very much your business to keep up that act, no matter what it cost Perle," I countered, needing to defend her.

Derek had the audacity to shrug. "They had a good thing going. People liked Henrik and Perle almost more than they liked just Perle. We were about to make a huge leap in visibility with the wedding thing. What a man tells the woman he wants to marry isn't really up to me. I didn't run Perle's personal life."

I remembered the failed engagement I'd found in Derek's background and sent a good-call mental message to whoever had cut herself free of this cad.

Frank set down his coffee. "How did you find out?"

"I got a letter," Derek replied. "Ostensibly from a reader, but I doubt this person would qualify as a fan. 'Opportunist' might be a better word. Ninety percent of letters I ignore, but this one had enough facts that I contacted Henrik."

"So you've gotten letters about Henrik before?" I asked. Recalling some of the heartless remarks I'd heard outside the shop the night Perle was killed, I didn't find that so hard to believe.

"Not about him specifically, but mail like that comes more than you might think. Some people get a thrill out of tearing down their heroes."

Or killing them, I added in my head.

"You got a letter from someone implying Henrik was a fake." Frank clicked his pen and pulled out his notepad.

"More or less. 'A discredit to Perle and all she stands for.' Some high-minded language like that."

I didn't consider that language high-minded. More like spot-on.

"So you took that accusation to Henrik?" Frank asked. "Not Perle or both of them?"

"I figured Henrik would agree with me that we had a good thing going that should be protected. We wrote a little check—well, maybe not so little—and the problem went away. That's usually how it works."

I really didn't care for the look on Derek's face. As if he was schooling us small-town folk on the finer points of high-powered dealings. This from a man who'd just tried to sneak out on his hotel bill.

"But that didn't work because Perle found out," I said, now sure of my theory. I fought the urge to quote one of Mom's favorite sayings: "The truth always finds its way out into the open."

Derek set his coffee on the desk. "I don't think she knew. I thought Henrik's idea to propose before she did find out was a smart move. Perle was a sensitive sort. She'd have overblown something like this. Henrik might be a first-class pain in the ass, but he grounded her. Kept her focused and moving forward." He crossed one leg over the other, loosening up from his earlier agitation. "Not that it's my place, but he really does love her, you know. He made her very happy—personally and professionally."

"You were in favor of her building a marriage on a *lie*?" My sharp tone resulted in Frank's hand on my arm.

"She'd had the idea for the book a year back, before Henrik told me he was going to propose. The way I saw it, a once-in-a-lifetime publicity opportunity was falling in my lap, and she seemed to love him. I figured they'd work it out when things came to light."

I had known Perle only a short time and I already could tell that such a loss of integrity would have been devastating to her. She'd have felt compelled to admit the falsehood. Publicly. She'd have renounced her claim to the Norwegian culture that had been at the core of her career. No wonder the beginning of her speech sounded like a permanent goodbye. That's exactly what it was.

"Marital bliss aside, if Perle's career gets cut short, you lose out. Isn't that true?" Frank pressed.

Derek ran his fingers across the edge of the desk. "I'll admit we're going to take a hit, yes."

"Enough to kill for?"

"No," Derek shot back. "My career is bigger than one knitter and her Viking poster boy. And that hit I'm going to take pokes a hole in your little plotline, Chief. If Perle was important enough for me to kill for, isn't killing her just as damaging to my career? If not more so? We both know I've nothing to gain and quite a bit to lose by her death. I've no motive here."

"Would Henrik kill to keep it hidden?" Gracing Harold Emery with the name Henrik gave me an unpleasant taste in my mouth now that I knew the truth.

Derek slowly took a sip of coffee before he replied, "I think he's capable of it, yes."

"Does that sound like 'He really does love her' to you? So why did you go to such great lengths to point us toward Nolan? That whole business with the trees." I had the sudden, ugly thought that Derek might have considered the unbombing a great publicity stunt worth the money, too.

"Because I do think he did it. I said I thought Henrik was capable of it and that he loved her. Neither's the same thing as guilty. Nolan? He's guilty, I'm telling you." Derek shifted in his seat. "None of this explains your sudden interest in Henrik's genetics. Aren't you supposed to be solving a murder, not barking up family trees?"

I looked at Frank, unsure as to what he was going to share. If he wanted to turn the heat up on Derek, this was a chance to do it.

"Because of the lab results on the blood we found on the needles at the murder scene." Frank fixed Derek with a firm glare. "They tell us the blood isn't from someone of Nordic descent."

I knew that was still an educated guess, but Derek didn't. "Up until now that would have helped to clear Henrik," I added. "So if you're confirming that Henrik isn't who he says he is, he's no longer cleared."

"And as far as I'm concerned, neither are you." Frank let that sink in for a moment. "And only one of you was trying to slip out of town this morning."

Derek swallowed hard. "What about Nolan? The kid disappeared. Twice."

I imagined Nolan wouldn't take well to being referred to as "the kid." "Nolan is Danish—at least partly. He's the son of Perle's sister, remember? So as of now, he's the only one who gets cleared by those lab tests."

"It gets that specific?" Derek asked.

It struck me that the specific distinction between Danish and Norwegian was at the very heart of this whole mess. Perle was highly aware that her Danish heritage didn't hand her rights to Norway's cultural treasures. That—and, I hoped, love—was why Henrik was so important to her. So important that she was ready to give it all up rather than continue on a pretense once she discovered it. How many people in the world are there anymore with that kind of integrity?

The man in front of me wasn't one of them. He and Henrik seemed all too eager to keep the charade going. If Henrik had gotten the chance to pop the question, would it have been a true proposal or just an emotional security deposit? Did Derek and Henrik really think that somehow when the ugly truth surfaced it wouldn't matter just because marriage vows had been spoken?

Then again, hadn't Sterling thought the same thing? I saw parts of him I never knew existed after the "guarantee" of our marriage enabled him to ease up on his facade. Maybe that was why the deception in all this cut me so deeply. I had my own wounds from lies told by someone I loved.

Frank loomed over the table. "I'm gonna ask you one more time. And I'll remind you that things will go far easier if you cooperate now. Did you or did you not strangle Perle Lonager with a skein of red yarn last Friday?"

Derek swallowed again, and for a moment, I thought I was going to be surprised by his confession. After all, I was still sure down to my bones that it was Henrik.

"I did not kill Perle Lonager." Derek gave a clear, defiant edge to his words.

"And why should we believe you?" Frank pressed.

"Because I'm about to tell you where the last page of the speech is, and her killer wouldn't do that."

CHAPTER TWENTY-THREE

My mouth surely hung agape in astonishment as Derek walked over to his suitcase and opened it.

"You told us you didn't know where the rest of Perle's speech was," Frank challenged.

"I don't think this is all of it, but trust me, it's enough."

"We have a missing page," Frank admitted.

Derek paled a bit, perhaps worried that his ace in the hole wasn't as valuable as he thought. "I'd like to see it."

Frank glared. "Show us what you have, Mr. Martingale. What you should have shown us earlier, I might add."

"I was in need of some insurance at the time. Henrik doesn't know I have this, and I thought it best to keep it that way."

"How did you find it?" I asked.

"When I found the first pages of Perle's alternate speech in her hotel room, I put two and two together and figured out she'd learned Henrik's secret. It didn't take much imagination to then figure out what she had planned and why she was so insistent that I be in the audience that night."

"You knew she was going to expose Henrik in front of you and everybody. Which meant she could expose that you knew about it and paid to keep it quiet," Frank confirmed.

"Perle had once made a joke about hiding things in needles. Did you notice there was a pair of the large ones she was knitting with in her hotel room?"

I hadn't. I must have been too stressed to catch that detail. Then again, it wouldn't have been at all odd for Perle to have a knitting project around her, so why would I?

"While you all were over at the theater, I pulled the ends off them and found the one page," Derek went on.

"But not the other page," I cut in, "because it was in a different set of needles at the theater." Poor Perle. She'd been cautious enough to hide both pages in completely separate locations.

"It could have happened that way. Or it could be that you pulled it out of the other needle at the theater before or after you killed Perle." Frank's alternate theory earned a dark glower from the publisher.

Derek slid his hand behind the lining on one side of the expensive-looking suitcase. He produced a plastic bag containing a single folded sheet of paper. It looked just like the other handwritten pages of Perle's speech.

"Even if you're not guilty of murder, you're guilty of a lot of other things, including withholding evidence. You're not off the hook yet, son, not by a long shot."

Derek bristled at the chief calling him "son" as if he were no older than Jake Davis. He removed the page and tossed it onto the coffee table in front of Frank and me. Something close to a sneer slid across his face.

I recognized the handwriting as Perle's. In a way, we

were staring at her last words—hearing her voice from beyond the grave. She died for whatever was on that page.

I picked up the paper, deciding to read from it out loud as the last memorial I could give her. The words started mid-sentence, clearly a continuation from the page I had seen earlier: "'. . . owe you more than that. So little in this world can be called authentic. I have always tried to be authentic with you. In my art. In my life. In the beauty I hoped to create and'"—my voice caught on the next words—"'leave behind after I'm gone.'

"'We've been lied to, you and I. By the people we should have been able to trust. I fell in love not only with the Norwegian *Selbu* and other knitting traditions, but with the Norwegian man you see beside me.'"

A vision of Henrik standing beside Perle in my shop flashed in my mind. She must have known then. No wonder she looked as if she couldn't hold it together. No wonder she was so fastidious about every detail of the event—she was planning her professional funeral.

And it had become the actual end of her life.

"'This man will never be my husband, because I could never knit my life to someone who has lied to me—and to you—on so deep a level. The man beside me isn't Norwegian. He isn't even Henrik. He is an actor named Harold Emery, who saw an opportunity in claiming a heritage that was never his to claim. In claiming a heart that should have never been his to claim.'"

The pain in her words, however eloquent, cut through me. This must have been why I had been so drawn to her, even without knowing her for long.

"'Nor can I knit my craft to a publisher who would knowingly further this lie. I can no longer, will no longer, profit from a culture's precious traditions that are not mine to claim. This all has started to change me in ways I can't allow. There will be no more books, no more patterns, no more events.'"

How horribly prophetic those words turned out to be. I felt as if I were watching a soul being stripped of all it held dear. Had she been alive to deliver these words, I would have rushed the stage to pull her into a huge protective hug. And while I don't think I would have truly had the nerve to do it, I would have wanted to give the lying Henrik a solid slap across the face.

"'You all have meant so much to me. I don't know where things go from here. So much has gone wrong. But we know what to do when the stitches have gone all wrong. We rip them all out, undo them all. So that is what I've done. I've dismantled all the work now wasted and wound it back into a simple ball of yarn. I want to believe it can become new stitches, a new creation. But that is not now. Not yet. Farewell.'"

I wiped my wet cheek with the back of my hand. Beside me I heard Frank push out a troubled breath, but I couldn't quite look up from the page yet. There must have been a full minute of stunned quiet. Finally, I forced my eyes away from the heart-wrenching handwritten words and glared at Derek.

"How could you keep this?" I saw no point in hiding the rage building deep in my chest. It boiled up in the silence that followed until I couldn't hold back from nearly yelling, "How could you do this to her?"

"We would have continued to publish her, you know." Martingale said it as if it absolved him. "Had she not gone and done this, we would have figured something out. I don't think anyone would have really cared whether he was Henrik or Harold or Houdini."

"She cared!" I yelled. "Doesn't that matter at all?"

Martingale offered no answer.

There was a time when I dreamed of being part of the "kniterati," the famous, sought-after designers who authored books and made appearances and got to make their lives in the fiber arts world. What I just saw soured that dream instantly. I dearly hoped I was looking at the worst example, that there were more Perles than Dereks and Henriks. That the world was filled with other people and publishers and shops who loved the craft and those gifted artists who perfected it. All my shop regulars were dear to me, but in this moment they became doubly dear.

As did my craving to see justice for Perle.

Frank rose, clearly done here.

"Am I free to go?" Derek asked.

"No. You are to remain at the inn until an arrest has been made for the murder of Perle Lonager. Unless you'd like to pull another stunt and earn some time in our accommodations over at the station." He reached down and drained his cup. "The coffee is nowhere near as good over there, so I'd consider carefully." Frank pulled at the sheet of paper I was still clutching tightly in my hands. "This stays with me."

I hated the idea of Perle's impassioned words tucked away in a plastic evidence bag, but I understood. I handed over the page—even though it felt like saying goodbye to Perle as I did it—and we left Derek Martingale to his phone calls. And his conscience.

I clutched my coffee mug for warmth and comfort as I sat in the Perfect Slice, filling Margo in on all that had happened. "It's driving me crazy that we don't have enough to charge Henrik with Perle's murder. He did it. I know it. I just can't prove it." I was hoping a proper breakfast would help me find the patience Frank asked for, but it wasn't working.

"Wow," Margo said, choking up at the poor summation I had given of Perle's beautiful words. "That's so sad. And so wrong." She passed me a slice of quiche she'd whipped up for me while I was at the police station. I often wished I was as good at anticipating Margo's needs as she was at guessing mine. Hot coffee and warm quiche went a long way to soothing my wounded and impatient spirit.

"Henrik did it," I said for the tenth time. "But we still can't prove it."

"That's Frank's job," Margo replied. "And you've done a ton to help him do it. Now you just have to let him do what you know he's good at." She put a hand on my arm. "Perle will get her justice. I believe that, and so should you."

"I hope so," I sighed, the high emotions and lack of sleep catching up with me. My back ached and my eyes were bleary despite all the coffee. I still had a whole day at the shop ahead of me, even though the morning hours dragged by as if it had been years since I spent last night glaring at my computer monitor. "It's just taking so long. Too long. Why can't those lab tests tell us more? Faster?" I complained. "If we could just get word on whose blood is on the tips of those needles . . ."

"Well, we know it can't be Perle's, right?" Margo refilled both our coffee mugs. "The police didn't find any wounds on her body. Frank told us she was killed by the yarn around her neck, not the needles in her hands."

"That's true. Everyone is working on the assumption that Perle used the needles on her attacker in defense." That got me to thinking. "So someone out there is walking around with wounds from those needles. And we're pretty sure it can't be Nolan, because he's half Danish."

"Those were big needles. Wounds like that would be hard to"—Margo's hand stilled with her coffee mug in midair—"hide." Margo's eyebrows furrow in a crazy way when she gets a wild idea. I saw it happen before she invented butterscotch shortbread bites for my birthday this summer.

"What?"

"Henrik."

"He has no scratches." Not that I had seen, anyway.

Margo blinked at me. "His shirt."

"Yeah, I know—it's always some crisp button-down open far too wide. Seems to me Henrik wants to make sure we see his broad, manly chest."

"Or not." Margo's brows furrowed even more. "Did you notice what Henrik has been wearing lately?"

I groaned. "How can you be a Henrik fan now?"

"His shirt," she emphasized. "As in the shirt he *hasn't* been wearing. No wide-open shirt. Henrik's been in a turtleneck since the day of the event."

I could almost have laughed. "I didn't even know the man owned anything that didn't button down so he could leave it open." Truth be told, I hadn't paid a lick of attention to Henrik's wardrobe. Who had time for that kind of detail lately? But now that I thought about it, he *had* been in a turtleneck when he came to the shop before, demanding I give him the needles.

"A turtleneck," Margo repeated, cuing me to some sort of conclusion I was too tired to draw.

And then it hit me. I felt a jolt surge through me as I

caught on to Margo's brilliant line of thinking. "You think Henrik's hiding his chest? Because it's got scratches on it from Perle's needles?"

She sat back in her chair. "I can't think of another explanation. And it makes sense."

The more I pondered the idea, the more it sounded right. "He had just gotten out of the shower when we went over to the hotel to look for Perle."

Margo nodded. "Washing off the blood, perhaps?"

"I don't think Chief Reynolds can force Henrik to take off his shirt, can he?" The concept of taking a man so prone to showing off his chest and compelling him under police order to take off his shirt made me laugh.

"If you confront him with that and the false-identity thing, he'll have no choice but to confess."

I shook my head. "I sincerely doubt he'll just suddenly crack and admit his guilt. That only happens on television. But if he does have a pair of scratches, it would be awfully hard to explain away alongside his deception. Those two facts make him look incredibly guilty. He *is* incredibly guilty." I had to admit to a fair amount of satisfaction that we were piling evidence up against Henrik. Still, I hated the idea of someone Perle had once loved doing her so much wrong.

Sure, Derek and Nolan had both behaved badly. But there's a mile of difference between misbehavior, misdirection . . . and murder.

I pulled out my phone. "Do you want to tell Frank about your brilliant observation?" Margo ought to be credited for her clever sleuthing, especially if it led to Henrik's confession and arrest.

Margo looked at her watch. "I've got to open in a few minutes. I'll be okay if you have all the fun."

I don't know that I would have classified any of this as fun. But even witness interrogation was more fun than the scowling face of George Barker currently peering in Margo's window. "I think you have a customer," I warned her.

Margo looked at George. "I don't think he's here for me." She pointed to the strands of yarn clutched in George's irritated fist.

With the practiced cheer of someone who's dealt with undercaffeinated early-morning customers her whole life, Margo rose and unlocked the shop door.

"Good morning, George. You've never been my first customer before."

George walked right past her to stand over me as I sat at the little table in Margo's shop. I had the instant urge to gobble down the rest of my quiche before he launched into whatever was sure to sour my stomach.

He tossed the strands of yarn down on the table. "I cannot believe it. Again? There's yarn everywhere. Collinstown Yarn Day," he said with infuriating contempt, "is long over. Get that ridiculousness off the trees immediately."

I don't take kindly to calling anyone's handiwork "ridiculousness." Certainly not after the morning I'd had. After the week I'd had. I was about to launch into an ill-advised rebuke when Margo cut in.

"It deserved to go back up. It's beautiful. *I'm* in no hurry to see it taken down."

George ignored her. I could tell he'd been brewing up a speech on the whole drive over here, and God Himself couldn't hold back the tide when George gets worked up. "Our beautiful main street is not your personal playground. I see no reason why the tree in front of *my* office needs to advertise *your* shop."

"Oh, really, George? That's just petty," Margo scolded.

I had some other words clanging around in my head and was using my last available nerve to keep them tamped down. I needed to be on the phone with Frank, not standing here listening to George's whining. "I don't really have time for this, George."

George puffed himself up to full-blown Chamber of Commerce presidential pride at my dismissal. "You should make time. No one approved this," he pronounced, pointing a thick, angry finger at me. "The whole Yarn Day nonsense was bad enough, but no one okayed double rounds of vandalism."

"Art," I corrected, losing my patience. "It's art."

"Your *art* has already resulted in criminal activity. I know about Jake Davis. The whole thing is connected to your store." His face pinched tight and I steeled myself for whatever final blow George was about to deliver. "We never had this kind of trouble before your shop opened."

The accusation that I had brought this on Collinstown sent me over the top. I'd choked down enough of George Barker in the months leading up to the store opening and with the way he strutted around Collin Avenue like he owned the place. No one called him King George behind his back for his diplomatic prowess.

His Majesty didn't realize what he'd just done. To even my own surprise, that man had just handed me the ultimate motivation to knock the crown off his head. I rose up from my seat. "Are you saying this is my fault? That some lovely young woman's senseless murder is on me?" I stepped closer to him. "Is that what you're saying, George?"

"Well, I wouldn't go so far as to—"

"Oh, but you would," I cut him off. Normally I try never to rise to George's bait, but something had come unleashed in me. He was going to hear what I thought even if it made our blood boil. "I will *not* apologize for the trees. Either time. They're beautiful. People have told me how much they like them. It wasn't even my idea, you know. But I will tell you what *is* my idea."

"What?"

"I think I've had about enough of you. I think the Chamber of Commerce can do better. Loads better. So right here, right now, I'm officially declaring my run for Chamber president."

If George were a horse, he would have reared back. I'm sure he considered himself Chamber president for life. Out of the corner of my eye, I saw Margo break into a wide grin. After all, she'd been trying to convince me to run for months. Margo couldn't have predicted that George would be the one to convince me.

"Well . . . I . . . ," George stammered. A nobler woman would not have enjoyed his shock as much as I did. But true to his nature, George didn't stay stymied for long. He straightened his tie and jutted his jowly chin out. "I suppose that's your right, even after all I've done for this town."

We stared—or, more precisely, glared—at each other for a minute, until Margo chimed in sweetly, "Will you be wanting a cup of coffee to go, George? Some shortbread, perhaps?"

George merely grunted and turned toward the door. He clearly wasn't here to patronize the Perfect Slice. He'd come in purely to have another dig at me. I've butted heads with George any number of times, and this felt like the first time I'd come out on top. That was a win worth savoring, given all that had been happening.

If George heard the whoop Margo gave after he closed the door, I couldn't bring myself to care. "There you go!"

Margo said as she pulled me into a jubilant hug. "I've been waiting for that for a long time. When did you decide?"

"Just now." I stared at the door, trying to catch my breath after just declaring war.

She grinned. "I never thought I'd see the day I'd be glad at how George pushes buttons." She stared out the window as we both watched George stomp across the street in the direction of his office. He stopped in front of Y.A.R.N.—or, more precisely, in front of the wildly decorated tree in front of my shop—and for a moment I thought he was going to kick the tree. Instead, he hunched over and continued his prowl down the sidewalk.

"That is one irritating man," Margo said. "I predict a landslide victory." Her face brightened further when she said, "When are you going to tell Gavin?"

A flurry of what-have-I-done? ripples traveled through me at the thought of how I'd just further complicated my already complicated life.

"That will have to be tomorrow's problem." I grabbed my phone and handbag. "Right now I'd better go talk to Frank and see how we can prove your theory."

Margo rubbed her hands together in glee. "Today just keeps getting better."

I hadn't made it fifty feet down the sidewalk when I saw Gavin coming toward me. At a determined clip, eyes full of surprise.

Seriously? Had George even waited until he got back to his office to call in this news? Today had more twists and hurdles than a spy novel, and it wasn't even nine a.m.

"Is it true?" Gavin asked.

"Is what true?"

Gavin gave me a don't-mess-with-me glare. "I just got off the phone with George."

I must have really pulled the rug out from under that man. "That was fast."

Gavin looked at his watch. "And early. What's got you up and out and staging Chamber of Commerce coups at this hour?"

I tried not to look smug. "A free and democratic election is not a coup."

"Tell that to George. Between this, Yarn Day, and the trees again, he's pretty put out." Gavin's face changed. "Seriously, though, is everything okay?"

"That remains to be seen." It occurred to me that I wouldn't mind a little moral support for what I was about to do. "Have you got a half hour to go see Frank with me?" When he nodded, I said, "I'll fill you in along the way."

CHAPTER TWENTY-FOUR

I had to give Frank credit. This was the first time he looked truly bewildered in all of this. "You want me to bring Henrik in here and make him take off his shirt."

"Essentially, yes. Unless you can think of another way to get a clear look at his chest, or back, or wherever it was that Perle struck him."

Frank pinched the bridge of his nose. "Look, I believe the guy is guilty. But I don't want to give him even an inch to weasel out of this on a technicality. We don't have enough to arrest him yet, and I can't order a strip search—which is basically what you're asking—unless he's under arrest. Not without suspicion of him hiding drugs or a weapon."

"No one wants Henrik to strip." Heavens, the man was so proud of his physique, I couldn't say he wouldn't readily comply. Unless, of course, Margo's theory was right. And I knew in my bones it was. Henrik was our murderer. The existence of those wounds would simply give us another way to prove it.

"We seriously don't have enough to arrest the guy?" Gavin asked. Now that I'd filled him in on everything, Gavin was as convinced as I was that Henrik was guilty.

"The name thing is enough to bring him in for questioning. But I can't force him to take a DNA test without a warrant, and I can't make him take his shirt off without one, either. Margo's theory doesn't exactly qualify as probable cause."

"What about a medical examination?" Gavin suggested. "Can you force him to undergo one of those?"

"I don't have sufficient grounds." Frank scratched his chin. "What we have here is a collection of incriminating evidence, but it's still all circumstantial."

"He's guilty." I couldn't seem to say it enough times.

"Not yet," Frank replied. "Remember, the law is weighed heavily on the side of the suspect, and for good reason." He began flipping through papers on his desk. "I can try to get a warrant, but the earliest it could come through would be tomorrow. I'll see if I can light a fire under that specialty lab for the DNA results."

"I don't want him to get away with this!" I probably shouldn't have shouted.

Frank and Gavin both raised up their hands in calm-down gestures. "Nobody wants that," Frank said. "But he might do just that if we botch a technicality because we rushed."

"He did it," I declared with all the certainty I could muster.

"Well, then, our best bet is to get him to confess."

I didn't want to wait another second. "So bring him in and make him confess."

Frank's face suddenly changed. He glanced up at the clock on his office wall, and then he looked at me. "I might have a better idea. Your shop doesn't open until ten, right?"

"Yes."

"Call Henrik and ask him to meet you at the shop as soon as he can. Before it opens."

We were going to confront Henrik. I held up my phone like a sword raised for battle. "Gladly."

Seventeen minutes later, the man who called himself Henrik walked through my shop doorway. His striking blue eyes first went wide with alarm, and then narrowed with annoyance when he saw who was with me. It did feel rather like an ambush. A justified ambush, but one just the same.

With a sick mix of satisfaction and dread, I noticed he was indeed wearing a turtleneck. It was a gorgeous display of needlework, gray with black designs of large snowflakes and small zigzags. Tiny white x's ran along the shoulders, cuffs, and hem. It was clearly Perle's work—traditional, yet with a dash of contemporary flair. In what I hoped was fortune smiling on us, it was a zip-front turtleneck, with the zipper traveling from the bottom of the sweater all the way to the high neck under his chin. It burned me that Henrik was, for all intents and purposes, hiding under Perle's craftsmanship. For a millisecond I had the foolhardy urge to rush up to him and yank down the zipper.

"What's going on?" he demanded, standing defiant with his feet wide apart. "You said you wanted to talk about the needles. Why are they here?" he added, nodding at Frank and Gavin.

I had lured him with that, but we were going to talk

about the needles—sort of. "I have some questions I want to ask you, and I thought they ought to be here when I did." Frank's brilliant idea was to question him here so Henrik didn't get the impulse to refuse and "lawyer up" the way he would at the station.

The man's size intimidated me as it always had. This was going to be a tricky business, and I didn't feel especially ready to play interrogator. Still, my desire to get to the bottom of this—and the presence of two men I knew would protect me, should things get out of hand—overrode the shaking of my insides.

I injected a hospitality I didn't remotely feel into my voice as I gestured to the shop's front table. "Why don't we all sit down?"

I'm not at all sure why I went through the absurdity of setting out coffee and treats. *Just your friendly neighborhood amateur sleuth hoping to nail you for murder. Cookie?*

Everybody sat down, but no one touched the coffee. Frank nodded at me. Honestly, I felt like I was auditioning for *Yarn Shop Cop*—the worst idea ever for a reality show, if you ask me.

I made it a point to be sitting where I could see Perle's mittens still up on my wall. Instead of the displays of love and fidelity *Selbu* mittens ought to have been, now the colorful wool "hands" seemed to hang in judgment over the man seated across from me.

Under any other circumstances, I might have opened a conversation by commenting on the beauty of Henrik's sweater. Few things make me happier than the chance to compliment knitters on their handiwork. While I still could find it in myself to admire Perle's skill and talent, I could see this particular garment as only tragic and ugly.

"I'll get right to the point." I opened a file I had set on the table and removed a few sheets of paper containing printouts and screenshots I'd made at two this morning. I laid them out in the center of the table facing Henrik. "Are you Harry Emery?"

It startled me how easily I could watch the shock hit him. While he quickly covered it up with his usual Viking swagger, the flash of fear was unmistakable. I felt a flash of my own, a surge of redemption that my hunch had been correct. Usually I love being right, but I took no enjoyment at all out of this.

"Why would you ask something like that?"

"Because I don't believe you were born Henrik Emilsen. I don't believe you are Norwegian. I don't believe Perle knew you are Harry Emery. At least not until recently." I pulled in a fortifying breath. "And I don't believe you are innocent of her murder."

Henrik turned to Frank. "Are you going to sit here and let her accuse me like that?"

Frank crossed his hands over his chest. "As a matter of fact, I am."

Henrik shifted in his chair, then stood up. "I don't have to answer that."

"Technically, no," came Frank's amazingly calm voice. "But if I were you, I'd think hard about being cooperative right now. Lab results on the ethnicity of blood found on a pair of needles, not to mention a court order for your DNA test, are being rushed to my office as we speak. I figure it'll take my guys an hour, maybe two, to churn through the paperwork. Not that it matters, since a few hours ago your buddy Martingale sold you out. So not much point in lying now. We already know."

I'm not quite sure where the confidence in my voice

came from when I repeated, "Are you Harry Emery? Did you decide to become Henrik Emilsen to boost your chances of landing a role on *Ice and Fire*?" I chose to let him establish that before we got on to the uglier business of his lies to Perle.

Henrik's legendary chin stuck out in defiance for a full minute before he grumbled, "That part should have been mine. It would have made me a star."

Gavin, Frank, and I traded looks around the table. "That's not an answer to the question," Frank pressed.

"It's not a crime to have a stage name. I could show you half a dozen actors who don't use their real names."

"In a police investigation?" Frank prodded.

Gavin stood up, and for the first time, I realized he was even taller than Henrik. "Are you Harry Emery?" Gavin used a slow, demanding tone that was even lower and more serious than his Mayor Voice.

"Last chance . . ." Frank pulled out his phone as if one call could send a SWAT team swarming over the shop in a matter of seconds.

Henrik wiped his hands down his face. "Yes." His voice held none of the dash and swagger. All Harold and no Henrik. The whole thing struck me as pathetic.

Step one had been achieved. Henrik had admitted to being Harold. Step two was to get him to admit he hadn't told Perle, and maybe had never planned to. "But you didn't get that part," I went on. "So you decided to use it to get Perle instead."

His eyes grew pained. It caught me for a moment, until I remembered this man was an illusion, just like the design of the scarf on my desk at home. If he had any performing talent, this was the worst way to use it. "It wasn't like that," he almost whispered.

Henrik's gaze traveled to the display still in my front window, and then around the shop until it found the photograph of himself and Perle that I had removed from the window. It was as if he said the next words to her and not to us in the room. "I fell for her. The moment I saw her. That hair, those eyes, the passion she had for life and art. Her frailty. How could I not fall for her?"

He believed he loved her. And yet I could not see how any kind of love allowed for what I believed he had done.

Henrik put his hand over his heart. How he managed to make the gesture look both genuine and theatrical was beyond me.

"I suppose you could say I wanted to impress her." He went on, his words slow and soft. "She seemed so taken with the atmosphere of the show. If I am guilty of anything, it's trying to be the person she wanted."

"You lied to her," I challenged. "You dreamed up a whole heritage just to suit her fascination. How is that love? Perle got nothing except your deception while you got what you wanted. Perle made you a celebrity."

Those last words snapped him out of his stupor. "We made each other," he declared sharply. "I took her talent and transformed it into something people craved. Something they lined up for. I was the key to her success as much as she was the key to mine." He began pacing the shop, holding his head in his hands, and I braced for another dramatic Henrik outburst.

"Do you know who convinced her to go after that first publishing deal?" He stopped pacing, turned toward me, and brought one fist to his chest in a very Viking-like gesture. "I did. I believed in her long before she believed in herself. Way before Martingale. If you want to talk about someone who exploited my beloved, let's have a conversation about *that* man."

Mercy, he was good. Even my rock-hard conviction that he was guilty began to tilt a little at the power of this performance. *He's acting,* I reminded myself. *He's just very good at lying.*

"Let's keep the conversation on you," Frank replied. "And let's keep the theatrics to a minimum, please. Sit back down."

"You deceived." I said it as much for myself as to him. "You lied to her, to all her fans, to everyone. How could you claim to love her and do that to her? How?"

Henrik sank down into the chair, deflated. "I was going to tell her."

That sounded way too much like one of Sterling's hollow apologies. More remorse at getting caught than at doing wrong. "When?" I questioned. "*After* you were married?"

"I started to a million times. And then I'd convince myself she couldn't love Harry Emery from Tennessee. Not someone like her. She was too extraordinary for anyone ordinary like me." He looked at me intently. "But you know how it goes. The longer you hang on to something like that, the harder it is to let it go. You just sort of . . . believe it, even when you shouldn't."

I felt a tiny, inexplicable pang of pity for him . . . until he said, "And really, who cares about authenticity anymore? Not them." He motioned out the windows as if the unwashed masses of my customers were out there ready to welcome his grieving self into their arms. "I don't think Martingale gave a damn what was on my birth certificate as long as it sold books and won Perle fans."

That was it. I'd had just about enough. Henrik had admitted that he had lied about his identity and that he'd lied to Perle. I was tired of waiting for his third strike. Pitching all of Frank's tactics to the wind, I stood up, leaned over the table, and gave that Viking the darkest glare I could summon.

"Take off that sweater."

Frank and Gavin turned to me in disbelief.

I wasn't backing down. "That intricate hand-knit sweater I'm just betting Perle spent hours making for you. Take it off. Now. Or so help me, I'll take it off you myself."

Henrik looked at Frank. "She's kidding, right?"

"I don't think she is," Gavin said.

Henrik bounced his gaze back and forth between Gavin and Frank, thinking they'd step in and stop this nonsense. "I won't do that. Why should I do that? I don't have to sit here and listen to this."

He started for the door, but Gavin calmly stepped in front of it and stood his ground.

"That's a ridiculous thing to ask," Henrik protested.

"It's a simple thing to ask," Gavin said. "Unless you've got something to hide under there."

Henrik looked at Frank. "Are you going to stop this?"

"I probably should," Frank replied without saying that he would.

We were pushing the limits of things, and I felt a pang of regret for backing our fine police chief into a legal corner. But we were too far into it to go back now, and I could feel my conviction lighting a fire under my courage. "Of course you don't want to take it off. For the same reason you've been wearing turtlenecks since Perle died. Instead of those wide-open shirts you're so famous for. You're hiding your chest." I started to come around the table.

"Stop her!" Henrik shouted.

"That probably would be a good idea." Frank's tone didn't match his words at all. He wasn't going to stop me. But his eyes told me I had to be careful.

"This can't be legal." Henrik's voice began to pitch up in alarm.

"If you want to file a harassment complaint, I can leave you alone with these two while I walk on over to the department and get the paperwork."

"Are you afraid to take that sweater off?" I challenged.

"Of course not. I don't have anything to hide. But I don't have to be shaken down by the likes of you."

Shaken down. What a telling choice of words. He was getting anxious, angry even, which just made me all the more bold. "I think you won't take the sweater off because there are wounds on your chest. Ones made by Perle as she tried to defend herself. With her own needles. When you strangled her. Because she was about to announce to the world what a fraud you are. You found the start of her second speech and realized what she was going to do. You were about to lose her. You were about to lose everything, including your control."

I don't know what came over me. Instead of heading straight toward Henrik, I walked over to the boxes of Perle's stock and picked up two of the needles the exact size of the ones now sitting in Frank's evidence room. "If there's no scratch on your chest, prove it. Right here, right now. Come on, *Harry*." I wielded his name like the weapon I knew it was. "Prove you're the hero Perle thought you were."

His face contorted at the sight of the needles and the use of that name. "I made her," he shouted. "She was nobody when we met. All talent and no business sense. You're right—I became the hero she needed. And look what happened. Look what she became."

Out of the corner of my eye, I saw Frank straighten up. I also saw Gavin move close behind me, ready to step in between Henrik and me.

Henrik's hand went to the top of the zipper as if he had to hold on to it to keep it from coming undone on its own. He began pacing again. There comes a point in every drop-stitch pattern where you let loose one stitch, pull a bit, and watch an open gap unfurl itself clear down the rows. An unraveling of sorts. And even when you know it's coming, even when you've planned for it, it still startles you a bit to see it happen. I had the clear sense of watching Henrik unravel in front of my eyes.

"We were so good together. People loved us. You saw it. I gave something to her work no one else could. She became who she is because of what *I* did for her career." He stared at me, a maniacal disbelief widening his eyes. "Nobody thought it had to stop. Why stop it? Why throw it all away for such a tiny thing no one cares about?"

The disbelief began to harden into slowly building anger. "She didn't get to decide for both of us. She didn't get to throw it all away in front of everyone like that. It wasn't all-or-nothing. It never had to be all-or-nothing." He flung his hands wide, long fingers jabbing into the air. "I had to stop her because she wouldn't see that. Why wouldn't she see that? Why did she make me have to stop her?"

I suppose some part of me thought I ought to feel sadness. Pity, maybe. Yet as my hands gripped Perle's beautiful needles, all I could think about was how Henrik's pride and ambition had cost Perle her life. Had cost all of us the things she might have created. He'd not only ended her life and career; he'd robbed her of the chance to do the right thing. To pull out the wrong stitches and start over, just like she had written in the speech Henrik had stolen her chance to give.

Frank reached for the handcuffs at the back of his belt, the ones I'd never seen him use before today. He had what he needed, which made waiting for court orders unnecessary. He started toward Henrik.

"Wait," I said. I'm not quite sure why I dared to do it. Perhaps I was a bit numb from the shock of it all, but my voice was remarkably steady as I said, "Henrik, take the sweater off."

Frank gave me a look, as did Gavin. It seemed an unnecessary request to both of them, I'm sure. But it had become vital to me.

Henrik muttered something under his breath, followed by "What's the use?" In a single motion, he yanked down the zipper and sloughed the sweater off his shoulders. He let it fall to the floor with a dismissal that cut into my heart. It was as if he was tossing away Perle and all her work as he tossed away the garment.

There, starting at his left collarbone and running in dual red lines, was a scabbing-over set of scratches. Instead of clean swipes, they were jagged, in fits and starts as they ran down his chest. Signs of struggle. My own breath came in short gasps as I imagined Perle's attempts to fight back as her air supply dwindled.

Nauseated horror made me unsteady on my feet as I walked up to Henrik. I held the two needles together in my hands and laid them up against the scratches. The distance matched perfectly.

Henrik flinched at the contact, and I felt Gavin come right up behind me. I'd alarmed Frank and Gavin—I knew that—but somehow I also knew Henrik would not hurt me. The room was still for a grieving moment, save for my lurching stomach and Henrik's short, defeated breaths.

"Harold Emery, do you confess to the murder of Perle Lonager?" Frank's question was low and serious.

Henrik didn't really nod; he merely lowered his head. He'd loomed so large all the time I'd known him, and now he struck me as small and lost. Very lost.

"Say it out loud, son," Frank said. The words might have been kind, but the tone was unmistakably commanding.

"Yes." Henrik more moaned the word than spoke it. With a sudden sense of desperation, he added, "But I loved her. I really did."

No, I replied in my mind. *That's not love.*

The saddest part of all was that I was sure Perle had loved him. Once.

CHAPTER TWENTY-FIVE

I can't say I would have minded if Frank had paraded Henrik down the block in handcuffs. It seemed as theatrical an ending as the man deserved. Instead, Frank had a squad car pull up to the shop and take Henrik into custody. Frank's nod as he got into the front seat felt like satisfaction enough.

As Gavin and I stood outside the shop watching the car pull away, I began to feel pieces of my world slide back into place.

. . . Until I felt Gavin's tight grip on my arm. He turned me toward him, planting both hands on my shoulders as if he'd sink me into the sidewalk.

I couldn't read his expression. Fear mixed with admiration and anger—a dozen emotions flashed through his eyes as he stared intently at me.

"Don't . . . *ever* . . . do that again."

I was both touched and peeved. Sure, I'd taken a mon-

ster of a risk goading Henrik like that, but I was proud of
my courage and even prouder of the payoff.

"What?" I asked innocently, daring more of a teasing
attitude than the serious one the situation called for. "Confronting a murderer and pulling a confession from him?
Armed with nothing more than a pair of knitting needles
and my wits?"

Gavin's hands lifted off my shoulders to flail in exasperation. "You had no idea. . . . He could have . . . Anything
could have happened in there."

"Justice for Perle happened in there. Peace of mind for
all of us happened in there."

Gavin got that look men get on their faces when they
have a dozen things to say but know all of them will get
them into trouble. He settled for "Libby . . ."

"I'm fine," I assured him, even though parts of me still
felt as if they were shaking. "I'm better than fine actually. I
think I needed to do that. I needed to take back what I'd lost
from everything that happened." Dramatic as it sounded,
that was exactly how I felt. I'd needed to do this for Perle
and for me. I didn't even realize the level of fear I'd been
carrying around until it disappeared.

"He could have hurt you."

I did know that on some level. "I don't think you or
Frank would have let that happen. I wouldn't have been
foolish enough to do that without either of you here."

"Good." After a second, he added, "But don't ever do
anything like that again."

Now I was feeling a little coddled. "Does that line work
on Jillian? Because it's not working on me."

"Honestly, Libby, you—"

I cut him off before he could work himself into a lather.
"Stop worrying. I have no plans to make a career of stuff

like this. I just want to run my shop in peace and not have to worry about homicidal Vikings."

"We all want that for you." There was an awkward pause when I thought he was going to say more. Something more personal—something that I both wasn't ready to hear and maybe wanted to hear. We'd been through a lot together in the past week, and things were tumbling around in my chest I couldn't safely sort. Certainly not with him standing so close and looking the way he did.

"Besides," he said, breaking the moment, "if something happens to you, who will dethrone King George?" He reached for the shop door, opening it for me. "You're really going to do that, aren't you?"

In fact, I felt more courage to take on George than ever. "I am." After a murderous, deceitful Viking, how hard can one self-absorbed, egotistical real estate broker be? Maybe I could give every town business its own day. "Who knows? I might even stage a few middle-of-the-night yarn bombings myself."

"You wouldn't," he called as we walked inside.

"No, I wouldn't. But you never do know about Mom and the Gals."

Gavin shook his head. "I'd better get back to the office and get a statement ready."

I smiled. "The proud mayor declaring Collinstown's streets safe again."

I laughed, and then he laughed. A piece of my jumbled life settled back into place.

"Tell Jillian I look forward to our next lesson. She's a sweet, smart cookie, that girl." I dared to add, "I have a feeling she gets that from you."

Gavin didn't reply, only tipped his head and walked out the door.

I had ten minutes of silence in the shop to ponder everything that had just happened before Margo came barreling in.

"Did I just see what I thought I saw?"

"Henrik being arrested for Perle's murder? You did." I grabbed a pair of coffee mugs. "Sit down and I'll tell you all about it."

I helped Nolan put the last box of Perle's needles into the trunk of his car Sunday morning.

"What will you do with them?"

Nolan sighed and ran a hand through the white spikes of his hair. "Chief Reynolds gave me all the needle business paperwork they found in Perle's hotel room." He smiled a bit. "Along with a long lecture about respect for law enforcement."

"Frank's a good man. And that's good advice."

Nolan shrugged. "I was able to get into her website last night and check the in-box. There was a pile of orders for needles. Enough to run through all these, I bet. Maybe more."

I didn't doubt it. Except for the set that Perle had given me, I'd already sold clean through the stock I'd purchased from her earlier. Sure, there was a little bit of sensationalism behind some of the purchases, but most were for the reasons why I'd loved the needles in the first place—they were beautiful. Lovely to hold and a pleasure to use.

"Will you make more? Continue on?" I dearly wanted him to, but wasn't sure it was my place to say.

Most of the time I'd seen Nolan, he'd looked frightened and confused. In that moment, standing at the open trunk of his rusty Jeep, I saw a glimpse of passion and purpose in his eyes. And in that moment, he looked very much like his aunt to me. I found that comforting. "Yeah, I think I will. Kinda what I ought to do, don't you think?"

"Yes," I replied, glad to be able to admit it. "I'd like to be your first customer to keep carrying the line, if it's all right with you."

"She'd set you up to be one of the first stores to do it. I don't see why we can't keep it that way."

I put a hand on Nolan's shoulder. "I'd be honored."

Nolan ran fingers across the tattoo on his arm. "I still can't believe he did it. I mean, I never liked him, and I even thought he did it, but to find out he actually . . ." He looked at me. "I know that makes no sense. It's just . . . the thought and the real act. Killing her. I think some part of me just wanted to believe it wasn't possible, you know?"

I stared in the direction of the police station. "I'm not sure how Chief Reynolds does it. Seeing the darker side of what people are capable of. How far people will go to achieve their own aims." I have always considered myself an optimist, but I'd be lying if I said it wasn't taking a little extra effort these days.

"I don't feel like I ever really got to know her. Not like I would have if she and Mom had been closer." He touched the pair of *Selbu* mittens I'd given him as a gift. I wanted to make sure that each of the dozen of Perle's knitted patterns we had hanging in the shop went to someone special. Not just stored away in some box in our shop storeroom, but given as a gift, as mittens were meant to be. I'd picked the most masculine of Perle's designs and told him to give them to his boyfriend when they "got serious"—or whatever people his age are calling it these days. After all, that's what *Selbu* mittens were for.

"I didn't spend much time with your aunt, but I do feel

like I know her. So much of who she was showed up in her work. You can know her that way."

His eyes returned to me. "You don't think Henrik ruined that, did he? Lying about everything? Will they hate her now?"

I touched his arm. "No. I don't think Henrik—Harold— ever had that kind of power, even though he thought he did. Oh, people can get angry about the silliest things, but I like to think that knitters are a pretty forgiving kind. Perle was always trying to do the right thing. Even up to the end. Now it's your job to help them see that." I'd given him a copy of Perle's final speech pages, and Nolan had decided to publish the text on Perle's web page. She'd get the chance to say goodbye. It made me happy to think that, try as he might, Henrik wouldn't succeed in silencing her in her brave effort to tell the truth.

There was a stray end of this I hadn't woven in yet. "Do you mind my asking one last thing before you go?"

"Sure."

"What is between you and Derek? You said you hadn't met before this, but I got the feeling you had some history with him."

Nolan leaned up against his Jeep. "I hadn't met him. But you're right. There's a . . . history there."

Derek had paid a hefty fine for his theft-of-services charge and retreated to New York in the company of his attorney. I didn't know what Gibson House Publishing would do about his collaboration with Henrik, and part of me didn't want to know. "You don't have to tell me," I replied to his reluctance.

"No, it's okay. We were almost related. Well, sort of." He made the pronouncement with distaste. I understood—I'd seen enough of the man to never want an opportunity to work with him again.

"How?"

"A couple of years back my boyfriend's sister was dumb enough to be engaged to him. That was before we met, but there are stories. The whole family hated him. Not hard to see why, is it?"

No wonder Nolan had been eager to see Perle get the truth from the man she was going to marry. "Well, no, he isn't my favorite person."

"I couldn't believe he was Perle's publisher when I figured it out, but that gave me the nudge to try to connect with her again. So I suppose, in a weird way, I kinda owe him."

Margo came out of the shop across the street, a trio of bakery boxes in her hands. "No one should drive back to Ohio on an empty stomach. It's not a Tom's cheeseburger, but it ought to get you through Pennsylvania."

Nolan smiled. "Thanks." He looked up to see Hank with both paws up on the shopwindow as if to wave goodbye. "See you later, boy." He raised an eyebrow at me. "I may just have to get myself a dog."

"I recommend it," I replied. "You meet the most amazing people when you walk your dog." He rolled his eyes at my wink, but I didn't mind.

Margo handed off the goodies, which Nolan put in the passenger seat of his car—for ready access, I imagine. The three of us stared at one another for a minute, the goodbye suddenly feeling awkward. After all, we'd been through a murder. It's not the kind of thing that makes for a normal relationship. I couldn't escape the feeling, however, that I'd made a new friend. I liked the solid way that settled under my ribs.

"Would it be weird if I gave you a hug?" I asked. The lost-boy look in his eyes tugged too hard on me to pass the opportunity by.

Nolan gave me an embarrassed look and a shrug. I decided that meant "Sorta, but do it anyway."

I expect I held on too long, but when I was ready, I pulled back and said, "Take care of yourself. Go be great and do marvelous things."

As Nolan walked around to the driver's side of his car, he paused at the tree in front of the shop. He studied it for a moment, then pulled at one loose stitch. A strand of red yarn unraveled for about half a foot, then came loose. Nolan took the stretch of yarn, wrapped it into a small coil around two fingers, and tucked it into his pocket.

"I left something for you in the shop," he said as he slipped in behind the wheel. "On the blackboard."

No gift could have made me happier. I confess I got a bit choked up as Margo and I waved goodbye to Nolan. We stood for a moment watching the Jeep head for the road leading to the highway. Ohio and the rest of his life awaited him.

"Shall we go see?" Margo suggested.

Together we walked into the shop to scan the blackboard. It took a few minutes before we found it, tucked in a high corner, surrounded by a design that echoed both his tattoo and the needles: *Y not Ask 4 Radical Ndings?*

Margo laughed. "I think he bent the rules a bit."

I felt my smile widen. "Seems like something he would do. He doesn't strike me as a color-inside-the-lines kind of guy."

"I think he'll do okay," she said. "I think you will, too."

"I'd do better with a slice of strawberry rhubarb," I teased. "Got any?"

Margo grinned. "As a matter of fact, I do. Be right back."

CHAPTER TWENTY-SIX

Dog Sweater Day didn't have the same ring to it as Collinstown Yarn Day, but I loved it anyway.

It had been Linda's idea—an offhand comment about all of Perle's sweater kits that had been sold and all the happy, cozy pets that must have resulted. It took us only about thirty seconds to decide to throw a Dog Sweater Day, complete with a four-legged fashion show. After all, it had been three weeks since Yarn Day and we had lots to celebrate.

We'd commandeered one of the prettiest sections of the park, one with a gazebo by a picturesque bend in the river. The makeshift fence Chief Reynolds had erected barely held the canine chaos at bay as dozens of colorfully clad dogs romped, barked, and generally enjoyed themselves as much as their owners enjoyed showing them off.

"How many are here? The shop could never have held all this!" Mom shouted over the happy yaps of the Yorkie currently in her lap. While quick to admit she didn't want the commitment of a dog of her own, she was a ready grandma to Hank and any other pooch that would have her.

"You're right on that count," I replied, feeding the little dog yet another special-for-the-occasion dog biscuit Margo had provided. Dog bones wearing frosted Nordic sweaters—what could have been more adorable? "We sold forty-seven kits in all, and thirty-three of them are here. Oh, my goodness, will you look at that?"

I pointed to where Jeanette was walking across the grass with a basket. Inside was her adorable kitten, now astonishingly clad in a Nordic sweater.

"You won that bet," Linda teased.

The kitten seemed none the worse for his attire, and Jeanette beamed. I couldn't help but smile, won bet or not.

As everyone cooed over the kitten, a yearning expression lit up Margo's eyes. "That woman over there showed me a photo of her new litter of chocolate Labrador puppies. Hold me back."

Carl playfully clutched his wife. "On it. You don't want a dog. You only *think* you want a dog because it has chocolate in the name."

"I'll lend you Hank whenever the urge overtakes you," I offered to Margo. She had, in fact, watched Hank overnight once or twice when Mom wasn't able to dog-sit.

"Milo!" I called in greeting as Caroline and Milo walked up, the latter clad in the dapper blue and yellow sweater from the kit she had picked out the afternoon of Perle's event. Caroline's sunny yellow cable-knit tam matched perfectly. She'd quickly become one of my favorite customers—and one of those deep, instant friends.

Caroline looked around the delightful mayhem. "Why

on earth don't you have a television crew here? It's the happiest thing I've seen in weeks."

"I'd prefer a low press profile for a while. Thanks." I was indeed happy for the mundane nature of my life since Henrik's arrest. Justice, I discovered, could be exhausting.

As if she'd read my thoughts, Caroline gave a small sigh. "She would have loved this. Perle. All the colors, and the knitters admiring one another's work."

The warmth of my smile filled me as much as the crispness of the fall sunshine. "She would have."

"It's going to be a lovely holiday season," Mom said as the Yorkie jumped off her lap to go chase a herd of loud Chihuahuas. She looked at me. "Will you help me get the decorations up? I don't want to bother that fellow down the street again this year."

Margo caught my eye for a split second. This was the third time we'd had the conversation about my helping Mom with her holiday decorations. I'd already agreed twice. I simply smiled and agreed a third time.

"How's the store looking for the holidays?" Caroline asked brightly, catching on to the exchange of glances between Margo and me. "I love all the programs and projects in your newsletter, but you've got to stop. I need to keep my job, but you keep distracting me with yarn."

The shop had, in fact, recovered remarkably well. Whether my regular YARNies had doubled their holiday-knitting-project purchases because of my clever marketing or their sympathetic support, I neither knew nor cared. We wouldn't post a great quarter, but it wouldn't be nearly as bad as I'd feared. Weathering the crisis had bolstered my courage, as if Y.A.R.N. could survive anything if it had survived Perle's murder.

Whether I could survive next year's campaign for Chamber of Commerce president? That was yet to be determined. Still, I felt bold and ready, bewildering George with a wide smile every time I saw him.

"And look who's here!" Mom called as Monty, Jillian, and Gavin walked up. "Martin looks dashing. Doesn't he, Elizabeth?"

"Monty," Jillian corrected her.

"I don't know. He looks like a Martin to me." Mom leaned down to give Monty a vigorous petting. "That name will just be our thing, then, Martin."

"Hold out a treat, and you could call that dog Archibald and he'd come running," Gavin laughed.

I pointed with admiration at the hand-knit scarf Gavin was wearing. "Jillian gave me an early birthday present," he said, catching my eye and touching the scarf with a smile.

I broke the moment by peering down to look at the black and red sweater Monty wore. "Monty's sweater turned out fabulous. Jillian, look at you adding a bit of your own design down there by the tail."

Jillian beamed. "Do you like it?"

"The best knitters make every pattern their own." Jillian had amassed excellent skills and a terrific eye for design. I fully expected to be hosting her own design events one of these days. Nothing would have made me happier.

"Can I get a photo of you and him?" Jillian asked, raising her camera. "For my Instagram account. It's all Monty and my knitting."

I happily posed with Monty while Jillian snapped a few shots, bringing Mom and Margo in for a couple as well.

Gavin watched with an unreadable expression on his face. Our relationship had changed—deepened a bit—but I still hadn't decided where I wanted things to stand between Gavin and me. That wasn't helped by the fact that Jillian and Mom never lost an opportunity to let me know where they thought things *ought* to stand.

As I stepped out of the impromptu photo session, Gavin pulled an envelope from his jacket pocket. "I've got another declaration in here."

I put my hand up to stop him. "We barely recovered from the last one."

One corner of Gavin's mouth turned up in amusement. "You may not ever recover from this one." He unfolded the sheet of paper. "This is your official declaration to run for Chamber president against George."

I balked. "I have to sign a declaration?"

"Three actually. There's a whole formal procedure. George created it."

"Why am I not surprised?" I tucked the papers in my tote bag. "Am I about to declare war?"

"You might want to when I tell you George convinced the Chamber that you have to"—he searched for the right verb—"unyarn every tree but yours. By Thanksgiving if not earlier."

I had taken it as a personal victory that the trees were still decorated. George was not going to give up on this. Gavin was right. I was in for a battle. "The little rat."

Gavin still held a smile I didn't quite understand.

"What?" I pressed. "You're not on his side, are you?"

"Of course not. I like the trees. Jillian loves the trees. Which is why I'm so proud of her for getting the last word."

"Meaning?"

Gavin's face displayed an amusing mix of prankster and proud papa. "Jillian overheard me trying to talk George out of his campaign to take the yarn down off all the trees. So at school yesterday she launched a campaign of her own."

I knew I liked that girl. "Which is . . . ?"

"Jillian convinced the student council that the trees around the school absolutely need to be yarn-bombed in their school colors."

I now understood Gavin's expression completely. In fact, I couldn't say my own face didn't hold a smirk of pride. "You raised her right, Your Honor. That's brilliant."

Gavin's smile faded just a bit. "Well, I confess she didn't *quite* come up with it all on her own."

I suddenly knew where this was heading. "Mom?"

He nodded. "She and her Gals have already volunteered to help. A whole battalion of seventh graders and grannies off to do"—he couldn't seem to think of the word to do it justice—"whatever it is you call it."

"Art," I told him with no small amount of satisfaction. "Like I've told George—over and over—it's art."

ACKNOWLEDGMENTS

Every book represents the efforts and support of many more people than just the author. I'm blessed to have a whole team that makes my life easier and my writing better, and enables my books to reach new readers.

First thanks always go to my husband, Jeff, who puts up with a lot of "authorial tendencies," like discussing characters over dinner as if they were real people (wait—they aren't?), odd research adventures, and a creatively dramatic personality that can be equal parts good fun and royal pain.

My good friend and writing colleague Virginia Smith had no idea what she was launching when she called me one day and asked, "Do you think you could write a mystery?" I owe you, Ginny, for sending me down a path I hadn't yet seen for myself but now love.

Enormous thanks go to the talented Starla Williams of Starla Knits, who immediately caught my vision for Perle's Nordic dog sweater and created a fabulous pattern. She exceeded all my expectations and I couldn't be happier with the result. If any of you knit the sweater, by all means send me a photo at allie@alliepleiter.com.

I am blessed to have not one but two agents. Karen Solem and Sandy Harding, both of Spencerhill Associates, not only help me craft my career but also offer me wise counsel and the not-so-occasional "Stop worrying."

Thanks go as well to my marvelous editor, Michelle Vega at Berkley, as well as the team of sales, art, and production professionals who made this book the thing of beauty that it is.

My assistant, Michelle Prima, helps me to keep all the details corralled and the e-mails running. Her skill with a gorgeous social media post is a huge asset to me.

For this particular book, I had some marvelous expert help. My thanks to Kristen Quain for her review and assurances that I'd managed to get most of the Norwegian knitting and culture details right. And to Janet Avila of String Theory Yarn Company (my local yarn shop) for putting me in touch with Kristen. Any craft or cultural missteps in this book are on me, not on Kristen's assistance.

I'm also grateful to Jim Hickey, who patiently answered scores of police procedure questions and headed off numerous newbie errors. Again, any mistakes in this book belong to me, and are not the result of his generous help.

And it goes without saying that I'm grateful to you, dear reader, for this visit to Collinstown and Libby's Y.A.R.N. shop. I do hope it's the first of many.

PERLE'S NORDIC DOG SWEATER

Written by Starla Williams

MATERIALS: Rowan Pure Wool Worsted, 219 yards per skein. Or any other worsted weight yarn. Approximately 75, 100, 170, 190, 240 yards each of the main color and 50, 75, 110, 140, 175 yards of contrasting color.

NEEDLES: Size 7 and 8, single point or circular, or any size needed for the gauge. Size 6 dpn and/or circular for leg and body ribbings.

GAUGE: 5 stitches and 6.5 rows, 1 inch in fair isle pattern.

OTHER NEEDS: Large safety pin markers or 3 small stitch holders, tape measure, crochet hook, tapestry needle. Small amounts of waste yarn for crochet chain cast-on and harness hole.

MOST IMPORTANT OTHER NEEDS: coffee, chocolate, will to knit, and an awesome pup to knit a sweater for.

SIZES: Use chart to determine size. If in doubt, match the chest measurement as close as you can.

SIZE	NECK	CHEST	LENGTH*
X-SMALL ADULT TOY	8"	11–12"	9–10"
SMALL	11"	13–15"	11–13"
MEDIUM	14"	16–18"	13–15"
LARGE	16"	19–21"	16–17"
X-LARGE	18"	22–26"	18–20"

Lengths may be adjusted, as each breed is different. Instructions on where to adjust length are written in the pattern.

GLOSSARY

EDGE STITCH: First and last stitch. Allowed in the pattern to make seaming the fair isle pattern together easier. Always knit first and last stitch.

M1R: With working needle, pick up the bar in between needle from front to back and place it on the needle to be worked from front to back. Knit this stitch through the back loop.

M1L: With opposite working needle, pick up the bar in between the needle from back to front, knit the stitch from front to back.

SSK: Slip next two stitches one at a time, as to knit. Slide tip of opposite needle in the front of the two stitches just slipped and knit the two stitches together.

E-WRAP: With the strand of working yarn, take your index finger over the strand and then back under, making a loop around your finger. Slide the tip of the knitting needle into this loop, transferring the strand from finger

to needle. Remove index finger and give the working
yarn a slight tug to tighten the e-wrap you just made.

IMPORTANT THINGS TO KNOW: The pattern is written for
single point needles, then blocked and seamed. Leg ribbings will be added after knitting the body.

Knitting starts at the neck, with a crochet chain cast on.
Neck ribbing will be added later and worked in the round
instead of seaming ribbing. If preferred, a *loose* cast-on
may be used.

Increase by using an M1R after the first edge stitch and
an M1L before the last edge stitch.

LET'S START: Starting at the neck, with a crochet hook and
waste yarn crochet a chain of at least 43, 55, 71, 79, 87
stitches; attach safety pin marker in the last stitch made.

Return to opposite end of crochet chain. With main
color, pick up 43, 55, 71, 79, 87 stitches in the bumps of the
chain and purl one row. Do not cut yarn.

Starting with a knit row, work 0, 2, 2, 2, 2 rows, stocki-
nette stitch.

Change to size 8 needles.

Work fair isle charts **at the same time** while shaping
neck and leg openings. Please read ahead and consolidate
these steps for your size.

FAIRISLE CHARTS

SIZES X-SMALL, SMALL: Following Chart A, A, start with
row 3, 1. Work leg openings on row 17, 21, finishing
chart. Go to snowflake section.

SIZES MEDIUM, LARGE, X-LARGE: Following Chart B, start with row 3, 1, 1, work through row 14, 14, 16, then work chart A, A, A, starting with row 1, 1, 3. Work leg openings on row 9, 9, 17, as you finish chart A. Work snowflake section.

SNOWFLAKE SECTION FOR ALL SIZES: Work chart C on next 8, 13, 19, 23, 32, PM; work snowflake chart on next 19 sts, PM; work chart C to end of row. Work through charts as set, slipping markers as you go.

After completing the snowflake section, work Chart B, starting with row 4. Large and x-large sizes repeat chart B as needed.

AT THE SAME TIME,

shape neck as follows:

ALL SIZES: M1R at the beginning and M1L end of row (inside edge stitches), every row, 3, 1, 1, 1, eight times. Then on right side every other row 5, 8, 9, 11, eleven times, incorporating new stitches in charts.

59, 73, 91, 103, 125 stitches.

LEG OPENINGS: Work across 7, 8, 10, 11, 12 stitches. This is the left side. Knit next 5, 6, 7, 8, 9 stitches for leg and put them on a large safety pin marker or small stitch holder. Work center 35, 45, 57, 65, 83 stitches following chart. This is the back. Knit next 5, 6, 7, 8, 9 stitches for other leg, and put them on a holder; knit remaining 7, 8, 10, 11, 12 stitches. This is the right side.

Turn.

Work next 9, 11, 11, 13, 15 rows on 7, 8, 10, 11, 12 stitches following chart. Place stitches on holder. Cut yarn.

Join yarn to center-back stitches on wrong side and work across on appropriate row on chart.

If you want a harness hole, proceed through harness hole section. If not, work 8, 10, 12, 12, 14, 16 rows for leg opening.

HARNESS HOLE: Worked on row 22. Work to center 5, 5, 5, 6, 6 stitches. Drop yarn and with waste yarn; work the next 5, 5, 5, 7, 7, stitches. Drop waste yarn. Slip them back on needle to be worked again. Continue working with working yarn, work the 5, 5, 5, 7, 7, stitches again, and finish row. Work remaining rows of the chart for the back section. Cut yarn.

Join yarn on wrong side to the remaining left side stitches and work 10, 12, 12, 14, 16 rows, following chart. Do not cut yarn. Turn.

JOINING ROW: With right side facing you, work across 6, 8, 10, 11, 12 stitches, e-wrap cast-on 5, 6, 7, 8, 9, stitches. Work across 37, 45, 57, 65, 83, stitches, e-wrap cast-on 5, 6, 7, 8, 9, stitches. Work remaining 6, 8, 10, 11, 12 stitches.

Total number of stitches: 59, 73, 91, 103, 125.

If wish to make longer or shorter, adjust rows in the following section.

Continue working in chart until body measures 5.5, 6.5, 7.5, 9, 10.5 inches from beginning of neck, or desired length, before shaping the back of the sweater. If you need to adjust, please take into consideration that you will have 18, 22, 24, 28, 32 more rows to add to the length for tail shaping.

SHAPE TUMMY OPENING: Keeping to the chart pattern, bind off 8, 10, 10, 12, 14 stitches at the beginning of the next two rows. 43, 53, 71, 79, 97 stitches. You will not have edge stitches anymore. Place a safety pin marker at each end of the work. Be ready for a right-side row.

DECREASE ROW: K1, ssk, knit to last 3 stitches, K2 tog, k1.

NEXT ROW: work even in pattern.

Repeat last 2 rows 9, 11, 12, 14, 17 times more. 23, 29, 45, 47, 61 stitches.

Bind off 3, 5, 8, 10, 12 stitches at beg of next two rows. Leave remaining 17, 19, 19, 27, 37 stitches on holder.

FINISHING HARNESS HOLE: Return to harness hole and carefully release live stitches on 2 dpns. With the right side facing you, attach yarn and bind off stitches in the round. Secure ends to wrong side and work in the ends.

Work in all tail ends with tapestry needle.

Steam block flat.

Sew center seam using mattress stitch, using edge stitches as a guide. Sew from neck edge to tummy cast-off where you placed markers.

NECK RIBBING: If you used a provisional cast-on, return to the safety pin marker and release live stitches. If you just casted on, pick up stitches over cast-on stitches. Divide stitches on double-pointed needles and join in the round. With contrasting color, knit one round, decreasing evenly to 40, 52, 64, 72, 80 stitches. Work k2, P2 ribbing for 6, 6, 6, 8, 8 rounds. Bind off loosely in ribbing.

BODY EDGING: With right side of work facing you, starting at tummy and bind off. Join contrasting color and pick up and knit 17, 21, 18, 25, 27 stitches across tummy stitches 10, 16, 17, 18, 27; along decrease side 3, 5, 8, 10, 11, end bind-off stitches, knit across 17, 19, 29, 27, 37 end stitches from stitch holder 3, 5, 8, 10, 11, other end bind-off stitches, pick up 10, 16, 16, 18, 27 along decrease edge on other side. 60, 82, 96, 108, 140 total stitches. Work in K2, p2 ribbing for 6, 6, 8, 8, 8, rounds, loosely BO in ribbing.

LEG OPENINGS: Pick up 24, 24, 28, 32, 36 stitches around leg openings. Work, K2, P2 ribbing for 6, 6, 6, 8, 8, 10 rounds. Loosely BO. Repeat for second leg.

Please repeat the six-stitch charts as many times as necessary to complete rows. It may be helpful to some to place markers every 6 stitches to designate repeats.

RIGHT-HANDERS: *Read right-side rows from right to left. Wrong-side rows from left to right.*
LEFT-HANDERS: *Work opposite.*

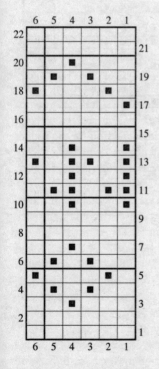

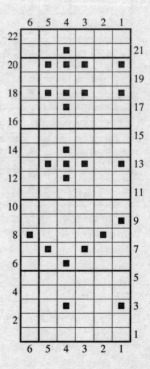

CHART A - SIX STITCH REPEAT   **CHART B - SIX STITCH REPEAT**

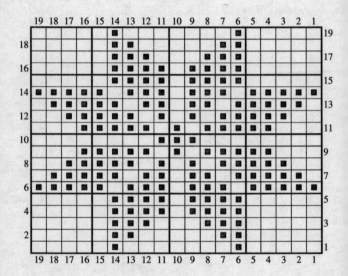

SNOWFLAKE

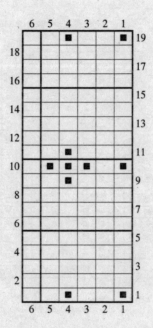

CHART C - SIX STITCH REPEAT-WORK
ON EACH SIDE OF SNOWFLAKE CHART

Ready to find
your next great read?

Let us help.

Visit prh.com/nextread